# A Sweethaven
# CHRISTMAS

## COURTNEY WALSH

**Guideposts**
New York, New York

*A Sweethaven Christmas*

ISBN-10: 0-8249-3182-3
ISBN-13: 978-0-8249-3182-7

Published by Guideposts
16 East 34th Street
New York, New York 10016
Guideposts.org

Distributed by Ideals Publications, a Guideposts company
2630 Elm Hill Pike, Suite 100
Nashville, TN 37214

Guideposts and Ideals are registered trademarks of Guideposts.

The characters and events in this book are fictional, and any
resemblance to actual persons or events is coincidental.

All Scripture quotations are taken from *The Holy Bible,
New International Version.* Copyright © 1973, 1978, 1984,
2011 by Biblica, Inc. Used by permission of Zondervan.
All rights reserved worldwide. www.zondervan.com

Library of Congress Cataloging-in-Publication Data has
been applied for.

Cover and interior design by Müllerhaus
Typeset by Aptara, Inc.

Printed and bound in the United States of America
10 9 8 7 6 5 4 3 2 1

# DEDICATION

For Adam.
Me and you.

# ACKNOWLEDGMENTS

During the writing and editing of this book, our family moved across the country for the second time in two years. Perhaps I'm weepier because of it, but it's left me with so much gratitude and taught me that there are so many good people out there. People who make it possible for you to pack up and move away and still get done the things they know are important to you. People who all play a part in making this dream come true. I hope one day I can return the favor.

I want to thank them with chocolate, but for now, I'll just list them here:

Sophia, Ethan and Sam. We've been on so many adventures the last few years, and you guys have been amazing with every single one. I'm so impressed by all of you, and I thank God every day for giving us each one of you. I'll try not to incorporate too much of your real lives in my writing . . . but I'm not making any promises. I love you guys.

My parents Bob and Cindy Fassler. For helping us get moved and settled and allowing us to crash their house for ten days between houses. Thank you for not letting us be homeless. Also, Mom, thank you for providing so much Christmas inspiration for me to draw from. Your house on Christmas? The best.

Sandra Bishop. Agent extraordinaire. It's a daily thing, my thanking God you're in my life. You always seem to know exactly what to say to help me—with my writing, of course, but also with pretty much everything else. Thank you for your prayers when I most need them, for your kindness and your friendship. I am most blessed.

Rachel Meisel. I sometimes feel like a stray puppy that was left on your doorstep. Thank you for taking me in and taking such great care of me. For your encouragement, your wisdom and your kindness, I am forever grateful.

Lindsay Stout. I feel so lucky I got to meet you before we got to work together. It's made me feel like we were insta-friends, and to me, that's the BEST kind of person to work with. Thank you for your excitement and all your help with this series. What would I do without you?

Buffy Cooper and the rest of the Müllerhaus team. For taking the vague ideas I had about the covers of these books and turning them into reality. You went above and beyond, creating gorgeous ART, and I couldn't be more thrilled with all three of these covers. Thank you. Thank you.

My editors Beth Adams and Lindsay Guzzardo. I still remember getting the call that Sweethaven was a go. I can't believe how much you both have taught me throughout this journey. I am indebted to each of you for sharing your knowledge and challenging me to be better.

Deb Raney. My mentor and friend. Thank you for the wisdom, advice and endless friendship, all things you give generously . . . and for talking me off many a ledge.

Lauren Wave. You are such a gift. You take the heaviest part of my burden and run. Thank you for planning my launch parties, organizing signings and spreading the word. I am most grateful.

Jeane Wynn. For your support, encouragement and friendship. Thank you for believing in me and in these books. I am so glad you're on my team.

The friends and critique partners who sustain me, encourage me, celebrate with me and get me out of the house (occasionally): Carrie Erikson, Ronnie Johnson, Mindy Rogers, Gwen Stewart, Carla Stewart, Kellie Gilbert, Shannan Martin, Jenn Schmidt, Lyndsey Lewis, Liz Hicks.

Brandin O'Neill. I'm eternally grateful to work with someone who gets it. You've taught me so much simply by being yourself. And as an added bonus, you've become such a great friend to me. I thank God for you daily.

To the friends, family, and even acquaintances and strangers who showed up in 106-degree heat to either move us out or move us in. I don't know what to say other than, "Wow." You've humbled and amazed me, and I'm pretty sure there aren't enough words to ever express the gratitude I feel. Thank you for showing our family that kind of love—it won't soon be forgotten.

To the readers of *A Sweethaven Summer* and *A Sweethaven Homecoming*. Thank you for your e-mails and messages to let me know you liked your visit to Sweethaven and for sharing it with your reading friends. Perfectly timed and always unexpected, I have been truly blessed by every word.

And, of course, my Heavenly Father, Who has blessed, challenged and taught me so much. I am constantly learning and praying You order every step. Thank You for Your *redeeming grace*.

Christmas waves a magic wand over this world and, behold, everything is softer and more beautiful.

—NORMAN VINCENT PEALE

ONE

*Lila*

"Why is that woman staring over here?" Lila shifted in the tall-backed linen-covered chair and nodded toward a blonde woman at the bar. Normally, Lila attributed the stares of other women to jealousy, but with her expanding stomach, she felt more self-conscious than usual. She hadn't begun to show, but she felt bloated and puffy.

Tom shrugged. "Maybe she thinks you're glowing." He leaned over and kissed her on the cheek. "Because you are."

Lila met his eyes and smiled, letting a hand fall to her belly.

"You *are* especially beautiful right now, Lila," Campbell said from across the table.

The three of them and Luke sat at The Grotto waiting for Mama and Daddy so they could finally start their Thanksgiving dinner. Lila hadn't seen her parents in weeks, and she'd been reluctant to agree to spending Thanksgiving with them, but Mama had insisted.

"We are your family, dear," she'd said. "And when that baby comes, you're going to be so overwhelmed and exhausted you're going to need us. Don't make me your enemy now."

Lila's jaw tightened. Hadn't Mama always been something of an enemy?

"Do you always eat out on Thanksgiving?" Campbell sipped her water from a sparkly crystal glass. She'd accepted Tom's invitation to dinner, even though she and Luke had had plans to spend the evening at Adele's Thanksgiving feast. So much less formal—more relaxed. Lila fought back her jealousy.

Lila forced a smile. "Mama insisted that this year neither of us needed the stress of cooking."

*And what Mama says goes.*

Before Lila's smile faded, she spotted her mother entering the restaurant. As always, Cilla Adler was the picture of Southern beauty. She'd obviously been to the salon, and her black cocktail dress hugged her curves in just the right places. Lila pulled her hand away from her stomach, suddenly even more self-conscious.

Daddy entered a few moments later, and Lila noticed the tension on both their faces. Most likely they'd had one of their fights in the car—probably the reason they were twenty minutes late.

But Mama never offered explanations or apologies.

Would Lila be the same kind of mother as Mama?

Lila stood as her mother approached, but as soon as she spotted her daughter, Mama's eyes widened. "You're already so huge!"

Lila's shoulders slumped and she felt Tom's body as he stood beside her. He wrapped a protective arm around her, and Lila forced herself to smile. "That's good, Mama. It means the baby is growing." But at only three months along, Lila knew any excess weight she'd put on had been the result of eating too many carbs to ward off morning sickness—not the result of a growing fetus.

"Oh dear, you better be careful. I wore my regular clothes until I was eight months along with you." Mama laughed. "At this rate, by the end you'll be wearing the curtains."

Tom squeezed Lila's shoulder and she bit her lip to keep from crying. She'd gotten more emotional with this pregnancy. And perhaps that had been an excuse to eat a little more than usual. Lila had never had to worry about her weight before, but this baby had her feeling like a whale already. How would she feel three months from now? And three months after that?

Mama turned her attention to Campbell, and Lila cringed. Mama could use Lila as a punching bag, but not Suzanne's daughter. Her mother smiled and extended a hand toward the girl.

"You must be Tom's . . . Campbell."

Campbell stood and shook her hand. Lila recognized the intimidation in her eyes. "It's nice to officially meet you, Mrs. Adler."

"Please, call me Cilla. We're practically family. Though I can't believe Lila's gotten over this whole thing so quickly." She turned her attention to Luke as Campbell's face went pale. Lila caught Campbell's eyes and mouthed the words "I'm sorry." Mama went on. "Where is your father? He got tied up talking to someone, I'm sure."

Lila followed Mama's gaze toward the entrance to the restaurant, where she spotted Daddy talking to the same woman who'd been staring at her earlier.

"Who is that?" Lila said.

Mama turned back to the table. She pressed her lips together and Lila could see her jaw tensing.

"Mama, who is that woman?"

Mama sipped her water and shook her head. "I don't know," she said.

Lila glanced back at Daddy, who now stood in the entryway of the restaurant alone. When he looked up, he met her eyes and put on a smile, but Lila knew something was wrong.

Daddy moved toward the table. As he sat down next to Mama, she stiffened at his touch. Lila glanced at Tom, who sipped his water, careful not to make eye contact with anyone.

Was this woman the latest of Daddy's conquests? Lila had long given up the hope that he would change his meandering ways, but how dare he flaunt it in front of them in public.

The waitress arrived and presented the menu—a classic Thanksgiving spread that Lila felt certain she could devour in one sitting. She'd refrain, of course, under Mama's watchful eye. They listened and then Lila spotted the blonde woman back in her seat at the bar.

The woman couldn't have been much older than Lila. She might even be younger. Had Daddy really stooped that low? If the woman didn't know he was married with a family and a soon-to-be grandchild, she knew now. Or maybe she'd come to expose the sordid affair. Could she be pregnant with Daddy's child—making the baby Lila's half sister—and she'd come to claim her fortune?

Whatever the reason, the whole idea of it made Lila's stomach turn.

"This is such a lovely place," Campbell said. Poor girl. She had no idea what she'd agreed to when she said she'd join them for the afternoon.

Mama smiled. "One of our favorite restaurants." She looked over at the woman on the bar stool. The woman's eyebrows rose, then she looked away.

Lila's throat went dry and she took another drink of water. It had always been like this. None of them talking about what was really going on. Pretending they were a perfect family, the epitome of Southern grace. But Lila had looked the other way for too long. Something about being pregnant had made her tired of pretending. She didn't want to bring a child into this kind of environment.

"Daddy, who's that lady?"

Victor Adler coughed. He wiped his mouth with his napkin and shook his head. "I'm not sure," he said. "She stopped me in the entryway looking for directions."

Mama lifted her chin.

"To where?" Lila stared at Daddy until he met her eyes. Behind him, she could see the woman walking in their direction, but Lila kept her eyes focused on Daddy. The woman drew nearer.

Finally, Daddy said, "Lila, she's no one important. No one you'd know."

The woman stopped and her face fell.

"Maybe you should tell her that." Lila glanced up at the woman behind Daddy.

As his words registered, the woman's demeanor changed, her eyes searching for understanding at the revelation that to Victor Adler, she meant nothing.

Daddy followed Lila's eyes to the woman's and then his jaw went slack. He stood and faced her. "I'm sorry—I didn't mean . . ."

The woman held up a hand. She shook her head and ran out, leaving Daddy standing alone, anxiety etched on his face.

Mama placed her napkin on her plate. "I'm sorry I can't stay for dinner. Lila, see that your father finds his way home." She stood, placed her purse on her shoulder and walked out.

Lila sat for a long moment, waiting for Daddy to say something—anything—to make sense of what had just happened. When he stayed silent she stood. "How could you, Daddy?"

His gaze remained downward.

"I'm sorry, Campbell, Luke, it looks like dinner is canceled." Lila picked up her purse and glanced at her father. "You can ask your girlfriend for a ride home."

Memories of all the years Daddy had chosen other women over Mama—and her—rushed back as Lila walked away. She spotted the restroom and ducked inside, hoping Tom would get the car and take care of Campbell and Luke.

She reminded herself that this wasn't her problem anymore. She'd married a man nothing like Daddy, despite her mother's best efforts to put them in the same category.

"Tom is no better than your father," she'd told Lila the last time they spoke. "He betrayed you and kept a secret from you for years. How does that make him a good man?" Lila couldn't deny she'd been betrayed. Earlier in the year, she'd learned that before she and Tom had married over twenty years ago, he'd had a brief relationship with her dear friend Suzanne, leading to the birth of their daughter Campbell. Learning about Campbell had devastated Lila, but it had also led to something completely unexpected—a strengthening of her and Tom's relationship.

Lila bent over the sink and splashed cold water on her cheeks. She glanced in the mirror and saw her red eyes fill with tears.

After all these years, something like this shouldn't upset her this much. It must be the hormones.

She turned the water off and the door to the stall opened. The blonde woman met her eyes in the mirror, and Lila's breath caught in her throat.

The woman looked away as she walked toward the sinks. "I didn't mean to . . ."

"To what? Rub it in my mother's face that Daddy's still unfaithful after all these years?"

The woman's eyes widened and confusion spread across her face.

"Never mind. This was a bad idea."

Lila put a hand on the woman's arm. "What are you doing here? What do you want?"

"I'm sorry I came. I just . . ." The woman stared at Lila for a full five seconds and then pushed past her and disappeared behind the slowly closing bathroom door.

Lila stood, unmoving, trying to make sense of what had just happened. In all the years of her father stepping out on Mama, none of the women had ever approached him in public like this. What made this woman different?

She had a feeling her father had a lot of explaining to do.

TWO

*Campbell*

In the safety of Luke's truck, Campbell finally released the tension in her shoulders, having spent the last forty-five minutes rigid. She sat with her purse on her lap, her coat pulled tight around her now that the weather looked toward winter.

"You okay?" Luke took her hand.

Campbell swallowed and tried to find words for the thoughts racing through her head. "No wonder Lila's so uptight."

Luke squeezed her hand. "You should hear some of the things Cilla has said to my mom over the years."

Campbell stared out the passenger window.

"Hey, what's wrong?"

"Is she right about me?" She turned to look at Luke. "Am I just a constant reminder of a terrible mistake? How does Lila still look at me, much less talk to me?" She felt her throat close around the knot of sadness. Her quest to find her father had been a bittersweet discovery Campbell couldn't fully embrace. She might never have gone through with her search if she'd known where it would lead her—to Lila's husband.

Still, Tom and Lila seemed happier than ever—on the cusp of starting their own family after years of trying, but what if Lila regretted ever meeting Campbell?

"Cam, now you're talking crazy," Luke said. "Lila loves you. We all do."

She pulled her attention from her folded hands and met his eyes.

He held her gaze, then scooted closer, taking her face in his hands. For a long moment, he stared at her, then finally met her lips with his own. His kisses had grown more familiar, more passionate the more time they spent together, and she couldn't deny she'd thought about their future, contemplated whether or not he was the one.

He pulled back and brushed her hair away from her eyes. "I mean it, Cam," he said. "I love you."

Her heart flip-flopped and she studied his eyes—expectant, waiting for her reply.

Why weren't the words coming? She did love him too. Didn't she? Why couldn't she say it? Instead, she leaned back into him and distracted him with her kisses.

A knock on the truck's window startled them apart, and Luke let out a laugh as he rolled down the window. Tom stood, looking lost.

"Do you think your mom would mind if I brought Lila over for Thanksgiving?"

"Are you kidding? She'd be mad if you didn't."

Tom stared toward the restaurant.

"Is Lila still in there?" Luke said.

He nodded. "I'm going to go check on her." Tom sighed. "Thanks, you two. I think being with her friends is what she needs most right now."

Tom walked away.

"See?" Luke said.

"What?"

"Don't let Cilla Adler make you worry about yourself or your place here. He wants to be in your life. And he knows Lila does too." He started the truck and pulled out onto the road while Campbell considered his words. All of them.

He loved her. He said so, right before they were interrupted by Tom. Should she bring it up again? He glanced at her and smiled, then turned his attention to the road.

After too many silent moments, Campbell finally settled on something to say. "Do you think this is how Lila feels?"

Luke's eyes remained on the road. "What do you mean?"

"If Cilla could make me feel this horrible in one meeting, imagine what it's been like for Lila growing up with her."

Luke nodded. "Couldn't have been easy."

His tone had changed. Or was she just imagining it? She could kick herself for her silence. She'd waited years to feel this way about a man. Why had she hesitated? She shook the notion away. Lila. She would figure out this situation with Lila. She reminded herself that feeling sorry for Lila wouldn't do her any good. But she couldn't help but feel responsible for so much of the woman's pain the past few months. After all, it was her fault the truth had come out.

"We're better for it now, Campbell," Lila had told her. "It's like almost losing each other made us realize how much we love each other."

Campbell didn't understand it. If she discovered some crazy secret in Luke's past, how could she ever move beyond it? But maybe that's what love was. Maybe that's why she couldn't say she loved Luke—because she didn't really know what love would take. Or maybe it had more to do with the fact that everyone she'd loved had let her down—or left her. And she knew she couldn't survive another heartbreak, not with Mom's death still at the forefront of her mind. She had to hold back to keep from feeling that kind of pain again.

Luke reached across the truck and took her hand from her lap. He held it for a long moment. Was he wondering why she hadn't told him she loved him back? Did it matter to guys the way it mattered to her? Maybe Luke told all the girls he dated that he loved them.

She glanced at him and smiled. As their relationship intensified, was she ready for the next stage?

And if not . . . then what on earth was she doing anyway?

## THREE

*Jane*

The Sweethaven Chapel bustled with activity as people drifted in for the Thanksgiving service. When Jane got the call a few weeks earlier that they needed someone to host the Thanksgiving festivities, she agreed, thankful for the chance to spend the holiday with good friends at Adele's. Graham had given her the news that morning that she'd be welcoming everyone to the service and reading a poem just after the music ended.

At first she protested, but she settled into the idea that she wanted to take on more of a leadership role. After her success with the ladies' Bible study, it made sense for her to be more visible. Especially if they intended to spend next summer in Sweethaven pastoring the little chapel.

Now, standing at the back of the church, Jane greeted old friends and new faces as people shuffled in to find their seats.

"Jane? Is that you?"

Jane spun around to find a thin brunette wearing too much makeup standing in front of her. Her pointed heels showed off muscular legs, and her low-cut wraparound dress looked like something straight off the runway. Coco Chanel would approve.

Jane stole a quick glance downward, struck by the plainness of her outfit and shoes. She'd opted for "sensible" and "comfortable," two words no fashion model knew. She returned her focus to the woman.

"Yes, it's me." Jane searched the woman's face for someone she recognized.

"It's Lori Tiller. Well, Lori Woodman now."

*Lori Tiller.* Jane's face heated at the mention of her name.

"I heard you were back in town, and I just *had* to say hello. I didn't know you were married to a pastor."

How would she? Jane had never wanted to see her again.

And yet, here she was.

Jane would have said she was over it, but suddenly she felt like that overweight twelve-year-old again wearing a large T-shirt on the beach.

"Yes, Graham and I have been together since high school."

Lori followed Jane's eyes to where Graham stood, just a few feet away. When she spotted him, her brows shot up. "Him?"

"Yes." Her voice sounded more like the squeak of a church mouse.

Lori turned back to Jane. "Jane, I must say. Who would've ever guessed you'd do so well for yourself?" Her tone dripped sugar and her smile contradicted her words.

Lori hadn't changed a bit. Jane landed on another memory. She was a teenager again, sitting on the aisle of the church pew. Lori, with her long, dark curls and thin, bronzed body, strolled past, stopping beside her.

"Careful, Jane, pews have weight limits." Then she'd smile and greet Jane's parents like she was campaigning for political office.

Now Jane stood in front of her wondering if her old nemesis had had work done. She wanted to ask but something stopped her. Instead, she caught Graham's eye and willed him to her side.

"Everything okay, hon?" Graham said as he reached her.

"You must be Graham," Lori said, holding out a manicured hand in Graham's direction. "I'm an old friend of Jane's."

"Oh?" Graham shook her hand and glanced in Jane's direction. She kept her eyes glued on Lori's paws, which were currently wrapped in her husband's hands. Finally, Jane's eyes met Lori's.

"I wouldn't exactly say we were friends," Jane said.

Lori's eyes seemed to gleam before she turned her attention back to Jane's husband.

"It's awfully nice of you to come back to Sweethaven for Thanksgiving and perform this service," Lori said. "We're all so thankful to have you here." She tilted her head to the side, her eyelashes batting a home run.

Graham maneuvered his hands away from Lori's and wrapped an arm around Jane's shoulder. "We love it here," he said. "Wouldn't have missed it." Then, to Jane: "You should get ready, hon. We're about to start."

"Jane, are you speaking?" Lori laughed. "I imagine it'd be hard to be up on stage for everyone to scrutinize." She flashed a smile. "We'll be cheering for ya."

Jane tensed at the thought of Lori "cheering" for her.

Graham took Jane's hand and led her away from Lori, concentrating on the look on Jane's face. "Are you okay?"

"I can't believe she's still coming here after all these years. I didn't see her once this summer and now she's here to ruin Thanksgiving. Did you see the way she came on to you?"

Graham laughed. "Honey, you're overreacting. She's a little pushy, yes, but you have nothing to worry about. Now, get ready to read. You're going to be great." He kissed the top of her head and took his place on the stage, leaving Jane to stew. Now she had to get up on the platform. In front of everyone. To be scrutinized.

Graham began the service and as he spoke, Jane glanced at Lori. The woman sat in the front row, her ample bosom propped up like it was on a shelf, nodding at Graham with a red-lipped smile. Jane suddenly understood what it meant to feel her own blood boiling. She scanned the three kids sitting next to her and reminded herself that Graham was the most loyal person she knew. No matter what Lori tried, she'd be shot down like a duck over open water.

"And now I'd like to ask my beautiful wife Jane to come to the stage with a reading to get the service started."

Jane smiled as she met Graham's eyes. She stood and walked toward the platform, reminding herself to breathe and avoid Lori's stare. Jane reached the podium, steadied her voice and read Langston Hughes's poem, which she'd read so many times before.

*When the night winds whistle through the trees and*
*blow the crisp brown leaves a-crackling down,*
*When the autumn moon is big and yellow-orange and round,*
*When old Jack Frost is sparkling on the ground,*
*It's Thanksgiving Time!*

One look at Lori and she stepped down. It was then Graham ushered her over to a chair on the stage-left side.

"I should go sit with the kids."

Graham smiled. "Everyone's who's speaking is sitting up here," he whispered. He left her standing awkward and alone. As he took his spot behind the podium, Jane took a deep breath and sat down in the rickety chair on the edge of the stage. As she did, she heard a crack as the chair gave way. It snapped in two like a board over the knee of a karate master.

As Jane fell to the ground, the splintered chair dug into her skin and her face flushed with the heat of embarrassment. The gasps from the crowd eventually died down, leaving nothing but silence in their place. Graham rushed over and helped her to her feet, but the damage had been done. The chair now lay in pieces on the stage. She tried to avoid the stares of the crowd, tried to stay focused on the goal of reaching the door that led out of the sanctuary, but she heard the slight snicker coming from the brunette Barbie doll in the front row.

Jane looked over her shoulder and found Lori's face lit with amusement, her hand covering her mouth, her eyes fixed on Jane's backside.

Jane returned her gaze to the door, inhaled a shaky breath, and smoothed her dress pants. But as she did, she discovered they'd split up the back. Now she stood on the stage with her back to the entire church—and Lori—with her undergarments exposed.

Tears sprang to her eyes and Jane rushed off the stage, Jenna following close behind.

"Mom, are you okay?"

Jane covered her face with her hands for a moment, then swiped her cheeks dry.

Jenna pulled her into a hug, but it didn't console her. For the rest of her life, Jane was sure she would relive the horror of that moment over and over again.

The scene was playing like a movie in her mind, one in which she'd forever see Lori in the front row, eyeing her husband and smiling at Fat Jane's expense.

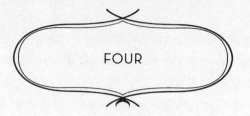

# FOUR

*Meghan*

"Thank you for agreeing to meet with me on my last day in Nashville. I know we're all trying to get home for Thanksgiving."

The music executive, Dan, grunted. "Yes, let's get to it then."

Meghan stared at Dan, who had almost as much vested in the success of her current album as she did. Beside him, a well-dressed woman named Judy stared at her underneath a raised brow.

Dan cleared his throat. "I'm not going to pretty it up for you, Meghan. Your career is in jeopardy. Sales—well, they aren't good."

"You need to concentrate on your image," Judy said. "I'm sure that doesn't come as a surprise to you. Duncan's been telling you that for years."

Meghan's stomach dropped at the mention of her former manager. He was doing his best to tell his side of the story to anyone who'd listen as to why they'd parted ways. True to form, his version of the events was more fiction than fact.

"Duncan is the one who's largely responsible for the state of my image, ma'am," Meghan said, willing herself to stay calm, forcing aside the memory of the way he'd leaked decades-old nude photos of her to the press. "And I can assure you, I am seeking new—better—management."

Dan cleared his throat. "We'd hate to have to drop you from the label." He stared at her for a few long moments and then stood. "We'll be in touch."

The two of them left Meghan alone in the room, contemplating whether any of this was even worth it anymore.

The flight back to Sweethaven had been turbulent. Fitting, since her entire trip to Nashville had been turbulent. She hadn't expected the meeting to go well, but she also hadn't planned on hearing she was in danger of being dropped from the label. While she'd done a lot of soul-searching the past few months about what was really important, Meghan didn't want to lose her career.

After all the money she'd made them, how could they just throw her away without a second chance?

Who was she kidding? This was business. Things like loyalty had nothing to do with it.

Meghan sighed and unbuckled her seat belt, thankful to see Lake Michigan out the window. So many years the lake had haunted her dreams, but she'd finally come to terms with it. Now, it was a welcome and familiar sight.

Nick and the kids waited for her in the airport, an even more welcome and familiar sight.

The twins ran to her, and she was greeted by bear hugs and laughter.

"We missed you, Mama," Nadia said, throwing her arms around Meghan's neck.

No matter how much she loved her career, she knew she'd made the right choice coming home to her family. In that moment, there was nowhere else she wanted to be—maybe giving up life as a celebrity wouldn't be so bad. She smiled and squeezed both of her children and then turned her attention to her husband, whose lazy grin warmed her all the way to her toes.

"How'd it go?" Nick said.

She shook her head as he picked up her suitcase, and she and the twins followed him to the car.

"That well, huh?"

She didn't want to think about Nashville or Duncan or stuffy music executives or poor sales. She'd much rather pretend for a little while that everything was just as it should be, but how often were things as they should be?

As they drove back to their little yellow cottage on the lake, the twins happily chattering in the backseat, Meghan stared out the window, and a feeling of grief washed over her.

"Maybe I'm just done," she said.

Nick glanced at her. "What do you mean?"

"I mean, I've had a good run, but I don't know if you can have everything. I think you either have a family or you have a career. How does anyone do both?"

"People do it all the time."

"Duncan is turning them all against me, Nick." She sighed. "I had three meetings yesterday and in each one I was told that I'm too much of a 'wild card.' Which is exactly what he used to say to me." She could still recall the last time she'd spoken to him, days after she found out he'd leaked the photos of her and stirred up so much trouble in her personal life.

He'd called wanting to explain himself, but Meghan wouldn't hear it.

"Publicity is publicity. No matter what you think, those photos sold albums," he'd said.

"Those photos could've ruined me, not to mention what they did to my kids. How could you do that without telling me?"

Duncan scoffed. "I did a lot of things without telling you, Meghan, and it never mattered to you before."

"It matters to me now." Meghan resisted the urge to hang up on him.

"You know you can't do this without me," he said. "I rebuilt your career. I'm the reason anyone even knows who you are."

"I can't trust you, and I can't work with someone I can't trust."

"You'll regret this, Meghan."

When she hung up, her stomach twisted in a knot. "He'll ruin me," she told Nick.

"We won't let him."

But now, with a failed trip to Nashville under her belt, she wasn't so sure.

"What is it you need exactly?" Nick asked as he turned off of Main Street and headed out into the country where their cottage hid.

"Publicity. The new album isn't selling very well, and I need to fix the damage I did by going off grid when we were, you know, going through our mess. They're talking about dropping me from the label."

Nick stilled. "Would a nationally broadcast television show help?"

Meghan laughed. "Yeah, but I don't have any contacts in television. Duncan had all of them."

"I know a guy."

She glanced at her husband, who kept his eyes on the road.

"Nick? What aren't you telling me?"

"Do you remember the Miller house? The one with the outbuildings and the big yellow barn?"

Meghan nodded.

"A guy from LA bought it a couple of years ago—said he wanted a place to get away from everything."

Meghan frowned. "So he picked Sweethaven?"

"He's from the Midwest. Reminded him of home." Nick looked over his shoulder before changing lanes. "I did some work for him on the house. He liked it and gave me his card. Said if I ever needed anything, to call." Nick shot her a look. "I called."

Silence hung between them and Meghan tried to make sense of what Nick said. "What did he say?"

Nick laughed. "I pitched the idea of a Christmas special. A Sweethaven Christmas with Meghan Rhodes."

"I'm sure he jumped right on that."

He looked at her and smiled.

"He liked it?"

"He loved it."

Meghan tried not to get too excited. Nick had never done any managing for her—why should she expect that he'd understand how to put together a deal like this?

"Said he's a huge fan of yours and that he wants to talk to you about it. He'll be here tomorrow."

Meghan's heart sped up.

"I hope it's okay. I could tell by the tone of your voice the other night on the phone that it wasn't going well."

Meghan tossed a look over her shoulder at the twins. Finn glanced at her and grinned what she called his "hammy grin."

"Maybe I could be your stand-in manager for a while."

"You and I working together? I'm not sure that's a great idea." Nick was a contractor—not a music industry mogul.

"I run a very successful business, which I built from nothing."

True.

"And is there anyone you trust more?" He pulled the car to a stop in their driveway, then turned to face her. "I think having someone who really is on your side is the most important thing here, Meg." He lifted a hand to her cheek and brushed his thumb across it.

"No kissing!" Finn yelled from the backseat, where he now sat with his hands over his eyes.

Meghan brought her gaze to Nick's and smiled. "All right, Nick Rhodes. Let's see what you're made of."

# FIVE

*Adele*

Thanksgiving had been one of Adele's favorite holidays when Teddy was alive. In recent years, it had been one of the more depressing holidays. Luke would come over to humor her, but the table in her dining room was meant to be filled with family—and seeing it nearly empty had been one of the saddest sights she'd known.

But this year, finally, she'd have a full house again.

Excitement washed over her at the thought of it. A day that combined her love of family with her love of food had surely been crafted specifically for her.

Adele had pulled out all the stops this year, and her body was paying for it. Two straight days of cooking, cleaning and decorating and she had the spread she'd imagined. A traditional turkey dinner with all the fixin's and, of course, an array of desserts she couldn't wait to share. Apple, pecan and pumpkin pies, all made from scratch, along with a Texas sheet cake for the chocolate lovers.

Her reasons weren't purely about the joy of entertaining, though. She considered this special day research for a new project—a dream-come-true project she could hardly wait to tell everyone about.

She smiled at the thought of it.

Just before her guests were set to arrive, she stood back and admired the table. Tears sprang to her eyes as she thought about how different this Thanksgiving would be than it had been in the years past. She had her family back, and soon her home would be filled with the sounds of laughter, conversation and the giggles of her grandchildren.

"Thank You, Lord," she said out loud, trying to untie the knot in her throat. "I am so blessed."

The door sprang open, signaling the start of the holiday, and she knew she wouldn't get a moment to stop and breathe until the last person walked out the door tonight.

And that was just fine with her.

Campbell and Luke arrived with Meghan and Nick close behind. Her heart filled at the sight of them—her family, all together under one roof. She kissed Finn and Nadia, who ran upstairs to play in Meghan's old room where many of their toys now lived.

"We'll call you down for dinner soon," Meghan called after them.

"Tom and Lila may show up," Luke told her. "Can we set a couple of extra places just in case?"

Adele nodded and handed him the place settings, deciding not to ask any questions.

When Jane walked in, Adele pulled her into a tight hug. "Darlin', that poem you read at the service was just beautiful. Always makes me tear up."

Jane refused her eyes.

"Never mind the rest of it," Adele said. "Bet it felt a lot worse to you than it did to the rest of us."

Jane shook her head and looked like she might cry. "Excuse me," she said, rushing toward the bathroom.

Campbell frowned. "What's wrong?"

Adele wouldn't allow Jane's humiliation to become a topic of conversation—not today. "Oh, it's nothin'. Would you mind giving me a hand in the kitchen?"

Campbell glanced toward the bathroom, then back at Adele. "Of course. Whatever you need."

Before they could get started, Tom and Lila arrived. Campbell's face fell.

"What's wrong?" Adele asked.

Campbell shook her head. "Dinner with Lila's family was, shall we say, tense?" She moved toward the couple in the entryway, and Adele followed.

"You okay?" Campbell asked.

Lila nodded. "I'm so sorry you had to witness the Adler family dysfunction." She hugged Campbell, then took off her coat. Lila, usually the picture of beauty, looked tired. Maybe the pregnancy—or her mother—had worn her out.

Her girls needed some TLC, and she was prepared to give it. Nothing she loved more than comforting the ones she loved.

Lila met Adele's eyes and smiled, but her eyes stayed sad. "Thank you for letting us join last minute. We picked up a pumpkin pie." She took it from Tom.

Adele raised a brow.

Lila smiled. "It's for Mugsy. Poor dog looks pathetic out back."

Adele laughed. "You knew better than to bring a store-bought pumpkin pie into my house for Thanksgiving." She squeezed Lila, then Tom. "And you're always welcome here, you know that. Especially on Thanksgiving."

Lila swiped a tear from her cheek.

"Come on, now. Everything should be ready." Adele led them into the dining room where Jane now stood between Meghan and Graham. Adele had to choke back tears at the sight. Only a few short months ago these two old friends weren't speaking. The accident that claimed Jane's son's life had been a wall between them—between all of them—and finally, the Lord had answered the deepest prayers of Adele's heart and brought them all together again.

Could she get through grace without tears?

"I know we have a pastor among us, but I'd like to offer thanks today," Adele said as they all took hands. "I can't tell you in just a few words how much you all mean to me, but having you here at my table to celebrate this holiday blesses me more than I can say." Her throat tightened.

"We love you too, Mama," Meghan said and squeezed her hand.

Adele nodded. "And help us to remember to thank You for every precious day. Not just on Thanksgiving, but throughout the year."

A chorus of "amens" flitted through the room.

Adele waited a few seconds until everyone quieted. "All of you—my family—are such blessings to me. Jane, your sweet spirit and kind heart are a welcome gift in a world of people who are too focused on themselves. Lila, I am so thankful for your quick wit and the beauty you bring to my life." She glanced at Campbell. "And we're so happy we've added you to our family. It's like having a piece of your mama right here at the table with us—only even more special because we've gotten to enjoy Sweethaven through your eyes."

She squeezed Meghan's hand. "And you. My prodigal daughter." Adele closed her eyes. How could she explain all that she felt? Her girl was home—where she belonged—and her heart didn't have room to contain the emotion.

"It's okay, Mama," Meghan said. "I know."

Adele looked at her through clouded eyes. "I'm proud of you." She wiped her cheeks dry.

"You know the food's getting cold, right, Ma?" Luke winked at her from across the table.

Adele gasped. "Oh my stars, yes. Sit. Eat."

"And you can say great things about me before dessert," Luke said.

The room filled with laughter and chatter and the sounds of clinking forks on her good plates, and Adele closed her eyes to let her senses take it all in.

She never wanted to forget that moment.

After everyone had tasted the food, the compliments started rolling in, and Adele not only relished them but made mental notes on what people liked.

"These potatoes are perfect, Adele. They're so creamy. This pregnant woman could eat a mixing bowl full of them," Lila said, scooping up another helping.

"Thanks, darlin'," Adele said. "I am quite proud of those. Me-maw showed me how to make them when I was a girl, you know."

Amused glances crisscrossed the table.

"What are y'all giggling about?"

Jane smiled. "We love to hear you talk about Me-maw, Adele."

"Every time we eat." Meghan's tone was sarcastic.

Adele raised a brow at the lot of them. "Is that how it is, girls? I thought you'd outgrown makin' fun of me, but I see I was wrong."

"I like your Me-maw stories, Adele," Campbell said.

Lila threw a little piece of a roll across the table at her. "You kiss-up."

Adele laughed. "She's my favorite, girls. Campbell is the only one who gets dessert."

"You know we're just teasing, Mama, but you really should stop giving Me-maw all the credit. We know most of these recipes are yours."

"I guess that's true." Me-maw had taught her the basics, but Adele had tweaked and changed every recipe to get it just right.

"And I've got some related news, I suppose." She watched as all eyes turned her way. The excitement inside her had been bubbling like a geyser about to explode. She wanted to wait for the perfect time to tell them, and here they were, all together over plates full of her food—it didn't get much more perfect than that.

"Mama, you look like a fox in the henhouse. What's the big secret?" Meghan laughed and scooped up a bite of creamed corn.

Adele held their attention for a few moments longer, letting her excitement spill over and build up their own. "Well," she said, "I've been asked to write a cookbook."

"A cookbook?" Jane squealed. "Of course you have! It will be so wonderful."

"Mama, that's fabulous," Meghan said. "How on earth did you keep this to yourself? How long have you known?"

"Well, it was just the darndest thing," Adele said. "I brought a few cobblers over to the café last week."

"You knew about this?" Meghan shot Luke an annoyed look.

Luke shrugged. "I just do what I'm told."

"And I told him not to breathe a word. I wanted to tell y'all myself. Anyway, I plopped the cobblers down on the counter and this woman was sittin' there, having a cup of coffee. When I took the lid off, she asked me what I put in it, so I told her."

"You didn't tell her everything," Jane said.

"Of course not. I don't give away all my secrets." Adele laughed. "But I told her enough."

Luke jumped in. "So the two of them sat there for *two hours* at my counter rambling on and on about cooking and baking and spices I've never even heard of. I couldn't get rid of them."

"Oh, stop. You were eavesdroppin' and you know it."

"'Course I was, but it wasn't easy. You guys sounded like a couple of cackling hens." He imitated the two women in two high-pitched voices at breakneck speed.

"So who was she?" Lila asked.

"Turns out, she is an editor, and after our conversation she asked me to submit some recipes. She said she's been looking for a down-home cookbook."

Jane gasped. "It's just so wonderful. God really set you up, Adele." She smiled.

"I think you're right."

"So you sent her your recipes?" Meghan asked.

"Oh no, darlin'. No handwritten recipe was going to do justice to the magic I can create in the kitchen. I invited her over to sample my best work."

"So, why isn't she here today?" Campbell said.

"This is my preaudition. I need y'all to tell me your favorite dishes so I can create a menu and just knock her socks off."

The chatter began to build as they all recounted their favorite dishes.

"Braised pork ribs."

"Mama's meat loaf. That has to be in there."

"Strawberry rhubarb pie with homemade ice cream."

Each person had a vote, but Adele couldn't make out who was saying what. "Just wait now." She held up her hands. "I'm going to pass around scratch paper for everyone to write a favorite dish. This'll be a group effort."

"I just know she's going to love whatever you make her, Adele. That cookbook deal is as good as done." It was good to see Jane smile. And Adele knew she'd find support in this group.

Bless their hearts.

She stood and found a stack of scratch paper and passed paper around the table. "Now, I might need some taste testers. I want to make sure every recipe is perfect. You know most of what I do is from my memory." Adele laughed. "And that's not the most reliable source."

"Adele, I am happy to taste test anything you put in front of me," Campbell said. "I'm so excited for you."

Luke stood, scratch paper in hand. "I think I need to think over my options while watching the football game." He glanced at Graham and Tom, who both stood and followed him into the living room where seconds later the television blared.

Finn scooted off his chair next and handed Adele a piece of paper with a picture he'd drawn. Adele stared at the big circle with dark, colored-in dots on it.

"Is this what I think it is, Finn?"

He smiled. "I like everything you make, Me-maw, but you know my favorite."

"Monster cookies."

"Do you have some here?"

"Of course I do," Adele said.

"Not until later, though, Finn." Meghan stood and started clearing the table. The others followed suit and with their troops mobilized, they'd cleaned the kitchen and the dishes before Adele had a chance to push her way into the kitchen.

She couldn't deny it was nice to have help on the back end.

Once they finished, the girls returned to the table, each with her own dessert selection, all still buzzing about the opportunity in front of Adele.

"Was it something you always wanted to do?" Lila asked.

Adele shrugged. "I guess I never really planned for it, but I admit, it's got me very excited." She walked over to the bookshelf. "I was thinking about it this week and I remembered I used this little journal to keep all my recipes safe when Me-maw was teaching me how to cook." She pulled the small journal from the shelf and brought it back to the table.

"I've never seen this before," Meghan said, taking it in her hands. The book had been rubber-banded together to hold all the stray papers and note cards inside.

Meghan removed the band and opened the book. In her hands, it looked frail and old, and it was, she supposed, though she hadn't thought so until that moment.

"Mama, there are pictures in here—and handwritten notes." Meghan turned the pages gingerly as the girls leaned in for a peek.

"This is a scrapbook," Jane said, pointing to a black-and-white photo of Adele and her me-maw.

"I suppose it is," Adele said. "I never thought of it that way. Me-maw taught me everything I know about cooking and baking. We'd spend hours in her little kitchen coming up with all kinds of new things to try." Adele smiled at the thought of it.

Me-maw had been a soft-spoken woman who used food to tell her story. As a girl, Adele had loved spending time with her grandmother, right there in that same Sweethaven kitchen. "Things were different back then," Adele said. "Sweethaven was different."

Her thoughts spun backward in time, landing squarely on The Commons, the original Byron Colby Barn, before the fire. The town council hosted dances there every Friday night, and Adele could still remember the first time she'd been asked to dance. It felt like yesterday and a lifetime ago all at once.

"Who's this?" Lila snagged a small black-and-white photo with a scalloped white frame around it. She held it up and the memories rushed back. *Henry.*

Her parents hadn't approved. Henry was a good boy, but Adele was young—too young to be thinking about boys. At least that's what her parents believed.

But Adele had a hard time following the rules when it came to Henry. She might have been young, but her feelings were real, whether her father wanted to believe it or not. "Adele, you're blushing," Campbell said. "He's cute. Who is he?"

"Henry Marshall." At the mention of his name, Adele let the nostalgia of those days wash over her, remembering what it was like to be fifteen, feeling a flutter in her heart as she awkwardly moved across the dance floor in Henry's arms. "I suppose you could say he was my first love."

Knowing glances ping-ponged around the table, and Adele noticed. "Stop it now, girls, let's not romanticize this. We were just kids."

"Sometimes love is never stronger than when it's your first love," Jane said. "Graham was my first love and I still feel all sappy about him."

Adele brushed her off.

"Why haven't you told me about him before, Mama?" Meghan said, taking the photo from Lila.

"There was nothing to tell. Like I said, we were kids. We grew up." They didn't need to know all the reasons she and Henry didn't work out.

"It looks like you guys were in a band," Campbell said, her eyes fixed on the little book. "I didn't know you were a singer."

"It was a long time ago," Adele said. "A lifetime."

"Mama was a brilliant singer. She only stopped because she got pregnant with me," Meghan said.

"That's not true. It was an exhausting lifestyle. I still don't know how you do it," Adele said, her memory fluttering around. She'd loved the stage once upon a time. Loved the way the crowd responded to her. Loved singing as Henry backed her up on the piano.

"Whatever happened to him?" Jane asked.

Adele shrugged and took the photo. She ran a finger over Henry's face. "I don't know."

She'd wondered about Henry a lot over the years, but especially since Teddy passed away. She wouldn't trade her years with Teddy for anything in the world, but in her lonely moments, she thought of Henry. What had become of the boy she'd loved all those years ago?

"We could find him, I bet." Campbell's words jarred her back to reality.

"We definitely could. Let's look online." Meghan pulled her phone from her pocket and began moving her fingers across it.

"What? No." Adele's nerves kicked up like leaves on a windy autumn day.

"Adele, you're blushing again," Lila said, exchanging a glance with Campbell and smiling.

"This boy was obviously important to you. Let's just see if we can find him," Meghan said, not looking up from her phone.

Adele struggled for an argument and then settled on the truth. "I don't want to know." What she meant was, *I don't want to know what my life could've been.* There was something painful in the wandering of her memories.

"Surely you must wonder about him," Lila said.

"Of course, but I've imagined a whole beautiful life for Henry. What if he fell on hard times or worse, what if he's gone?" Adele sighed. "I know too many people who've been taken from this earth too soon. I like believing Henry's still out there, living it up and laughing that laugh of his."

Jane pushed the open journal in front of her. "Adele, this boy was important to you." Adele glanced down at the pages of her own handwriting surrounding an old photo of her and Henry at the Country Fair Dance in the Commons. The whole town had gathered for the traditional fall festivities—tourists often returned to enjoy the changing colors and cool temperatures of autumn in the little town. The dance was the final event of the weekend. "What if he's alone out there? You two could rekindle what you had all those years ago."

"Girls, you're romanticizing this. It's not that simple. There were reasons Henry and I didn't end up together." Adele hated those reasons. Hated thinking that she'd hurt Henry. At a time when he needed her most.

"Here. I think I found him. Henry Marshall, right? Lives in Grand Falls." Meghan looked up, turning the phone around to show the screen.

Adele gasped. "Grand Falls? That's only an hour away."

Meghan wagged her eyebrows. "Shall we pay him a visit?"

Adele grabbed her phone and looked at the page in front of her, then pulled it back as her eyes adjusted to the small words. "What is this? How'd you find him so easily?"

"It's Facebook, Mama. You want to set up a page?"

"What on earth would I do with a Facebook page?"

"Maybe rekindle an old romance?" Lila grinned.

"You girls are out of your minds." But as Adele stared at the photo on Henry's Facebook page, she couldn't hide her smile. He was still so handsome, though his hair had gone white and he'd bulked up a bit. She tried to pull her eyes from his image, but it drew her in, just like he always had.

*What kind of life did you have, Henry Marshall?*

Adele blinked back tears that caught her by surprise. How could she be so emotional over a man she hadn't seen in decades? She didn't know him anymore.

"You have a computer. What do you have to lose?" Jane nodded toward the old PC that Adele hadn't turned on in a month.

"I got that because Luke didn't need it anymore. He thought I could use it for the store." Adele scoffed. She had no idea what to do with it. She had someone who did her books for her, and she'd never found another reason to have a computer, yet there it sat.

"You have it all hooked up and ready to go. And you'll have to be on it a lot to write that cookbook. What do you think you're going to do, write it with pen and paper?"

She looked at Meghan, whose raised brows told her that her daughter's question was not rhetorical.

"You're such a smarty-pants," Adele said.

Meghan hopped up and flipped on the computer. It sounded like an old vacuum cleaner. Next she turned toward Adele and held up her phone.

"Smile, Mama."

"What are you—"

Before she could get her hand in front of her face, Meghan had snapped a photo. Moments later, it popped up on the computer screen and she'd been signed up for an account on that blasted Web site.

Seconds after that, Meghan announced she'd sent a "friend request" to Henry.

"I don't even know what that means," Adele said.

"It's okay, Mama, we're here to bring you into this century."

Adele felt like she'd just lost control of her own life.

"You girls are too much," Adele said. "What am I supposed to do now?"

Jane smiled. "Now, you wait."

"What am I waiting for?"

"For him to accept your friend request and write on your wall," Campbell said.

"My wall? What in the world? You girls are going to make a fool out of me," Adele said, peering over Meghan's shoulder.

"Once you get the hang of it, you'll be as addicted as the rest of us," Campbell said.

"Right, and then you'll feel like a teenager all over again, waiting for the boy you like to call you on the phone." Meghan smiled.

Adele sighed. These girls had just turned her whole world upside-down and they didn't even realize it. She took another peek at the computer screen.

Now, she waited.

And waiting wasn't her strong suit.

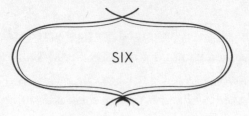

SIX

*Lila*

Days passed, and in spite of all efforts to try to forget what had happened on Thanksgiving, Lila kept replaying her conversation with the blonde woman over and over.

"You seem lost in thought," Tom said. The two of them sat in the three-season room, supposedly to enjoy a quiet cup of coffee, but Lila's mind was making too much noise.

She sat, face free of makeup and still wearing pajamas and a robe—something she never would've done even a year ago. How was it that nearly losing her marriage had brought a new comfort between her and Tom?

"That woman from the other day," Lila said.

Tom's face lit up. He'd asked her repeatedly what was bothering her, but something had kept her from sharing. Before she could explain, Mama walked in and sat across from her on the sofa.

"Lila, I hope this isn't how you're going to spend the rest of your pregnancy," she said, taking a drink of coffee.

Lila smacked the words away in her mind, willing them not to seep in.

She grabbed Mama's glare and decided to challenge her. Her pregnancy really was making her bolder. "Mama, do you know who that woman was?"

Lila detected only the slightest bit of surprise. "What woman?" She took another drink, holding Lila's gaze.

Lila wrapped her robe around her tighter, remembering the few times she'd stood up to Mama. It never ended well. "You know who I'm talking about."

Mama waved her hand as though she was swatting an imaginary fly. "You know your father."

Yes, she did. But the blonde didn't seem like Daddy's other mistresses, and Lila couldn't figure out why one of his mistresses would show up at their Thanksgiving dinner. Besides, there was something desperate in her eyes—Lila almost felt sorry for her.

But surely she couldn't have been the first mistress to fall in love with Daddy. How had her family escaped the emotion of the others?

One glance at her mother and pity washed over her. Mama had put up with Daddy's indiscretions for her entire marriage—but had she ever come face-to-face with one of his conquests before? And in such a public way? In spite of all her shortcomings, Lila didn't want to crush her mother.

"Lila, you need to learn here and now how to tell the difference between a legitimate problem and a woman who will make up lies to get at our money. Your father is a successful man. This isn't the first time some woman has shown up with a ridiculous claim."

Lila studied her mother. Had other women crawled out of the woodwork over the years?

"What kind of claim? What does she want?"

Mama shifted. "I think you should spend less time worrying about that woman and more time taking care of yourself, Lila," Mama said, picking up the newspaper and scanning the front page. "Think about Tom. Don't give him a reason to let his eyes start to wander. Am I right, Tom?" She glanced at Tom with a raised brow.

Tom shifted in his seat, then turned to Mama. "I think she's more beautiful today than she was the day I met her."

Mama stared at him for a long minute and then burst out laughing. "But what about the extra pounds creeping on?"

"She's pregnant, Cilla," Tom said.

"Her face isn't pregnant," Mama said with another wave of her hand.

Tom squeezed Lila's shoulder, but the damage had been done. Lila stood.

"Oh, Lila, don't get emotional. You know I only want what's best for you."

Neither Tom nor Lila spoke, and finally Mama sighed. "You're so sensitive these days." She set the newspaper down, stood, then walked out, leaving Lila stunned silent. She wrapped her arms tighter around herself, plopped back in her seat, and blinked back fresh tears.

Tom knelt in front of her, pulling her into his arms. "Don't let her get to you, sweetheart," he said. "Do you see what she just did?"

Lila shook her head.

"You were about to bring up something humiliating to her—so she turned all the attention back to you. And she's wrong. I'll always think you're beautiful. You're carrying our child." He swiped her tears from her cheeks and smiled at her.

All of Mama's spite threatened to change the way she felt about herself—to turn this pregnancy into something other than joyful, but Tom loved her, she could see it in his eyes.

"Maybe we should go back to Georgia," she said.

"I thought you wanted to spend the week here." He propped himself up on the coffee table but kept his hands on her knees.

"I did, but not like this." Lila looked around the lake house. Adele's house had been more familiar and comforting than her own parents' house.

Tom sighed. "I've got a flight out of Chicago in a few days. Wouldn't make much sense to fly back to Georgia just to fly right back here."

She frowned. He had a point. But the thought of being cooped up with Mama for even another hour filled her with anxiety. She inhaled deeply to calm her quickening pulse.

"Here's a crazy idea." A smile spread across his face. "Why don't we find our own cottage?"

"In Sweethaven?"

"We shouldn't let your parents ruin this place for us. I want our child to spend summers here, in the place where we fell in love. Don't you?"

Lila nodded. "Ever since Suzanne died, I realized how important this town is. It's made me slow down and appreciate what I had here." She let her thoughts turn to her earliest memories on the beach down by the lake. Mama would sit in her beach chair under the umbrella and Lila would run around with Jane and some of the other girls, digging in the sand, making castles and venturing out into the water. It had been a simple, idyllic way to grow up. She wanted that for her own child.

That, minus the entitlement.

"What do you think? We could spend the rest of the week looking," Tom said. "Let's just see what we find."

Lila smiled, warming to the idea. "I think having our own place, our own piece of Sweethaven, might be exactly what I need."

Tom leaned forward and kissed her. "And stop worrying about that mystery woman. Whoever she is, she's not your problem—she's your father's problem, and you don't need the extra stress right now." He folded the newspaper and stuck it under his arm. "I'm going to see what cottages I can find for sale."

He left her sitting there alone with the sinking feeling that this woman wasn't going away any time soon—and Lila had a feeling she wasn't in this for money.

This woman had come to expose the truth about her father. And Lila had half a mind to help her.

SEVEN

*Jane*

The humiliation of the Thanksgiving service hadn't even begun to dwindle, and if Jane could've come up with a valid reason, she would've left Sweethaven for home in Iowa Thanksgiving night. But she'd promised to meet Meghan for coffee, the girls planned a shopping trip, and Graham had made plans to spend a few days focusing on guy stuff with Sam.

Plus, she had lamented her embarrassment to Graham to the point where he and their children had announced they wanted to give her an early Christmas present: they loved her, but she didn't love herself, and they wanted her to stay in Sweethaven until Christmas to focus on her health.

"What's so crazy about that?" he'd said. "I think you should do it."

"What about the kids, Graham?"

He raised a brow. "You don't think I can handle a few weeks alone with the kids?"

She scrunched her nose at him. "I really don't."

He laughed. "We'll come up on the weekends. You need to do this, hon. For yourself. I want you to be healthy, and getting rid of distractions is important right now."

She'd thanked him a hundred times since, and while she knew she'd miss her family, a part of her was grateful for the chance to tackle this problem once and for all.

She smiled at the thought.

The Christmas decorations had already come out, and as she walked toward the café, Jane saw a group of people hanging lights and ornaments on a tree in the Square, just in front of the gazebo. December in Sweethaven promised a certain kind of magic for young children who still believed in Santa Claus—and adults who wished they did. The Luminary Walk, the lighting of the Christmas tree, and the Christmas Concert in the park were just the beginning of the holiday season. It had been years since Jane had spent a Christmas in the little town, but as she watched the antique light posts receive their oversize red bows and greenery, Jane longed to let that magic fill her once again.

Inside the café, she waved at Luke, busy with a customer, and perused the restaurant for any sign of Meghan. Nothing.

Her mind whirled back to the last time they were supposed to meet for coffee. Meghan hadn't shown, instead leaving Jane to sit alone looking more pathetic with every check of her watch.

*Please don't let her do that again.*

She spotted a booth in the back, near the fireplace, but as she made her way through the maze of chairs, she heard her name off to the right. She turned, expecting to find Meghan, but instead spotted Lori sitting with two other women. Perfectly groomed and color coordinated, all three of them hurried their eyes away from Jane, but not before Jane heard the words *How embarrassing* escape Lori's lips.

Her face heated and she looked back toward the booth, but someone had slipped into it, leaving no other empty seats. As Jane turned around, a small boy skidded in front of her. She tripped and nearly toppled over him.

"Oh, I'm sorry," Jane said, her face hot with distress.

A burst of laughter from Lori's table echoed out, and Jane apologized three more times to the mother of the young boy. Even though if he'd been sitting in his seat, she never would've tripped.

A table opened up near the front of the café, so Jane rushed to it, plopped down on the chair and stared out the window—away from the critical eyes of the Sweethaven population.

"You okay?" Luke stood beside her, tall and handsome like he'd just stepped off a movie screen.

Jane sighed. "I seem to be something of a mess lately." She looked away.

"You meeting Meghan?" He sat down across from her. If he was taking pity on her, it made her want to give him a hug.

Jane nodded. "I hope she shows up this time."

"She's right there," Luke said, nodding out the window where Meghan was handing a notebook and pen back to a group of teenage girls.

"I told her she could come to my house, but she insisted on getting out."

"I think she likes the attention," Luke said, laughing. "It's partly why she became a singer."

Jane shook her head and watched as Meghan entered the café. "A part I'll never understand. I hate having people stare at me."

Heads turned toward Meghan as she opened the door, her face half-covered by oversize sunglasses, yet still recognizable as Sweethaven's most famous resident.

Maybe the people in the café would forget all about Jane when they saw Meghan Rhodes sitting with her. Meghan waved when she saw her and rushed over to the table.

"You're in my seat, little brother," she said as Luke stood.

"He felt sorry for me," Jane said. "Sitting here alone."

Luke put a hand on Jane's shoulder. "That's crazy talk and you know it. I'll send Delcy over to take your order."

"Thanks, Lukey." Jane flashed a smile and tried to remember the people who really mattered in her life weren't the ones who cared if she broke a chair or tripped over a little kid in the middle of a crowded restaurant.

"You look upset," Meghan said, taking her coat off.

Jane shrugged. "It's nothing."

"I heard about the chair." Meghan's eyes were filled with empathy. Not pity. She'd missed her old friend. How thankful she was to have mended fences with Meghan after all they'd been through. "Once I was onstage and the heel of my shoe broke in the middle of a song, and I slipped and fell flat on my butt."

Jane gasped. "Were you okay?"

"Hurt my pride pretty good." Meghan laughed. A little girl with long red pigtails walked over to their table with a small notebook.

"Mrs. Rhodes, can I have your autograph?" she said, her blue eyes wide. The girl's mother stood off to the side, holding a fluffy pink coat.

"Of course, sweetheart. What's your name?"

"Emily." The little girl smiled a toothless grin.

"Emily, do you know my friend Mrs. Atkins has a daughter named Emily? It's one of our favorite names." Meghan signed the paper and handed it back to the girl.

"Thank you." Emily walked back to her mom and showed her the notebook, the grin on her face lighting up the room.

"You just made her whole day," Jane said.

Meghan smiled. "You still look upset."

"It's hard, Meg. Being the big girl. I've always been the big girl. It's just frustrating."

Meghan frowned. "That's not true, Janie."

"Yes, it is. Don't you remember junior high?"

"Sure, but I also remember high school. You were so thin. And at your wedding? Tiny."

Jane shook her head. "I've never been tiny."

Meghan's brows shot up. "Do me a favor. Go home and find some old pictures from high school and college and tell me honestly if you see a heavy girl in any of them."

Jane felt relieved when Delcy appeared beside them with two plates. "A grilled chicken salad for Jane and the pulled pork sandwich with french fries for Meghan. Can I get you anything else?"

"No thanks, Delc," Meghan said. "Tell Luke this is on him."

Delcy smiled and headed back toward the kitchen.

"How can you eat like that?" Jane stared at Meghan's huge plate of food.

"I have a fast metabolism," she said. "And a personal trainer. You should come work out with me sometime."

Jane scoffed. "I've had all the embarrassment I can handle for one week, thank you very much."

After lunch, Jane left with Meghan's suggestion still stuck in her mind.

Most of Jane's old photos and mementos were back in Cedar Rapids. She ended up wandering across the street and into the Sweethaven Art Gallery where Campbell was hanging new art. "You getting ready for Christmas?"

"Sure am. I figured some holiday-themed art would be perfect." Campbell smiled.

"This place sure does suit you," Jane said, looking around. At the center of the room, their old scrapbook sat on display—part of Campbell's first showing, "The Treasures of Sweethaven."

Jane walked toward it, trying to visualize the high school photos she'd find in the pages.

"Do you mind if I take a peek at this, Cam?"

Campbell followed her. "Of course not. It's yours. I suppose we should figure out a way to get it back to all of you."

Jane thought about how they'd divided up the pages when Campbell's mom left Sweethaven all those years ago. Pregnant and scared to tell any of them, she'd vanished without an explanation. They'd divided the pages among the four of them because it seemed like the fair thing to do. But now, seeing it in its entirety again, Jane couldn't imagine it any other way.

"I think it's found its new home," Jane said. She took a chunk of pages—the ones they'd created in middle school—and flipped them over until she stumbled upon one of the layouts they made the summer after their sophomore year.

Campbell leaned in closer and looked at the page. At the center was an enlarged photo of the four of them at the beach—the same photo they took every year. They'd glued it onto a blue background with Suzanne's hand-drawn waves filling the lower half.

"You guys are all so beautiful," Campbell said.

Jane nodded, staring at her sixteen-year-old self. "We were, weren't we?"

She wouldn't have believed it, but Meghan was right. Jane had spent her entire life feeling overweight and out of place, but looking at this photo, she didn't see "Fat Jane."

Sure, she wasn't as slim as her friends, but she was a far cry from overweight. In fact, she wasn't all that much bigger than Meghan.

Had she only thought of herself that way because she'd been comparing herself to other people all these years?

"You look upset, Jane," Campbell said.

Jane closed the scrapbook. "No, I'm fine. Thanks for letting me look through it. I won't keep you."

Campbell looked puzzled, but Jane couldn't give any more explanation. Instead, she walked out into the brisk November air. As she walked down Main Street toward her car, she caught a glimpse of herself in the storefront windows. As she reached the darkened windows of an empty building, Jane stopped and stared for a moment, sad at what she'd allowed herself to become.

She'd gained weight in the aftermath of Alex's death. One sad day after another, she'd found her comfort in ice cream, cookies and cakes. And now, her body protested her choices.

*If she wasn't born to be fat*, she had to wonder, *could she get healthy again?* Could she change the way she looked at food? Or was she doomed to accept what she'd created for herself?

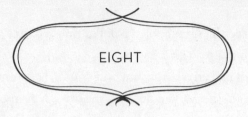

EIGHT

*Lila*

Only days after Thanksgiving, the streets of Sweethaven had been transformed into a winter wonderland. The forecast called for snow that week, and as a chill came over her, Lila remembered why she chose to live in Georgia.

Still, the oversize red bows and evergreen wreaths that had been affixed to Sweethaven's old-fashioned lampposts had their own charm. The stores on Main Street had begun the annual ritual of painting their storefronts or creating holiday displays for passersby to admire. They'd be judged as part of the town's Christmas festivities. Lila shook her head when she saw some of the attempts.

"Some people should not try to decorate," Lila said, protective of her profession. Not everyone had the talent or skill to bring a space to life.

Mama hitched her purse up higher on her shoulder. "Truer words were never spoken."

Lila hadn't wanted to spend the morning with Mama, but the guilt had been too much to take. Now, she had a bag full of knick-knacks she didn't need and at least another hour keeping the woman company. "The tree lighting is tonight. Are you going?" Lila asked as they carried their shopping bags down Main Street.

Mama shrugged. "I'm not one for sentiment, you know that."

"Even on Christmas?"

Mama scoffed. "It's not Christmas yet."

Lila refused to let Mama's bah-humbug attitude get the best of her. She only had a few more days in Sweethaven, and she didn't intend to let Mama ruin them for her.

This year, she wanted to let every ounce of Christmas spirit warm her to the bone. Maybe her mother didn't like sentiment, but it had grown on Lila.

Shoppers scurried down the streets, stopping in the little boutiques to find unique gifts for their friends and loved ones. Lila thought of her friends. Each one deserved something special this year—a thank-you for coming back into her life. But Lila hadn't mastered the art of gift giving. She'd always been more of a receiver.

An image of a photo Campbell had taken of all five of them at Thanksgiving popped into her mind. If she could get a copy of that, she could do something wonderful with it for all of them. Have them printed on a canvas or get them framed. She smiled, knowing it was the perfect idea.

She glanced across the street and spotted Campbell through the windows of the art gallery.

"I should go say hi," she said, watching her.

Mama followed her eyes to the gallery, then stiffened. "I can't believe you, Lila."

Lila didn't meet her mother's eyes. Instead, she lifted her chin. "Mama, I've accepted what happened. It's in the past."

Mama stopped. "Darling, you've clearly forgotten who you are."

Lila bit back her response.

"What Tom did was unacceptable."

"It was a long time ago—before we were married." The hurt feelings sprang back to the surface, the ones she'd worked so hard to bury.

"He's been keeping this from you all these years, and by your accepting that girl, inviting her to Thanksgiving and having coffee with her—you're saying it's okay what he did."

Campbell caught Lila's eye from across the street and her face lit up. She waved and Lila lifted a weak hand to return the gesture.

"You're in a mess now, being pregnant and all," Mama said. "I just hope you put that man in his place." She walked into the Gingerbread House—Sweethaven's Christmas store, leaving Lila standing on the street alone.

She'd certainly never known Mama to put Daddy in his place. Didn't she realize what a hypocrite she was?

She looked up and spotted Campbell running across the street toward her. Too late to hide now. She blinked back the tears that had pooled in her eyes and forced a smile.

"I've learned when to recognize your fake smile, Lila," Campbell said as she stepped onto the sidewalk beside her.

"Is it that obvious?" Lila swiped away the tear that slid down her cheek.

"I'm sorry," Campbell said.

"I think my being pregnant has made her even colder than usual. If that's possible."

Campbell reached up and put a hand on Lila's arm. "Can I do anything?"

"Give me some courage?" Lila laughed, but another tear slid down her cheek.

"What would happen if you stood up to her?"

Years ago, Suzanne had asked her the same question.

Lila met Campbell's eyes and thought about what Mama had said—what Tom had done *was* unacceptable, but if he hadn't done it, this girl wouldn't be here. And she'd grown to love Campbell over the past few months. Lila looked away.

"I have to get back to the gallery, but if you need anything, stop in later. I'm there all day." She smiled.

Lila nodded. "Thank you." She took a deep breath. Walking into that store felt like walking into a den of hungry lions.

The smell of cinnamon greeted her as she stepped inside the Gingerbread House. Christmas ornaments and decorations filled the shelves. There was a section for tourists looking to commemorate a stay in Sweethaven, a section for the lovers of all things vintage, and baskets of garlands in every color. The store only existed over the holidays, but it was a Sweethaven favorite and had been quite successful at drawing tourists.

On a small table in the center of the store, they'd created a serve-yourself buffet of wassail and Christmas cookies. Lila scooted through the crowd, maneuvering her shopping bags out of the way of the other shoppers. She smiled "hellos" to a few familiar faces, keeping her eyes open for Mama. She discovered her in the corner, speaking to someone she couldn't see.

"Don't think you're going to get away with this, darling," Mama said. "Think about what I'm offering. And then leave."

Lila took a few steps to the left and saw the woman from the restaurant standing in front of Mama. Her eyes darted to Lila, drawing Mama's attention to her daughter. Mama turned back to the woman, looked her up and down and then turned and walked away. As she passed Lila, she said, "Come on, Lila."

Lila stared at the other woman. The look on her face was one Lila recognized from the mirror. Shame.

"Lila!" Mama stood yards away and commanded the attention of the entire store. Lila turned, read the look on Mama's face and followed her back out onto the street.

Mama hurried toward the car, walking a few feet in front of Lila. As Lila followed her, she couldn't help but glance back and notice the woman watching them go.

NINE

*Meghan*

From the second-story window, Meghan watched as Martin Gould pulled up to the house in a black Lexus. He wore jeans, dark-framed glasses, a button-down with a suit coat, and black Chuck Taylors. Very LA. She listened as Nick opened the front door and made small talk, no doubt waiting for her to decide if it was safe to come down.

Meghan hated that, thanks to Duncan, she now entered business relationships with instant distrust. Maybe that suspicious nature had been evident to the music execs in Nashville.

No one wanted to overcome it. She had to.

Nick and Martin sat in the living room, talking about a renovation project Martin had planned for the summer.

"I'd love to get a quote when you've got time," Martin said.

Meghan reminded herself that this man wasn't like the others—he was one of Nick's clients, and for that reason alone she needed to give him the benefit of the doubt. The last thing she wanted was to destroy any part of the business Nick had worked so hard to build.

"Ah, here she is," Nick said when she walked into the room. "Martin, this is my wife Meghan."

Martin stood and smiled. Either the man had never had a sip of coffee or he'd recently had his teeth whitened.

*Meghan, it doesn't matter. Focus on what he can do for you.*

Meghan shook his hand and then sat down on the couch next to her husband.

"I've been a fan of yours for many years," Martin said. "In fact, I tried to book you once before."

"You did?"

"Talked to your manager—Duncan, was it?"

Meghan nodded.

"It was a charity event in LA. He said you didn't do charity events."

Her face heated. "Of course I do charity events." At the moment she couldn't think of a single one. "Or, I would have." She stilled.

Martin leaned back. "Duncan painted you like 'the bad girl of country music.'"

Nick slid an arm around her, instantly reminding her to stay calm. She took a deep breath and forced a smile. "That's not who I am, sir."

Martin laughed. "And I'm not a 'sir.'"

She relaxed. "Fair enough."

"I'm intrigued by this idea you two have come up with. Tell me more about it."

"This is Nick's idea." Meghan glanced at him.

Martin raised a brow. "A master carpenter *and* a music manager? Is there anything you can't do?"

Nick laughed. Modest to a fault, Meghan's husband had never known how to take a compliment.

"Tell me more," Martin said.

"Sweethaven is a slice of Americana—the kind of quaint town we all romanticize."

Martin nodded. "It's why my wife and I bought a house here. There's nowhere else in the world like the Midwest. This place helps us unwind from the pressures of normal life."

"We want to share that Sweethaven magic with the rest of the world, especially now, during Christmas. And Meghan is the tour guide." Nick cleared his throat.

"I'm performing at the Sweethaven Christmas concert in the park, and then there are all kinds of other events that are unique to this town—the Luminary Walk, the Reindog Parade, the ice-carving competition."

"So the thought is we could film some of those events with Meghan and our family and friends."

"I like it," Martin said. He leaned forward, and his eyes flashed, like he was imagining how it could work. "I do. Maybe we could even add in a live element too. We could get a crew in your house to film you around the tree doing traditional Christmas things— having dinner, singing carols, talking about Christmases from the past."

"Live?" Meghan's mind wandered back to the Shandy Shore debacle. "I'm not much of a fan of live television."

"This is about giving you the image you've been trying to get all along. I have no interest in making you look like something you're not, building a scandal or anything else. I want to show the world what a normal, wonderful family you have." When Martin punctuated his sentence with a smile, Meghan believed him. Something about this man was different.

"We'll set up a meeting with my producers and get this going. It's kind of last-minute, but I've been looking for this kind of show to fall into my lap, so the timing is perfect."

Meghan frowned. "Don't you have to tell someone or sell someone?"

Martin grinned. "I'm the someone to tell."

She felt her eyebrows shoot up as she realized Martin Gould wasn't just some low-level television guy—he was the big cheese. And she hadn't even offered him a cup of coffee.

Martin stood and shook her hand, then turned to Nick. "We'll see you at church Sunday. My wife and I decided to stay in town for a week or so."

Nick nodded. "Sounds good. Thanks for coming out today."

After Martin left, Meghan turned to Nick, with what she was sure was a bewildered expression on her face.

"Nice guy, right?" Nick said, as if the most normal thing in the world had just happened.

"You just booked me my own television special." She wrapped her arms around him, then pulled back to meet his eyes.

He smiled. "I want you to be happy."

Meghan stood on her tiptoes and drew him in, bringing her lips to his. "You do make me happy—TV special or not."

She wrapped herself in his arms and inhaled the scent of him, saying a silent prayer that somehow the two things she was most passionate about—her family and her career—really could coexist.

## TEN

*Campbell*

The week after Thanksgiving, the gallery buzzed with a steady stream of business during the Christmas Walk. Campbell hadn't expected so many customers, but she was thankful the Sweethaven tourism seemed to reach beyond the hot summer months. Why wouldn't it? She could already tell this town would offer a magical Christmas. Long strands of lights had been hung in a crisscross drape from one side of Main Street to the other. Store owners had decked out their windows in preparation for the window-decorating contest, infusing the downtown with small-town holiday spirit. In the coming weeks, Christmas events filled the calendar. Campbell could hardly wait.

Mom would've loved it here at Christmas. Campbell didn't see any indication in the scrapbook that she'd spent any Christmases here, but she wished they could walk arm in arm through the streets shopping for everyone on their list, drinking hot chocolate and admiring the decorations.

The crowd had started to die down when Luke appeared in the doorway. He said hello to the people walking out, then walked toward her, grinning.

"Nice to see all the people in here today," he said.

"How do you know? Were you spying on me?"

He shrugged. "Let's say I had a vested interest in your traffic flow." He handed her a newspaper. On the cover of *The Sweethaven*

*Gazette* was the headline: "Best new businesses this Christmas." She scanned the lower portion of the paper and found a photo and write-up of the gallery.

"How did I miss this?" she said, still reading.

"You were too busy to stop and read," Luke said, hopping up onto the counter. He pulled her toward him and kissed her forehead.

Realization washed over her. "A few people mentioned the newspaper ad. I thought they were just confused. Wait." She pushed herself back and leveled his gaze. "Did you have something to do with this?"

The lopsided grin returned.

"You got me in here?" Campbell smiled. "How?"

"I know a guy."

Campbell shook her head. Since the beginning of their relationship, Luke had always found ways to surprise her, and though initially he'd been unsure about her buying the gallery, once he got over the fear, he'd done everything he could to support this dream.

"From what I can tell, it paid off. Did you sell anything?"

"Luke, thank you," Campbell said. "And yes. I sold things and signed up lots of kids for the Christmas vacation art classes." She smiled.

"Are you ready to go? Dinner at my place? I've got everything ready."

"Let me get my stuff." Campbell locked the doors, turned the lights off and flipped the sign in the window to *Closed*. Before they left, she turned to Luke. She wanted to finally respond to his profession of love from the other day, but when she met his eyes, she froze again.

"You okay?" He brushed her hair away from her eyes and studied her face.

She nodded. "Just really happy." Luke's trips to Chicago on the weekends had slowed, and she had to wonder if that was yet another sign that he'd gotten more serious about the two of them. Maybe she was overanalyzing.

He wrapped his arms around her. His kisses had become cozy and familiar, but when accompanied with the echo of three key words in her mind, her insides went to mush. Would she ever be able to vocalize how she felt? When he pulled away, she held his gaze, the words *I love you, Luke* rushing through her mind.

"Luke, I . . ." She looked away. She couldn't say it.

"What's wrong?"

She shook her head. "Nothing, it's just . . . what you said the other day."

His brow popped up and he smiled. "The 'I love you' thing?"

Campbell couldn't hold his gaze. "Yeah, that." She cracked her knuckles. "Do you say that a lot?"

He stared at her, a look of amusement on his face. "You seem uncomfortable with it. Should I not have told you?"

She shook her head. "No, I'm just . . ."

"You don't have to have it all figured out, Campbell. You're bound to have some stuff to work through after losing your mom. I'm not going anywhere."

She let out a stream of hot air. "It's not that I don't, I just . . ."

He put a hand up to her mouth and forced her to look at him. "Let's go eat. I'm starving." And just like that, the moment passed.

Luke had the table set for two, complete with candles and a vase of flowers. She hardly noticed that the candle was scented and the flowers were still in their cellophane wrap. They ate chicken Parmesan and laughed as they discussed the customers that had been in and out of their businesses earlier that day.

As the conversation lulled, Luke stood, walked to the bookshelf and pulled down a wrapped gift she hadn't noticed.

"Luke!"

"I didn't want to wait till Christmas," he said. He handed her the box, then sat across from her, eyes expectant.

"I didn't get you anything yet."

"This isn't really a Christmas present. It's more of a 'just because' present."

"But it's wrapped in Santa paper." Campbell raised her eyebrows to challenge him.

He laughed. "Just open it."

When she pulled off the wrapping paper, she found a square scrapbook album and a stack of photos of the two of them, starting with the gallery showing the night they shared their first kiss. In less than a year, Luke had invaded every thought she had and taught her more about unconditional love than she ever hoped to know. He protected her and put her first. It was obvious by the way he acted that what he said was true—he did love her.

"I know you have the Circle and do pages for the group album, but I thought we should have one of our own," he said. "Do you like it?"

"Are you kidding? I love it, Luke."

*I love you, Luke.*

She swallowed the words again. They almost felt too big for her to comprehend. Maybe the truth was she didn't *want* to love him. Love meant putting yourself out there—exposed. And if it went south, the pain would be more than she could handle. "Thank you."

He leaned across the table and kissed her, then picked up the plates. "I'm just going to wash these really quick. Then we can watch a movie or something."

"Can I help?"

"No." He laughed. "You're the guest."

"I can still wash dishes."

"You can help by making my Christmas tree presentable."

Campbell looked at the poor excuse for a Christmas tree. "You need a real tree. Don't you want the smell of pine to fill this place?"

"They're too messy. Last year, my real tree fell over three times. Do you know how hard it is to get those needles out of the carpet?"

She laughed. "Okay, but I'm not sure I can make this one magical."

"I have faith in you," he called from the other room.

Campbell opened a box of ornaments and wondered what stories were attached to each one. In her house, Mom had bought her a new ornament every Christmas, and always as a reminder of something she'd done that year. In sixth grade, it was a bumblebee, to commemorate winning the school spelling bee. In eighth grade, a camera, to document her interest in photography. Her senior year, a tiara—to remind her how it felt to be named Homecoming Queen.

It was as if Mom had known her time would be short, and she made up for it by leaving reminders of herself everywhere.

Campbell pulled a strand of tinsel from the box and started wrapping it around the tree. "I didn't know anyone still used tinsel," she called to Luke.

"You're not allowed to make fun of my decorations," he said, eyeing her from the doorway of the kitchen.

"I can't make that promise," she said.

She worked on the tree in silence for a few minutes, and as she leaned around the back of the tree, she spotted a small black velvet box tucked behind a white envelope without a name on the front. Campbell tossed a glance back toward the doorway, and when she didn't see Luke, she picked up the box.

Metal clanged in the kitchen and Campbell hurried the box to its spot on the shelf, scolding herself for snooping and waiting for Luke to appear in the living room.

When he didn't, she picked up the box again, leaning across the armchair beside the tree. She pried it open, and a diamond ring sparkled in the light of the Christmas tree. Silver-colored and set in an antique style, the ring boasted one large diamond at its center, surrounded by a circle of smaller diamonds. More diamonds were set into the sides of the ring, and as she stared at it, Campbell's breath caught in her throat.

Was this why Luke had gotten so romantic lately? He was planning to propose?

She hadn't even told him she loved him.

Her heart raced, but she couldn't place the emotion that coursed through her veins. Excitement? Terror? Nervousness?

What if he planned to propose tonight? He said the album wasn't the real Christmas present.

"Cam?" Luke's voice called from the kitchen, and she snapped the box shut and set it back on the shelf.

"Yeah?"

"You want some ice cream?"

Campbell's mind raced, thinking of all the people she'd ever loved. Though the list was short, the results were always the same— and they weren't good. In seconds, she imagined herself right back at Mom's funeral, watching them lower the casket into the ground.

And before that, the one time she gave her heart to a guy, he returned it to her in pieces.

Campbell grabbed her purse and walked to the kitchen door. "I just remembered some stuff I need to do for the gallery before tomorrow," she said. "I'm sorry. Rain check on the movie?"

Luke turned from the refrigerator, a pint of ice cream in each hand. "Okay." Confusion spread across his face. "Are you sure?"

She nodded. "Yeah, I'm sorry." A quick kiss on the cheek and she turned around. "I'll talk to you tomorrow."

In the quiet of the street outside, she knew Luke most likely watched her from his apartment above the café, but she didn't stop to wave to him like she normally would.

Instead, she raced back inside the gallery and upstairs to her own apartment.

She tried—and failed—to pretend she hadn't fallen for Luke. She told herself to stop acting foolish because love only led to pain. She'd have to make sure Luke knew she wasn't ready for a proposal—and she wouldn't be for a long time.

But the image of the ring flashed in her mind.

Luke was going to propose, and in that moment she realized, if she said "no," she'd lose him for good.

ELEVEN

*Adele*

Adele sat in the dining room with a pen and a legal pad and made a list of recipes to include in the cookbook. The editor, Kathy, had told her to come up with an outline and list of recipes. So far, she had more than she could fit in one book and what she thought was the perfect idea for a cookbook. But just as the idea nagged at her, so did the memories it conjured.

The plan was to infuse the recipes with personal stories, and it didn't get much more personal than her friendship with Henry Marshall.

No, it was more than a friendship. She'd loved Henry. Despite her dad's beliefs that she was too young, she knew now that love was love. No matter what age she happened to be.

The little journal lay on the table. Adele pulled off the band and opened it. The pages were yellowed with age, and the ink had faded, but the memories were still intact.

"Henry." Adele ran a hand over a black-and-white photo of the two of them, dressed in their Sunday best for the Christmas dance at The Commons. The first night they met.

Adele's cousin Jerry had a band and had been hired as the entertainment, and as soon as Jerry spotted her in the crowd, he pulled her up on the stage.

"My little cousin Adele has a voice you all are going to rave about," he said into the microphone. Adele covered her face with her hands and giggled as she peered out over the crowd.

The band began playing "Unchained Melody" as the lights dimmed and couples paired off all over The Commons. While the song was written for a male lead, the band changed the key for Adele's strong alto voice, and as she sang, she lost herself in the music, closing her eyes and forgetting where she was.

Music had a way of transporting her to another time, and she let herself go—as if she had a choice. When she opened her eyes, the crowd seemed to part, and Henry Marshall stood at the back of the room, staring at her. She nearly forgot the words. She'd seen him around town. The girls were all crazy about him, but he was quiet and never even glanced in her direction.

The song ended and the couples in the crowd stopped and applauded her addition to the band. Jerry thanked her and Adele was swept back into a sea of faces until she found her friends waiting for her.

Seconds later, someone tapped her on the shoulder. When she turned, she saw the handsome boy two years her senior, the one she'd admired since the beginning of the summer. She'd always been too shy to say anything to him, and now here he stood. Inches away.

"I didn't know you could sing like that," he said.

Adele smiled. "I sing a little."

He laughed. "You sing a lot."

She looked away, her face feeling flushed after being under the hot stage lights.

"I'm Henry."

"I know." She met his eyes. "I'm Adele."

He smiled. "I know."

Her friends chattered on behind her, but she couldn't make out what they said. The rest of the room had seemed to go dim, as if she and Henry were the only two people there.

"Do you want to dance?" He held out a hand to her.

She glanced back at the girls standing beside her. All three wore grins like the Cheshire cat. Adele took Henry's hand and followed him to the dance floor. She stayed there, in his arms, for the rest of the night.

Now, Adele studied the photo that had been snapped that night. Beside it, she'd written:

*Spent the evening dancing with Henry M. Do you believe it? He kept telling me my voice knocked him off his feet, and he even told me I was beautiful. No one's ever said that to me before. I think "Unchained Melody" will be our song. Isn't that a good one?*

Adele's cheeks flushed at her childhood naïveté. She'd been so smitten after just one night. When Henry asked her if she wanted to be part of his band, she didn't bat an eyelash. And she would've been content to be in his band for the rest of her life.

But things don't work out like they do in love songs.

Adele glanced over at the computer. The girls said she had to wait, but what did that mean? Facebook didn't make a bit of sense to her, and she wasn't very good at waiting. She turned on the dinosaur of a computer and waited for the screen to show all the little pictures.

At the start-up, she double-clicked on the Internet button and waited. It took her two tries, but she finally found the Web site again. When she saw her own photo—the one Meghan had taken with her phone—she stared at the screen. Now what?

Meghan had explained to her about the friends and the wall, but she'd forgotten everything. She clicked on the word *Friends* and saw that she had four. Jane, Campbell, Meghan and . . . *Henry.*

Adele's pulse kicked up a notch. If he showed up on her page, did that mean he'd accepted the request? Of course she assumed he was happily married with lots of family around him now, but did she want to know the truth? Throughout her marriage to Teddy, she'd rarely thought of Henry, but once Teddy passed away, her lonely mind started reminiscing. Was it normal to wander down memory lane most nights?

Adele clicked on Henry's name. A photo of him jumped out at her from the screen. Older and more distinguished, but easily recognizable. Henry's dark eyes hadn't changed.

"Who's Henry Marshall?" Luke's voice from behind her back startled her out of her chair.

"Lucas Barber!" Adele's shrill voice startled him back.

"Sorry, Ma," he said, holding up his hands in surrender.

Adele hurried back to the computer and clicked three different buttons until she finally saw Facebook disappear. She inhaled and turned to face her son, whose raised eyebrows and slight smirk told her she'd been caught.

"Don't look at me like that, Luke," she said. She picked up the little journal, snapped it shut and propped it back on the shelf where it belonged.

"Are you going to tell me who he is or am I going to have to take his name to the sheriff?"

She turned to face him with a hand on her hip. "You will do no such thing. You have your own matters to attend to."

Luke frowned. "What's that supposed to mean?"

"What are you getting Campbell for Christmas?"

"Don't change the subject, Ma. I want to know who this guy is. You look a little flushed. Do you want me to open the window?" He grinned.

"Very funny." She sighed. "He's an old friend. The girls made me sign up for that ridiculous Web site."

"And you hope he writes?" He bit into an apple and plopped down in a kitchen chair.

She shrugged, then brushed it off, choosing instead to turn the attention back on her son. But even as they spoke, her mind flitted back to the Web site where the photo of Henry would greet her the next time she turned on the computer—and while she wouldn't let on, she knew without a doubt that yes, she absolutely hoped he wrote.

## TWELVE

*Lila*

Lila returned home from shopping and spent the rest of the evening hidden away in her room. She didn't like feeling like an outsider, and around Mama and Daddy it had come to that. They argued in hushed tones, just low enough that Lila couldn't make out what they said, but she knew there was something going on they weren't telling her.

And it had to do with this mystery woman.

A woman Mama had clearly intimidated in public. What was so important that this woman could cause such upheaval? If she was just another one of Daddy's affairs, Mama would've turned a blind eye like she always did.

No, something about her was different. And Lila hated being the only one who didn't know.

Tom's words from earlier that morning came back, and she reminded herself not to take on unnecessary stress. This pregnancy was the most important thing, helping to alleviate the pain of her miscarriages. This baby was their chance of a new life, a happy life, together.

Having spent the day on her feet, Lila now felt swollen and craved water. Despite the turmoil in her emotional life, she had to pay attention to what her body needed. Her hands fell to her stomach.

"You just stay safe in there, okay?" she whispered. "You're the best thing in our life, so take whatever you need from me." This baby meant everything. Her chance to be a different kind of mother than Mama had been to her.

In the kitchen, Lila found a bottle of water and then glanced into her father's study, where he sat in an old leather chair reading the newspaper. Like there was nothing wrong.

Like he and Mama hadn't just had it out. Like his own daughter could still look him in the eye without suspicion.

Why had she spent all evening locked in her room, stewing over this situation, when he seemed unfazed by any of it?

*Think of the baby. No unnecessary stress.*

But the longer she stood there, the bottle of water chilling her hand, the angrier she got. Didn't he see that his indiscretions had done this? They'd caused everyone pain—everyone except him.

Lila walked toward the door of the study, her presence pulling his attention from the newspaper.

"What's wrong, Lila? You look upset." His shoulders tensed.

She needed to stay calm. For the baby's sake. Lila took a deep breath. "Daddy, who was that woman in the restaurant? I saw you talking to her—she didn't seem like a stranger."

Her dad cleared his throat. "Lila, I don't know her."

"But she knows you. How does she know you?"

He stiffened.

Lila narrowed her gaze, trying to read his body language.

"Mama practically accosted her in the store today. So tell me what's going on."

"She what?" Daddy leaned forward. If Lila didn't know better, she thought he actually looked concerned—but about whom? "What did your mother say to her?"

"Does it matter?"

"It does to me."

"Why? Is it because she matters to you? What's wrong, did this one turn up pregnant?"

"Heavens, Lila. Stop it." Daddy stood and turned his back to her.

"Tell me."

Daddy stared out the window for a long moment, then, as if he'd gotten a hold of himself again, he turned around and faced her. "Lila, I have a lot of money. People are going to make up stories about me and try to get their hands on a piece of what I've worked for."

"My earliest memories are of you and Mama arguing in the kitchen over where you slept the night before. It's not a secret, so if this woman is trying to expose something about you, she'd have to have a bigger bombshell than the fact that you're a cheater. Because everyone already knows that."

Daddy hung his head and rubbed his face with his hands. "I don't like your tone."

"And I don't like your lies. I deserve the truth." Her voice broke. "For once in your life, just tell the truth."

Her father stood. "This is still my house, Lila. And I am still your father. You will respect me."

Her mind flashed back years. All the times he'd demanded respect, he'd never done a thing to earn it. And he'd never offered it to her in return.

"I think it's time you started respecting yourself," she said.

Daddy threw the newspaper on the couch and stormed out, the front door slamming behind him. She stood in the entryway and watched the car pull away, then turned back to the empty house and inhaled, fighting back the tears that threatened.

Daddy didn't deserve any more of her tears.

Lila went back into the study and started searching through the drawers of her father's desk. She didn't even know what she was searching for. Something—anything—to tie him to this nameless woman who'd turned their lives upside down.

As she searched, she tried not to put anything out of place, but the longer she found nothing, the more frustrated she became.

The sound of the front door startled her and she closed the bottom drawer of the desk as quietly as she could, then walked to the doorway.

Tom shook off his coat and hung it up. "Hey, what are you doing in your dad's office?"

Lila sighed. "Snooping."

He reached out to her, then pulled her into a hug. "You've got to stop this. The stress isn't good for you or the baby."

"He's lying, Tom. I don't know about what, but I know he is."

Tom pulled away and met her eyes. "Maybe he's embarrassed."

She scoffed. "He should be. The way he's chosen to live *is* embarrassing. But not just for him, and that's the thing that makes me crazy. It's like he has no regard for what his choices have done to the rest of us."

She pushed past Tom and went upstairs with him following close behind. She opened the door to her parents' bedroom and started shuffling through the dresser drawers.

"Hon, what are you doing?"

"Maybe there's something in here." She opened the hutch and then the vanity and then turned to the closet.

"I feel like I'm watching a movie where you know the person snooping around is going to get caught at any moment," Tom said.

"Then keep an eye on the door. Or better yet, watch out the front window for the car."

Tom sighed. "This is ridiculous."

She turned to him. "Could you be a little supportive? Just because you didn't keep evidence of your other life doesn't mean Daddy didn't."

The stunned look on Tom's face came at her like a slap across the face.

"You're comparing me to your father?"

She shook her head. "No, of course not. I didn't mean that."

He turned away.

She rushed to him and wrapped her arms around him, but he stiffened. "Tom, I'm sorry. That's not what I meant."

"I don't like being compared to your father, Lila."

"I know. I didn't mean it." She willed him to look at her.

He stepped back. "I'll watch out the window."

She stared at the empty doorway, wishing she could take back her careless words. Tom was nothing like Daddy. Daddy was a chronic cheater. Tom had made one mistake before their relationship became serious.

She'd have to find a way to make it up to him. Later.

Lila flipped on the closet light and peered up on the top shelves lined with shoes and purses, but there was nothing sentimental that she could see. No big surprise given how detached her mother had always been. She hadn't kept a single report card or childhood drawing of Lila's.

Over on Daddy's side of the closet, she spotted an old briefcase. She still remembered watching him carry it as he left for work in the mornings. How it had ended up here, she didn't know. He'd stopped carrying it years ago.

She pulled it out and clicked it open. Inside, she found a stack of business papers, but underneath was a red envelope addressed to her father. She turned it over and pulled out the card—a Father's Day card. When she opened it, a small photo fell out. Faded and orange, the photo looked familiar. Like one she'd seen of her and Daddy from one of her earliest birthday parties. But the little girl on Daddy's lap wasn't Lila.

The card had been signed in a child's handwriting. *Love, Charlotte.*

Lila's mind reeled, her thoughts frantic and frenzied. Charlotte. She wanted to believe she didn't know who Charlotte was, but there were too many red flags unfurling in her mind. Cold swept over her.

"Lila, someone's pulling in." Tom's voice carried into the closet where she sat, the contents of the briefcase spilled out on the floor.

"Lila? Come on." He stood in the doorway of the closet. "What is it? What'd you find?"

"That woman isn't Daddy's mistress, Tom." She handed him the photo. "She's his daughter."

In the quiet of her parents' bedroom, Lila half-whispered, half-yelled.

"He lied to my face, Tom. This is proof."

Tom frowned at the photo. "It does seem suspicious."

"That is my father and that is not me. It's not suspicious. It's proof."

"Okay, you need to stay calm," Tom said. He took her hand and led her down the hall to her childhood bedroom. "Listen, he must've had a reason for lying about it."

"All of this deceit is to keep up appearances. It's sickening. Families are dysfunctional. Why is it so hard for them to admit they aren't perfect?"

Tom started to say something and then closed his mouth.

"What?"

He held up his hands as if to surrender. "Nothing."

"You were going to say something."

"I hate to say it, but isn't that exactly what you did when you asked me to pretend everything was fine between us this past summer?"

Lila groaned. Not her finest moment. When her parents surprised her at the lake house, she panicked. She couldn't have Mama knowing she planned to divorce Tom, so she asked him to live with her for a few weeks pretending everything was fine.

She didn't know it would make her fall in love with him all over again.

"That's . . . different." She turned and walked a few steps away from him.

"My point is, we can't get in the middle of it. It's between your mom and dad and that woman."

"My sister. Charlotte."

Tom looked at the photo again. "She does seem about the right age."

"She seems to be about the same age as me." Lila glanced at her husband, who shook his head and looked away.

"Do you think Mama knows? If she doesn't, and if she's been defending him—lying for him—she's going to leave him for sure."

"Lila, stop." He pulled her eyes to his. "You have to calm down. The baby."

She knew he was right. She had gotten herself worked up—and for what? She couldn't let her parents' mess threaten to steal their last chance at being a family. Her doctor told her she needed to take every precaution. With her age and her previous miscarriages, Lila couldn't afford to get worked up about anything. Yet here she was, pacing the floor.

She plopped down on the bed. "I don't want to stay here anymore."

"I know, I'm trying to find us our own place."

"For tonight, let's go to the Whitmore or I can call Meghan—they have an extra room."

"Do you really want to do that?"

"Yes. Can you help me with my suitcase?"

Tom hesitated, but finally stood and helped her pack. She packed as if they wouldn't be back to the lake house. She couldn't be around her parents for one more second—not if they didn't trust her enough to tell her the truth.

Maybe leaving them would make them finally fess up.

They descended the stairs, the entryway dark as the sun had long gone and the moon was too new to give off much light. As they reached the door, Lila saw Mama in the front room, where she sat in her stiff wingbacked chair reading.

"What are you doing?" More of a demand than a question.

"Leaving," Lila said.

Tom kept his head down, unwilling to engage Cilla and probably praying for a quick exit.

Daddy walked in from the kitchen. "Leaving for where?"

"You're not going back to Georgia early, are you?"

Her parents planned to go back to Georgia in another day, which meant that no, she most certainly wouldn't be going back. "We're staying here through Christmas."

"What? Why?" Mama's eyes darted to Daddy, then Tom and back to Lila.

Normally, this was when Lila lost her courage. Her mother would shame her into submission. But not this time. She lifted her chin and faced Mama. "I can't be in a house with two people who refuse to tell the truth."

"What on earth are you talking about?" Mama's accent hung in the air.

"That woman from the restaurant." She turned to her father. "You said you didn't know her."

Daddy's eyes widened and he looked like he'd aged five years in the last few days. "That's right."

"Then why did I find this in your closet?" She produced the faded orange-tinged photo.

"You went through our closet?" Mama stepped forward and snatched the picture out of Lila's hand.

"It was in a Father's Day card." She held her voice steady. "So try to come up with a lie to explain that one away. Lucky for you I'm not hanging around to hear it."

Lila started to pick up her suitcase, but Tom grabbed it before she exerted herself.

"Tom, you can't let her do this." Mama grabbed his arm. "You know how dramatic she is."

Tom looked at Lila, then at her mother. "She's my wife, Cilla."

"But she's acting like a child."

"Demanding the truth sounds pretty adult to me."

Cilla scoffed and Tom pulled out of her grasp. "I think it's best to put a little distance between the three of you." He leveled Cilla's glare. "For the baby's sake."

Lila swiped a tear as Tom's hand pressed into the small of her back. He led her outside into the crisp December air.

He put their bags into the trunk of the car and pulled away, while Lila stifled unwanted sobs. In the quiet darkness of the moving vehicle, Tom held her hand and let her cry over the years of distance between her and her parents, over the family she was sure she'd just lost and over the fact that she hadn't earned the right to know the truth—even from her own parents.

"Where do you want to go?" Tom asked as they drove toward town.

She couldn't answer. Suddenly she felt like an orphan—homeless and betrayed. "You decide," she said.

When he pulled into Adele's driveway ten minutes later, something inside her stilled. In that house, she knew she'd find peace and comfort. Tom must've known it too.

Together, like two stray puppies, they walked to the door and knocked, and when Adele pulled the door open and met Lila's eyes, she ushered them in without asking a single question.

The way family ought to.

THIRTEEN

*Campbell*

Campbell lay in bed staring at the ceiling. She didn't want to look at the clock, knowing she'd see how few hours she had left to sleep. It would only stress her out about how tired she'd be tomorrow.

*I'll drink a lot of coffee. I'll be fine.*

She closed her eyes. The light of the streetlamp outside caught her eye. She turned over and faced the wall.

The heater kicked in.

She sighed. Useless. She might as well get up and work. At this rate, she'd never fall asleep. Still, she didn't move. She closed her eyes and the image of the ring popped into her mind. What would it look like on her finger?

What would it feel like to commit to someone for as long as they both should live?

What if, after only a few years, he discovered all her flaws and decided he couldn't live with her for one more day? Worse, what if something happened to Luke? She couldn't lose anyone else she loved.

Which meant, maybe she couldn't love anyone else.

Who was she kidding? Even now, losing him would be devastating. How had she let this happen? And what hope did she have of protecting herself at this point?

When morning finally dawned, Campbell felt groggy with the kind of headache that often accompanies a sleepless night.

As she readied herself for the day, her mind still spun with thoughts of the ring.

If Luke proposed and she waffled even a little, it could ruin their relationship. Worse, if she said she wasn't ready, he'd certainly be hurt.

But pretending she hadn't seen it wasn't going to work either, because she'd always been a terrible liar.

As much as she didn't want to love him, she didn't want to lose him either.

As she walked toward the front of the gallery, the door popped open and a group of people entered. At the center of them, Meghan. Her face lit up when she spotted Campbell, and Campbell forced a smile, though her stomach somersaulted at the sight of Luke's famous sister.

She reminded herself that no one knew how many times she'd imagined herself as part of Meghan's inner circle—not because of her fame, but because Campbell had never had a sister. If she'd already adopted Luke's family in her own mind, maybe marriage made sense. Maybe it was the next step after all.

"Hey Campbell," Meghan said. She turned to her assistant and two men Campbell didn't recognize. "You guys can wait here, I'll just be a minute."

Meghan approached the counter and rolled her eyes. "I'm sorry to bring them in here."

"It's fine. Maybe they'll sign up for a class." Campbell smiled.

"Nick worked out some crazy deal, and I'm going to have my own Christmas special on TV. Prime time." She grinned.

Campbell knew Meghan needed a break to repair her image after everything she'd been through. Maybe this was the break she needed.

"That's exciting."

"I know, and we're getting the whole family together at our cottage to go over how it's all going to go. It's live, so we need to rehearse."

*The whole family?*

Campbell didn't respond.

"I know it's short notice, but the whole thing is like that. Would you mind showing up? You and Luke?"

Campbell's mind came back to the ring. A camera crew and a Christmas special would be a unique way for a guy to propose. What if this was all part of the ploy to throw her off and keep her guessing?

"Campbell?" Meghan leaned in closer. "You okay?"

Campbell shook herself back to reality. "Of course, I'm sorry. It's just . . ." If she told Meghan about the ring, Luke would find out she snooped. "I'm not sure what I'll wear."

Meghan laughed. "Just not one of those hideous Christmas sweaters. I'm going to have a hard enough time making sure Mama doesn't show up in her Rudolph sweater. It actually has a reindeer with a light-up nose."

Campbell laughed. "You really don't have to include me in this, Meghan. I won't be offended if it's just your family." She studied the papers on the counter.

"What are you talking about? You're practically family already." Meghan smiled. "At least, that's what I'm getting from Luke."

Campbell's eyes darted to Meghan's. Maybe she did know something. Maybe Luke had confided in her or Nick. He and Nick were good friends. "Do you know something?"

Meghan frowned. "About what?"

"Nothing, never mind."

Meghan stared at her and Campbell shifted from one foot to the other, wishing she'd kept her mouth shut.

"You seem a little flustered. Is everything okay?" Meghan asked. "Oh gosh, you and Luke aren't fighting, are you?"

Campbell shook her head. "No, no, of course not. We're good. Everything's good."

Campbell could tell by the look on Meghan's face she didn't buy it. "Okay, well, I'll have Luke call you with all the details. I still don't know what time he's available." She turned to go. "You know how it is running your own business."

"Sure do." Campbell smiled and watched Meghan walk out onto the sidewalk, her handlers following close behind. The two men seemed to be setting up camera shots outside the gallery, and Meghan had pulled her phone out while they talked. Probably warning Luke that his girlfriend had gone crazy.

She wished she'd never opened the black-velvet box. At least then the surprise would let her answer in the moment rather than stewing about it. Across the street, Luke waved at Meghan, who walked over to the café. They talked for a few minutes, then both looked back toward the gallery. Campbell quickly buried her eyes in the paperwork on her desk, but all she could think about was whether or not Meghan had just implemented Luke's plan.

If she went to Meghan's Family Christmas Special, would she end up the main event?

And if so, would it be the end of the best relationship she'd ever had? She couldn't bear the thought of ruining what she and Luke had. Even if she hadn't quite defined it yet.

Deep in thought, she didn't hear the door open again, so when she turned and saw Adele walking toward her, she gasped.

"Sorry, darlin', did I scare you?"

Luke's family seemed intent on showing up today.

"Yes, but it's fine." She shuffled the papers around on the counter, avoiding her eyes.

"You all right? You seem flustered."

Campbell's laugh sounded nervous in her own ears. "Have you been talking to Meghan?"

Adele frowned. "No, and I need to talk to you."

Was she coming to warn her about Luke's plan?

Campbell took a deep breath. She was being ridiculous and she knew it. "About what?" She tucked the papers inside a folder and tried to look busy.

"Facebook."

Campbell met her eyes and saw pure panic in them. "What's wrong? Did something happen?"

"I think Henry said yes to bein' my friend." The panic intensified.

Campbell's eyes widened. "That's great, Adele."

"No, it isn't. I don't know what to do next." She dropped her purse on the counter and pulled out the little journal they'd all seen on Thanksgiving. "I know it's hard to believe, but Henry wasn't just a friend to me. I thought I was gonna marry him."

"That's not so hard to believe," Campbell said, forcing her thoughts to stay off of Luke and on his mom.

Was Luke Campbell's version of Henry? Years from now would she be looking him up wondering "What if . . . ?"

"I just don't know if maybe he's mad at me is all."

"For something that happened almost fifty years ago?" Campbell asked.

"You don't have to say it like that. Reminds me how old I am."

"Sorry."

Adele's eyes glazed over. "I loved my Teddy. He was a lot like Luke—kind, good with kids, and he treated me like a queen. I don't want any of this to make it seem like I was ever disappointed in the way things turned out."

Campbell watched Adele swipe a tear off her cheek.

"But I'm alone now, and I guess a part of me is wonderin' about Henry."

"And you feel guilty?"

"Like I'm cheatin'. On my Teddy."

Campbell covered Adele's hands with her own, grateful to have gained the older woman's trust.

"I'm sorry for unloading all of this on you. I can't tell Meghan or Luke—and you're practically family."

Campbell's face must've gone pale.

"What? Did I say something wrong?"

"No, no, of course not." Maybe Adele was referring to their friendship—because of her history with Campbell's mom. Not because of Campbell's future with her son.

"So, what would you do? If you were me?" Her eyes pleaded.

Suddenly, their lighthearted talk from Thanksgiving seemed like a mistake. To Adele, this man was so much more than a potential Facebook friend, and they'd all made light of it.

"Send him a note, maybe? The Internet just makes it easier."

Adele looked away. "Can you show me how?" It moved Campbell how difficult it seemed to be for her to ask for help.

"Of course."

They sat down at the computer and pulled up Adele's Facebook page.

"Now, if you want to send a note that anyone can read, you can go here." Campbell showed her around Henry's wall. "See, here, someone sent him a note about a chess game, and we can read that."

"I don't think I'd want anyone reading my notes to Henry." Adele stared at the screen.

"Then you want to send him a private message." Campbell showed her how to keep their communications private and then she clicked on his photo albums.

"He's handsome, Adele."

Adele smiled, eyes on the image of Henry holding two children.

They scrolled through the photos, and Campbell stopped on one of a younger Henry, arms around a small woman with dark hair. She leaned in and read what Henry had written about the photo.

"'Still miss her, even five years later.'" She glanced at Adele.

"I'm glad he found someone," Adele said. "I'm sure he made a great husband and they look so happy together." She quieted for a long moment. "I think I should wait."

Campbell stilled. "You don't want to say hello?"

Adele clicked on the Message button and chewed on her bottom lip. "Maybe."

"I've got a few things to do in the back room. You go ahead and when you're done, just click Send."

Adele nodded.

For ten minutes, Campbell pretended to work in the back room, but all the time, she kept one eye on Adele, who seemed to be deleting every word as quickly as she typed it.

Finally, Adele stood up.

"Did you send it?" Campbell asked, walking toward her.

"Yes. My hands are still shaking."

"It's always good to be kind to someone," Campbell said. "Think of it that way."

Adele smiled. "I like that. Join me for a cup of coffee?"

Campbell glanced out the window to the café. "Oh, I've got more work here, but you go ahead."

"You sure? Luke is probably anxious to see you."

"I wish I could." Campbell fidgeted with the bottom of her shirt. "Tell him I said hi."

Adele's eyes narrowed. But Campbell couldn't tell Adele what she suspected—or how it made her feel.

This was the kind of secret she couldn't admit. At least not yet.

But she'd have to make some sense of it sooner or later. Because she had a feeling Luke wouldn't wait around forever.

And that was exactly what she was afraid of.

# FOURTEEN

*Jane*

The doctor's office was white and smelled of disinfectant.

She glanced down at the paperwork the receptionist had given her to fill out.

*Why are you here today?*

Jane clicked the pen on the clipboard, then wrote "Routine checkup."

She couldn't write "I want to find out if there's a medical reason I'm overweight."

Jane hadn't exercised in many years. If she was going to start this weight-loss thing, she needed to make sure she wasn't going to kill herself in the process.

She finished the paperwork and returned it to the receptionist.

"It shouldn't be too long of a wait," the woman said.

Jane sat and flipped through a *Good Housekeeping* magazine dated eight months ago. Her eyes glazed over as she remembered the last time she'd been in Dr. Barry's office. Alex was five and his ear infections had gotten worse. The doctor rearranged his schedule to fit them in and prescribed the antibiotics to make her son feel better. She'd always been grateful for the way he treated their whole family. Often she wished their regular doctor in Iowa could sit down and learn from Dr. Barry.

They called her back and Jane hoisted her purse onto her shoulder. The young nurse wore pink scrubs and smiled as she greeted her. "Hi, Mrs. Atkins. How are you today?"

"Oh, fine," Jane said, dreading what came next.

"Just take off your shoes and step on the scale," the nurse said.

As she untied her tennis shoes, she glanced at the girl's name tag. *Amanda.* Amanda had no idea what she asked.

Jane removed her coat and dropped it in a heap on top of her shoes and purse. If only she could shed her midsection that easily.

She looked at Amanda, who stood, clipboard in hand, waiting to record Jane's weight.

"Okay, but don't tell me what it is," Jane said.

Amanda frowned. "Okay."

Jane knew what it was. She just didn't want the entire office to know. For some reason, nurses thought it was appropriate to broadcast those three numbers, as if it wasn't humiliating enough to see them flashing in front of you.

As she stood there, the cold metal of the scale stung her feet through her thin socks. Jane stared up at the ceiling as Amanda fiddled with the metal bar that tattled on her for too many nights spent with her old friends Ben and Jerry.

"Okay, you can follow me," Amanda said after the metal settled and she'd jotted down the sum total of Jane's self-worth.

Jane walked a few paces behind the young, thin girl, feeling like she should hang her head over what had just happened. How had it gotten this bad? And what would Dr. Barry say when she told him she wanted to get healthy? Would he laugh and say she was too far gone? It was how she felt most days.

"You can go ahead and undress and put this on," Amanda said, handing her a hospital gown. "Just flip this switch when you're ready and he'll be in shortly."

Jane thanked her and set her things down in the chair. Undressing in the doctor's office always brought its own batch of insecurities, and today was no different. She tied the gown around her quickly, then flipped the switch and scooted herself onto the table. A chill ran through her as she remembered the many times over the years she'd brought one child or another in to see Dr. Barry. He hadn't even met Sam, though with any luck there wouldn't be a need for that.

The light knock on the door pulled her back to the here and now and she waited for the doctor's face to appear. Dr. Barry looked the same—distinguished and older, with gray hair and kind eyes. Just as she remembered him, though he seemed slimmer.

She smiled, but inside she wondered if he was thinking the exact opposite of her.

"Jane, it's been too long," he said, extending a hand.

She shook it, nodding. "We've been away awhile."

He hugged the clipboard. The one with her weight written on it in bold, black ink. "I can't tell you how sorry we were to hear about Alex."

His office must've sent flowers or a card or something. Jane didn't remember. That entire month was a blur. That entire year was a blur.

"Thank you," Jane murmured and looked away.

"How are Graham and the kids? Did I hear right you have another son?" He smiled a warm smile, and Jane reminded herself that once upon a time she loved making small talk with this man.

"Everyone's good. And yes. Sam is our youngest. Quite a handful." She smiled and Dr. Barry turned his attention to her chart.

He sat on the little black stool in front of her. "So, it says you're here for a routine checkup? Is there anything bothering you?"

Jane's eyes filled with tears as she remembered the humiliating tumble she took on the stage of the church. Would he laugh when she told him?

"I'd like to take better care of myself," she said.

"That's always a good idea," he told her. His voice was kind.

Jane studied her hands in her lap. "I've always been heavy, but now it's getting out of hand." She thought about the photos in the scrapbook. She hadn't *always* been heavy. How did she change that perception of herself?

He flipped through the papers on the clipboard. "Yes, it does look like you've put on some weight," he said.

She forced herself not to internalize the comment. It wasn't an insult, just a statement of fact. "I know."

"Jane, I hope you're not beating yourself up. With what you went through, it's very common to put on weight. For some of us, stress and grief are a trigger to overeat and pick up some bad habits."

She nodded and decided not to let on that she'd put on fifteen pounds the summer before Alex died. His death and then the addition of Sam had served as excuses for the behavior she'd already adopted.

"Listen, let's run some tests and see where your health is. Afterward, we can come up with a plan." The doctor's smile was warm.

"So, I'm not a lost cause?" Her eyes fell, landing on her thighs. Seeing them, she certainly felt like a lost cause.

Dr. Barry rolled the stool closer to her. "Jane, there's no such thing."

She met his eyes and said a silent prayer of thanks that the judgment she expected was absent.

"I'd like to run a few tests," Dr. Barry said after the exam.

Jane frowned. "Am I okay?"

He smiled. "Of course. This is just routine. I'll need you to make an appointment with the receptionist to come back tomorrow morning for a glucose test. But I'll need you to fast for a full eight hours before the test."

Jane nodded and made sure to schedule the test for as early as possible the following day so she could eat a normal dinner and sleep straight through the fast.

The following day, though, she woke up ravenous. She hurried to get ready and get out before her family asked for breakfast. Graham could handle Sam, and the girls could make their own food. She knew better than to put herself in that situation.

Once she settled in for the test, the nurse gave her a fizzy orange drink, like a Fanta only sweeter and tougher to choke down, but she did it. Two hours later, they drew blood. An hour later, more blood. Jane wished she'd brought more to do.

The next day, when she finally got the results, Jane wondered if God had allowed that chair to break for a reason. Otherwise, she never would've known the truth.

"It looks like prediabetes," Dr. Barry told her on the phone. "Your blood glucose levels are higher than normal—high enough to cause some concern. It looks like you were smart to come in, Jane."

Her heart sank. "What does this mean?"

"It means you *do* need to make yourself a priority. You need to get in shape or this could become full-blown diabetes really quickly."

Jane sighed. If her life depended on it, would she be able to maintain an exercise regimen? Would the threat of diabetes keep her out of the fridge?

"I've made an appointment for you with a nutritionist, and you need to get some kind of exercise every day, or at the very least four days a week."

Jane listened to his instructions, but as she did, she thought about the holidays, only a few weeks away. The baking, the buffet-style meals, the family gatherings. They'd already made plans to join Adele and the others for Christmas—how would she resist Adele's treats? She'd been so looking forward to spending her favorite holiday in Sweethaven. It had been years since she'd done that.

"Jane?"

"Oh, I'm sorry, yes?"

"It's very important that you ease yourself into this, but it's time to make better choices with your health. We want you to be around to see your grandkids. Speaking from experience, you don't want to miss out on that."

"No, I sure don't."

Across the room a photo of her family caught her eye. How would she explain this sudden change to them? How would they react when she said she wasn't baking frosted sugar cookies this year? Could she deny them their orange cinnamon rolls on Christmas morning?

"Don't worry, Jane. We caught this early. You're going to be fine." Dr. Barry must've sensed her apprehension.

She thanked him and hung up, replaying his words in her mind. *You're going to be fine.* And she would be, but not without making a lot of changes.

And unfortunately, she didn't have the foggiest idea where to start.

After Dr. Barry's phone call, Jane drove herself back to his office where he'd set up a meeting with a nutritionist. She'd read everything that had ever been published on healthy eating, but somehow none of it stuck. Some skinny person in a doctor's coat wasn't going to change that. Even if she was at risk for developing diabetes.

Jane walked back into the waiting room, but this time she was led down the hall in the opposite direction to a corner office without a single window.

*How depressing. Just sitting in here all day would make me want to eat doughnuts.*

Moments later, the door opened and Jane turned, ready to meet the person who would solve all her eating issues once and for all.

"Jane!"

"Lori?"

"Dr. Barry told me he was referring a special patient. I had no idea it was you till just this moment. It's been so busy around here. How's that handsome husband of yours?"

Jane's face heated. In her hand, Lori held a manila envelope with Jane's test results *and* her weight, and now the rest of Sweethaven would have access to that humiliating information.

Jane stood. "I think this was a mistake."

Lori laughed. "Don't be silly, Jane. I'm a professional. I've been doing this for years. Dr. Barry is helping me get started up here in Sweethaven now that I've moved back for good."

Jane frowned. Why was Lori suddenly being so nice to her?

"So, let's look over your chart. Oh my, prediabetes. It's good you're here. I can help you." Lori smiled. "Sit down."

Jane hesitated, her pulse racing, but she forced herself to sit.

"As you can see, I'm at a healthy weight, but that's because I've taken the necessary steps to educate myself. What I'm going to do is share all that education with you so you can finally start taking care of yourself."

Jane frowned.

"I mean, we're not getting any younger, right? Best to get a hold of this thing before it spirals out of control. We don't want any more chair incidents, right?" Lori laughed. "Now, here's where we'll start—"

Jane's jaw went slack, but she couldn't find words.

"We've got your starting weight recorded here, but I want you to go home and take a picture of yourself in a swimsuit or bra and panties."

"Why?"

"Because we want to document your before and after transformation. Maybe you can even provide a testimonial about how well my program works." She smiled, and for a moment, Jane wondered if she truly had no idea how terrible her words were.

"Lori, I don't think I can do this."

"I know it seems daunting right now with *so* much work ahead of you, but trust me, it can be done."

"No, I know I can lose the weight. I just can't allow you to take credit for it." Jane stood.

"Jane—"

Jane rushed out of the office, started her car and sped off to the solace of her house. When she arrived, Graham was sitting at the kitchen table flipping through a new issue of *Sports Illustrated*.

"Hon, what's wrong?"

Jane peeled her coat off and hung it on the hook by the door. She met Graham's concerned eyes. She wanted him to see her only as a beautiful woman; how did she tell him the truth? That she'd paid so little attention to herself, she'd become what she feared most? And now her health was at risk because of it.

Jane sat across from him. "I haven't been completely honest with you."

He raised a brow.

"I didn't meet the girls for coffee like I told you."

"Okay . . ." He frowned, a question in his voice. She'd never lied to him before.

"I went to the doctor."

Graham closed the magazine and leaned forward in his chair, and Jane poured out the entire story from the glucose test to the prediabetes to storming out of Lori's office only moments before.

When she finished, she sat back, waiting for his disapproval—or his disgust.

"So, we need to get more active."

She threw him a look. "You play basketball three times a week and jog every other day. You're not the one who needs to be more active."

"Well, you don't have to do it alone is what I'm saying. Or we can do what we talked about before, and you can stay up here without any distractions." He smiled and took her hands. "You're beautiful. You've always been beautiful to me, but I'm not willing to risk losing you a moment before I have to, so I'll help you however I can."

Jane's eyes filled with tears. "Thanks, hon."

"So, where do we start?"

FIFTEEN

*Adele*

When Kathy the editor had asked Adele to see a few of her recipes, Adele had laughed and told her she'd do her one better. Before she knew it, she had a date to cook for a cookbook editor, and now, with Kathy's arrival imminent, Adele's nerves were not happy about it.

After tallying everyone's votes, Adele had finally settled on two complete meals. She'd keep Kathy out of the kitchen to prevent her from seeing what a tremendous mess she'd created preparing for her arrival.

"Mama? We're here!" Meghan's voice rang through the house. Seconds later, she and Jane appeared in the kitchen. The girls had agreed to help her serve the food so Adele could sit and answer Kathy's questions without stressing out about keeping the food from burning or getting cold.

Now, though, staring at the two of them, she realized she might not trust either one of them with her precious dishes.

"Oh my." Jane covered her mouth with her hand, looking across the spread of food. "This is terrible."

"Terrible? I cooked what y'all told me to cook." Adele's eyes darted from Jane to Meghan.

Meghan pushed Jane toward the living room, but her eyes stayed on Adele. "Mama, maybe this is a bad idea. Jane's on a diet."

"A diet? Whatever for?" Adele followed them into the living room, where Jane plopped down on the couch.

"Because I broke a chair in front of the whole church." Jane dropped her head in her hands.

"Darlin', you know everyone has forgotten all about that." Adele sat down in the rocker across from them.

"I haven't." Jane sighed. "It smells so good in here. Like heaven. I've been eating lettuce for two days straight."

Adele frowned. "That can't be good for you."

"The point is, Mama, I'm not sure this is a good idea." Meghan put a hand on Jane's shoulder.

"No, don't be silly. It's just food. I'll be fine." Jane seemed to put her brave face on. "I promised Adele, and I'm not going back on my word."

The doorbell rang and Adele gasped. "What do I do?"

Meghan stood. "Answer the door?"

Adele stifled a squeal. "I can't believe this is happening." She rushed through the entryway, smoothed her apron and pulled the door open, praying to the good Lord that the smells of her handiwork greeted Kathy.

But when she opened the door, a man—not Kathy—stood on her porch. He wore jeans and a peacoat, and his nose was the color of strawberries.

"Kathy sends her apologies," he said. "She got called away on a personal matter. She sent me in her place." He extended a hand in her direction. "I'm Seth."

She shook his hand, but her mind had already started spinning. She'd anticipated a lovely lunch with a woman she'd already met, but instead she'd be entertaining a stranger.

"Come on in," Adele said. "It's nice to meet you."

"It smells wonderful, and it's a great idea to provide a sampling of some of your best dishes. Gives me a good idea of what we'll be getting should we offer you a contract."

Adele's heart jumped. A contract. What would Me-maw say?

Seth took off the pea coat to reveal a crisp white button-down, sleeves rolled to the elbows.

"I can take your coat for you." Meghan appeared beside them.

"Oh, where are my manners?" Adele said, snatching Seth's coat. "Yes, here, Meghan, hang that up for the man, would you?"

Meghan widened her eyes at Adele, as if to say "Calm yourself down."

Adele smiled. "Seth, you might recognize my daughter Meghan—"

"Meghan Rhodes," Meghan said, shaking the man's hand. "And I'm sure he doesn't recognize me, Mama. He doesn't seem like my core demographic." She winked, then turned her back to Seth and whispered, "This is about *you*."

Adele nodded. "Of course."

"I definitely know the name. My nieces are big fans."

"Where are you from, Seth?" Adele asked.

"Chicago."

Jane appeared in the living room, face flushed but still in one piece.

"Wonderful," Adele said. "Why don't we head to the dining room?"

She showed the man to the table and disappeared into the kitchen, where Jane and Meghan stared at the spread of food.

"We don't know what to do with it all," Meghan said.

"I know what I'd like to do with it all," Jane said.

"Girls. What do I do? There's a strange man in the dining room."

Jane and Meghan frowned in unison. "What are you talking about?" Meghan asked. "Just feed him, just like if it was that lady editor."

"You don't understand, Meg. Kathy already *liked* me. This meal was just to seal the deal. This boy has no reason to recommend they give me a *contract*." She said the word as if they were giving her the Ark of the Covenant.

"Mama, get a hold of yourself. Get out there and charm the man like you always do."

"And let us take care of the food."

Adele eyed Jane. "Fine. I wrote everything down for you and labeled everything here."

They nodded and started with the salad while Adele returned to her guest.

"I apologize for keeping you waiting, Seth."

Meghan appeared at the doorway. "Here is my mama's famous Waldorf salad. I hope you enjoy it."

Seth looked at Meghan, then at Adele. "Do you mind if you bring out all of the food at the same time? I'm in a bit of a hurry, and I think I'll just sample everything and be on my way." He punctuated his sentence with a smile, but Adele couldn't hide her surprise.

Meghan rushed to her side. "Of course, Mama, let's go make up a sampler plate for Seth." She pulled Adele up off the chair and pushed her into the kitchen.

"Do you believe this man?" Adele hissed. "Coming in here asking for a *sampler plate* after I've been slaving away for two solid days making sure everything is just right."

"Quiet, Mama, he'll hear you."

"I don't care if he does."

"Yes, you do, Adele." Jane had placed an apple glazed pork chop on a plate beside a small helping of roasted red potatoes.

Adele grabbed the plate and walked back into the living room. "Here you have pork chops and potatoes, just the way my Me-maw taught me to make them." She plunked down the plate in front of Seth and forced a smile.

"It looks wonderful," he said. He took two bites of the meat and ate one potato. "You're clearly a gifted cook."

Adele raised a brow, still standing beside him. "Thank you for that. I'll get the rest."

Back in the kitchen, she grabbed the second plate from Jane, this one featuring Me-maw's meat loaf, garlic smashed potatoes and bacon green beans. She set the plate down in front of Kathy's poor replacement and watched as he tasted each item on the plate.

He nodded. "Wonderful, thank you."

Why did she feel like he was humoring her?

Meghan walked in carrying a plate. On it, two different desserts.

"There's a homemade apple dumplin'," Adele said, ignoring Meghan's glare, "and a Southern-style lemon cake with almond cream-cheese frosting."

Adele cringed when Seth pushed the two plates of barely eaten food away to make room for another wasted effort. He took two bites of each dessert and nodded. "Very good. I love your style, Adele."

She crossed her arms and stared at him. Meghan elbowed Adele, and Adele uncrossed them.

"Thank you so much for your hospitality."

Jane appeared in the doorway with Seth's coat. He took it from her, shook each of their hands and walked toward the door. Adele was too dumbfounded to speak. Her big chance and it was ruined by this child who wouldn't know a good meal if it crawled into his mouth.

"And I have to admit, Ms. Rhodes, I've been known to sing along with my nieces' Meghan Rhodes albums before," Seth said, glancing at Meghan.

Meghan started to speak but simply nodded instead.

"We'll be in touch, Adele." He closed the door behind him, leaving the three of them surrounded by uneaten food and staring at each other.

"I'm so sorry, Adele," Jane said, her voice hardly a whisper.

"He didn't say anything bad about any of it, Mama."

Adele plopped down into the chair. "That's because he didn't eat enough of it to even taste it. Do you believe the nerve of that man?"

She picked up his dishes, piled them on top of each other and shoved past Meghan into the kitchen.

Meghan and Jane followed her, watching as she dropped the plates into the sink and started boxing up the leftovers. "You girls have to take this food home. I don't want to be reminded of what a fool I was."

"What's foolish about going after a big dream, Mama?"

Adele stopped. "At my age? It's foolish."

Meghan took Adele by the arms and turned her around. "It's never foolish to take a risk—especially if it's something you've always wanted to do. You were so excited about this idea. If they're too blind to see how amazing it could be, then we'll find a new publisher."

Adele met Meghan's eyes. "It's easy for you to say. Your big dreams came true."

Meghan laughed and hugged her. "That man doesn't know what he's missing."

Maybe so, but one thing was certain—he'd wrecked Adele's confidence. She wouldn't tell Meghan, but she had no intention of going after another publisher. The only thing she'd do was close this chapter once and for all.

And try to get over what a fool she'd been. "Maybe you girls can stay for dinner?"

Jane frowned. "I wish I could, Adele, but being in your kitchen has me broken out into a cold sweat."

"Oh, darlin', I'm sorry. Let's go sit in the other room." She led them to the empty dining room table and forced herself not to dwell on the plates of uneaten food Seth had left behind.

Instead, something else caught her eye, the computer.

Like an obsessed teenager, she'd taken multiple breaks during her cooking marathon, looking for a reply from Henry.

"Mama?"

"What?"

Meghan smiled. "Do I have to be worried about you? You seem lost in your own world."

"Oh no, don't be silly. I'm fine."

"Were you thinking about Henry?" Jane's face brightened.

Adele tried to be casual. "I sent him a note the other day."

"You did?" Meghan looked shocked.

"I did. Just to see how he's doing."

"And?"

"He hasn't replied yet."

"Well, let's check it."

Before she could protest, Meghan had moved toward the computer, brought it back to life and now waited for Adele's page to load. "Mama, you have a new message."

Adele gasped and pushed Meghan out of the chair, staring at the screen, unable to move.

"Are you going to read it?" Jane stood behind her, waiting.

All those feelings of young love rushed back to her. Walking down the Boardwalk with Henry at her side. Waiting to meet him after he finished working on his parents' farm. The first time he slipped his hand around hers as they stared out over the lake at dusk.

"We're going to go get some water," Jane said. "We'll be back."

Adele heard Meghan protest as Jane dragged her into the kitchen.

Alone with the computer, she clicked and opened the message from Henry.

*Adele,*

*What a nice surprise to find your message waiting for me. I'm glad you're doing well. It looks like you have a beautiful family. I would love to catch up. I see you're back in Sweethaven. Would you like to meet for coffee sometime? We can trade stories. I'll be down that way next week and would love to see you.*

*Yours,*
*Henry*

Adele reached the end of the message and realized she'd been holding her breath. She re-read Henry's words two more times before Jane and Meghan returned from the kitchen.

"What's wrong?" Meghan asked.

"Is he okay?" Jane sounded concerned.

Adele pulled her eyes from the screen. "He wants to meet. Have coffee."

Jane's lips spread into a smile. "That's good, right?"

Adele scanned the words one more time. "Yours, Henry." But he wasn't hers. Not anymore. What was she doing? She wouldn't have the foggiest idea what to say if she met him for coffee. And, truth be told, she didn't want Henry to remember her old and plump—she wanted him to think of that girl he'd known all those years ago.

And how could she face him after the hurt she'd caused him back then? She'd been so terrible. This was a bad idea.

"Adele?"

"I'm not going to go."

"What?"

Adele clicked out of the Internet and walked away from the computer. They followed her into the living room.

"This is a good thing, Adele. If nothing else, the two of you could be friends. You were good friends, weren't you?"

Adele's mind wandered. They were friends, and so much more.

"You have that wistful look on your face again, Mama." Meghan sat on the couch. "Tell us about him."

Adele sat in her rocking chair and hugged a pillow to her chest. "It's ages ago now."

"We don't care." Jane spotted the little journal on the ottoman across from where she sat. She flipped open to a photo of Adele and Henry sitting at the Sim's soda fountain, one milkshake between them. "Tell us about this boy."

Adele took the little journal and studied the picture, remembering that day with stark clarity. "Henry and I were inseparable that summer. Once we met at the dance, we saw each other every day. This was taken a few weeks after that."

Sim's brought in the teenagers every afternoon. The ones who'd spent the day on the beach and were ready to come in out of the sun, and the ones who, like Henry, spent the day working and were off the clock and ready for a little refreshment.

They sat in a booth at the back of the restaurant, hoping for a little alone time, but it didn't take long before their friends spotted them. Soon, their party of two had become a small group and it seemed to be multiplying every second. Adele joined in the conversation with her friends, but Henry stayed unusually quiet. She met his eyes and thought he seemed upset about something—or unsettled. It worried her. Had something happened?

Had he changed his mind about her—about them?

She leaned across the table. "Are you okay?"

He took her hand and leaned forward. "Can we go for a walk?"

Adele held his gaze for a long moment. "Of course."

Together, they excused themselves and walked out into the steamy summer night. The moon led them to the beach, where Adele took off her shoes, letting the now cool sand squish between her toes as she walked alongside Henry toward the lighthouse.

"Is everything okay?" she asked after too many moments of silence.

"My parents were talking about the war again."

Adele glanced at him, then back to the sand in front of her. She didn't like thinking about the war. They'd already gotten word that Ronnie Jenkins had been killed last month. And for what?

"What are they saying?"

"There's going to be a draft." Henry sighed. "It's just got me thinking, is all."

"About what?"

Henry stopped and leaned against the railing of the dock. "About you and me."

Adele faced him, her heart pounding at his words. "What do you mean?"

"Everyone else pretends like everything's fine. Like there's nothing going on in the world. I can't do that. And when I think about it, I think about you and what you mean to me. I just . . ." Henry's voice trailed off, and Adele wondered what he wasn't telling her. Up until now, he hadn't made much sense.

He took her hands and pulled her a little closer. "I was thinking about Ronnie and how he never got the chance to say good-bye. If that was me—I'd want people to know how I felt."

"But that's not you, Henry. Ronnie was on the other side of the world in a terrible war. You're here. You're safe."

He reached up and put a hand on the side of her face. "I know, but I guess I just have a lot of time to think working on the farm."

His hand on her face stirred something inside and her breath caught in her throat. At sixteen, she was naïve and inexperienced. Henry was the first boy to ever show her this kind of attention.

"Most of that time I think about you." His hand cradled her neck now, the other hand wrapped around hers. "And I realized I haven't told you how you make me feel."

Slowly, she brought her eyes to his and found his intent stare unnerving. What had gotten into him? Had Ronnie's death caused him to examine his own life? They had been friends growing up.

"Henry, you don't have to say anything." Adele heard the slight shake in her own voice and realized how nervous he made her.

He took her face in his hands and leaned down, drawing their lips together. For a brief moment, Adele startled at the nearness of him. She'd never kissed anyone before, and his lips on hers felt soft and warm. She inhaled the scent of him, freshly showered after a full day on his daddy's farm. She pulled back and met his eyes, and her awkwardness melted away at the acceptance she found waiting for her there. Was it possible for her to love Henry after only a few short weeks?

She didn't know, but she knew he made her feel unlike anyone else in the world.

She leaned against him then, as he drew his arms around her and welcomed his kisses and the way they made her feel—like she was someone special. Because to Henry, she was.

"I still don't know what got into him that night," Adele said now, closing the book in her lap. "But I suppose there will always be something special between the two of us." She stilled. "I guess you could say he was my first love."

Jane smiled. "I had no idea, Adele. I always think of you with Teddy."

At the mention of Teddy's name, Adele straightened. She shouldn't let herself wander down memory lane like this. How unfair it was to Teddy.

As if she read her mind, Meghan leaned forward and put a hand on hers. "Teddy doesn't want you to be alone. You know that, Mama. He wants you to be happy—to live all the years you have."

Adele quieted. Teddy had always been the most selfless person she knew, and he wouldn't want her to be lonely. He would want someone to take care of her.

"Just think about it," Jane said, standing. "Graham's taking the kids back home first thing. I'm staying to 'focus on myself.'" She tossed a glance toward the kitchen. "Though I'm not sure I have the willpower to be in your house. I'm already terrified to be here for Christmas."

Adele's heart fell at the thought of everyone returning to their lives. She loved sharing her home with the people she loved, serving them her latest dishes, hearing their laughter fill the house. When Tom and Lila appeared on her porch the night before, she'd barely been awake, and yet her heart leaped with joy that she could offer solace in their time of need.

When everyone left, it would be quiet again, and the thought of it brought the loneliness back.

"I'm so happy you're staying until Christmas," Adele said as she followed Jane toward the front door, Meghan close behind.

"Me too."

Adele pulled her into a hug, then she turned to Meghan and gave her a squeeze too. "Thanks for helping me today, girls."

Meghan nodded and followed Jane out onto the porch. "Mama," Meghan said, facing her. "Think about Henry's invitation. For what it's worth, I think you should go."

"I will, darlin'. I promise." Adele waved as they walked down the steps toward Meghan's car.

Back inside, the quiet of the house haunted her. For someone as social as she was, the emptiness of that home was something of a curse.

She stood at the doorway of the dining room and stared at the computer for too many minutes, her mind spinning with ancient thoughts of Henry's touch—his kisses.

Then, without giving it another thought, she clicked open his message and hit Reply.

*Dear Henry,* she wrote, *I think getting together for coffee sounds like just about the best idea I've heard. . . .*

SIXTEEN

*Campbell*

The Monday night composition class would only meet for a few more weeks and then they took a break until after the New Year. With only six students, Campbell had been able to test her teaching skills, praying regularly that her mom's ease in front of an audience had transferred to her.

By now, months after that first nerve-racking class, she'd settled into her own groove and found that she enjoyed sharing what she'd learned about photography with her students. Most were hobbyists or young moms who were tired of their boring photographs. She'd grown to love them. Even Jed, whose camera was likely twice as old as Campbell.

The old man had proven to be a quick study, though—an artist who'd never blossomed, Campbell called him. Now, as she prepared to close the class and give them their assignment for the following week, the door at the back of the gallery opened and Luke walked in. Her students followed the distraction and her eyes in time to see Luke lift his hand in a slight, apologetic wave.

Campbell had been putting him off since the night of their dinner. The night her snooping had led her to the discovery of a ring she was not meant to see. At least not yet. He'd likely want to know why she'd been so distant. Her stomach turned at the thought of having the conversation.

She didn't want to jeopardize what they had, but something was stopping her from letting go completely. She couldn't even tell him how she really felt about him.

What was she so afraid of?

Campbell scanned the faces of her students. "Your assignment is to shoot low light at one of the community events this week. I'm planning to participate in this assignment myself." She could hardly wait to experience a Sweethaven Christmas for herself. Events like the Luminary Walk through downtown and the outdoor Christmas Concert in the Park promised to usher in the magic of the holidays.

"Which one will you be shooting, Miss Carter?" Jed asked from the back row.

"I'm going to try to get to all of them," she said, "but I'm most looking forward to the Christmas Concert in the Park."

"Then that's where I'll plan on going," Jed said, winking at her.

Campbell glanced at Luke, who raised an amused brow.

The others laughed and Campbell wished them all a wonderful week. As they left, her students chatted about their assignment, a few of them thanking her for such an enjoyable class.

She locked the door behind the last student and turned to find Luke leaning against the brick wall in the back. "Hey, stranger," he said. "I think I'm going to take this class next session."

She grinned. "Sure you are."

"You seem to be pretty comfortable in front of them."

"They're a good class."

"You're a good teacher." His eyes found hers, and she could see the question that lingered there. Had her absence, her distance, hurt him? Regret twisted in her belly, especially remembering how his absence, his distance with his consulting back in Chicago, had affected her at first. It had been unfair of her to react without any explanation, but the truth could do far more harm than good.

"You've been hiding away over here," he said.

She gathered her class notes and stuffed them in a manila folder. "It's been busy. Trying to get ready for next year's classes before the holiday break." She had to schedule everything to publicize the gallery in the local newspaper, and that had been time-consuming. But not nearly as time-consuming as she made it out to be.

He followed her over to the counter, where she filed away the class notes in the bottom drawer underneath the register.

"Looks like you've got a good system here."

She turned to Luke. "It's coming together, but you were right. It's a lot of work."

"Cam, is everything okay?" The pleading look in his eyes pierced her heart. Hurting him was not an option.

She put on a smile. "Of course, why wouldn't it be?"

"You tell me."

Her mind spun. What could she say? *I saw the ring and I don't know what to say if you propose to me.* Sometimes honesty wasn't the best policy, no matter what they taught you in Sunday school.

"It's just hectic, and, you know, it's the first Christmas without my mom." As soon as the words were out, she regretted them. How dare she use her mom's death as an excuse for her behavior? It should've been the reason, but it wasn't, and the idea shamed her.

His shoulders slumped then, deflating almost, and she imagined having a reason for her weird behavior had come as a relief to him.

She rationalized the thought and told herself that Mom had been on her mind a lot lately, though not because of the holidays. Because right now, she needed someone to talk her off the ledge—to tell her what to do, and she didn't have that anymore. Not really.

Still, had she deceived Luke by claiming Mom's absence as the reason for her own?

He sighed. "Cam, I'm sorry. I've been so insensitive about that." He took her hand and pulled her into a hug. "Do you need anything?"

She melted into him, wanting to stay there for the rest of the night, the warmth of his embrace all the comfort she needed.

"No, I'm fine." She pulled back and looked at him. "But thank you."

He kissed her forehead. "Listen, I have something I want to ask you."

Campbell's heart jumped. *Oh no. Not now.*

"I heard you say you're going to the Christmas concert?"

"Of course."

"Do you want to go together?" Luke grinned. "For me, it's the true beginning of the season, hearing them play all the Christmas songs, and this year Meghan's even singing at it—part of that special they're filming."

Her nerves quieted, though she couldn't explain the emotion that took their place. "Oh yeah, that sounds fun."

"You're up for it?"

"Of course."

He slipped his arms around her. "Good. I think you're going to love spending Christmas in Sweethaven."

Christmas at home had always been magical. Mom seemed to have so many friends without family nearby, and they'd all get together and feel less lonely, more like this was just as it was meant to be.

Would Sweethaven adopt Campbell the same way?

"I'm sorry you're missing your mom," Luke said. "I still miss my dad around the holidays."

His eyes melted her and for the briefest moment, she imagined herself letting go of these insecurities, of finally telling him how she felt. What if he did propose? What if she said yes? Maybe this was what she really wanted but was too scared to admit to herself.

"Thanks, Luke. I'm really looking forward to making some new traditions."

He smiled. "I'll pick you up here before the concert. We can walk over to the Square together. Dress warm."

"You don't want to keep me warm?"

He grinned. "Oh, I'll keep you warm. I promise it'll be the most romantic night of your life," Luke said, his eyes dancing in the dim light of the gallery.

She waited for more of an explanation, but none came. Only kisses—kisses she stopped herself from getting lost in.

Because in the back of her mind, she'd already started obsessing over Luke's words. The most romantic night of her life would surely include a proposal—in public, at the Sweethaven Christmas concert. Luke's way of adding to the holiday magic?

With every passing moment, and every threat of being swept away by his kiss, Campbell pulled herself back to earth with the reality that at this time the next night, she could be wonderfully engaged . . . or horribly single.

## SEVENTEEN

*Lila*

Even after a heart-to-heart with Adele, their night at the Whitmore hadn't brought any peace. Lila awoke with Tom at her side, the memory of the night before crashing back. The words she'd said to her parents had certainly put her out of their good graces, and while they weren't exactly in hers either, she imagined she took it to heart far more than they did.

"You feel like getting breakfast?" Tom asked when Lila turned off the hair dryer.

She couldn't sit around the hotel room all morning. "Sure."

After they got dressed, they walked down Main Street until they reached the café. They found a table in the back and one of the waitresses took their order. Lila hadn't been able to drink coffee after about a month into her pregnancy, and even now she wondered if the smell of it might upset her stomach.

"You okay?" Tom must've seen the green color of her face.

"Fine. Just need to eat something, I think."

Their food arrived and Lila had no problem eating her entire egg sandwich with a side of American fries. "I can't believe I spent so many years not eating this food."

Tom smiled. "You've been missing out."

They finished their meal, and just as they were getting ready to leave, her mother strolled in. Lila could tell she hadn't expected to see her there, but Mama quickly regained her composure and sailed through the maze of tables. She stood in front of Lila in a matter of seconds. Lila stared at the table.

"I wondered when I'd run into you," Mama said. "We need to talk. Tom, would you excuse us, please?" Mama glared at Tom, but Lila clapped a hand over his.

"If you want to talk to me, you can do it in front of my husband."

Mama drew in a long breath. Lila tried to brace herself for whatever Mama had planned.

"Fine." She sat. "I'm sure Tom would much rather remove himself from all of your drama, but if this is the way you want it, I suppose I can't change your mind."

"Say what you need to say, Mama. And then I have to go. We're looking at cottages this afternoon." She knew it would irk Mama if Lila bought her own cottage. They'd discussed the day the lake house would officially be passed down to Tom and Lila, but in light of recent events, Lila had no intention of receiving anything from her parents. When they outgrew it, her parents could put the lake house on the market—she didn't care anymore.

"Why would you do that?"

"I don't want to get into it here."

Mama sighed. "You were always so obstinate, Lila."

Lila's jaw went slack. Mama had always been cold, but with this latest development, it seemed to have gotten worse.

"I just want you to know that this is as much a shock to me as it is to you," Mama said, her eyes stony, her jaw tense.

Lila studied her mother for any sign of emotion but found none.

"When I saw that woman in the restaurant, I assumed, like you, that she was another one of your father's mistresses. He has a way of flaunting them around town, but I thought he'd have the decency to keep them out of our holiday celebration."

Mama pressed her lips together. "When I found out who she really was—that he'd been lying . . ." Mama brought her gaze to Lila's, then quickly looked away. "I'm just sorry any of this had to happen."

Lila had never seen her mother vulnerable. Would this be the thing to finally help them see eye to eye? With Daddy as a common enemy, the two of them could move past this, start over.

"So what will you do?" Lila resisted the urge to reach out and take Mama's hands. She didn't know where to begin to comfort her mother, but she was quite sure Mama wouldn't accept any empathy from her.

"Same thing I've been doing for years, darling."

Lila frowned. "How can you do that? How can you turn a blind eye over and over?"

Mama's eyes darted to Tom. "I would think you of all people would understand, dear daughter."

Lila felt Tom's hand on her knee, but she ignored it. "How dare you, Mama."

Mama's brows sprang upward and an innocent look washed over her face.

"Don't compare Tom and me to you and Daddy. Daddy's a chronic cheater."

"Once a cheater, always a cheater, my darling." Her glare hung too long on Tom, and Lila shifted in her seat.

"I think you should go, Mama."

"I understand the truth hurts, but eventually you get used to it. You accept the fact that men are not made to be faithful. And when something like this happens—something like Campbell happens—you learn to accept it and move on. It does me no good to leave your father."

Lila couldn't make sense of Mama's behavior. What if Mama really didn't care? Stopped believing she deserved a loyal husband?

The older Adler stood, smoothed her jacket and looked down on the two of them. "We all have our disappointments, Lila. But the important thing is that you're honest with yourself about them. I simply wanted you to know I had no part in this."

Lila watched her mother walk out the door.

"Hon, let it go," Tom said. "You know you can't listen to your mother. She's obviously a miserable person who doesn't love anyone but herself."

"Is she right, Tom?"

"About what?"

"Once a cheater, always a cheater?"

He closed his eyes and drew in a deep breath. "Don't let her do this to you, Lila."

Lila's mind spun with all the overnight trips Tom had taken over the years. Sometimes he'd be gone for a week or more. How did she know he'd been faithful? All those years they had problems—had he even once ignored the gold band on his finger?

She turned to face him. "Tell me the truth. You've had plenty of opportunity. Flight attendants, women you've met on planes. Tell me you've never slept with anyone else."

Tom held her eyes. "I've never slept with anyone else."

"The entire time we've been married?"

He brought a hand to her face and brushed away a tear. "Lila, I made enough mistakes before we were married. I wasn't going to keep making them afterward. I knew how it made me feel to have to keep a secret from you."

She wanted to believe him, but Mama had seemed so sure.

"I'm not your father. And you're not your mother. Thankfully. Don't take on their problems. You know me."

Lila let him hold her as she regained her composure, determined not to let herself fall apart in the middle of the café.

Mama wanted to believe that everyone else's marriage was as miserable as hers, but the old woman didn't know everything. She hadn't spent any time around them, so what could she possibly hope to do by casting aspersions in their direction? Finally, Lila had what she wanted, a happy marriage, a baby on the way—and Mama was determined to ruin all of it.

All because her own life had gone so sideways. Lila wouldn't give in. If she had to cut Mama out of her life altogether, she would.

She looked at Tom as they got in the car and drove toward the first house on their list.

No, Mama wouldn't convince her that her husband had been anything but faithful to her. They'd seen their fair share of troubles, but they were past that now.

So why had this nagging feeling lodged itself in her heart?

And how could she make it go away?

## EIGHTEEN

*Jane*

The annoyance of the alarm finally woke Jane from a dead sleep. Exercising the past few days had worn her out, and it hadn't gotten any easier to drag herself out of bed before the sun rose.

Jane had never been athletic. Any weight loss she'd achieved in the past had been due to extreme dieting, and had always been short-lived. So, asking her to suddenly learn to love moving her body was like asking a prisoner to suddenly enjoy his cell. Nothing about exercise appealed to her, but she'd done it two days in a row.

Before she got out of bed, Lori's condescending smile appeared in her mind. How was it possible she'd allowed Dr. Barry to set her up with a nutritionist whose name she hadn't bothered to get? "Just come to my office and give them your name," he'd told her.

Jane went blindly, and now she regretted it.

Still, as much as she hated to admit it, Lori was right about one thing. Jane did want to have some benchmark of her progress along the way.

She hauled herself out of bed and locked the bedroom door, her fear of being seen next to naked paralyzing her. The same fear that had caused her to insist on a dark room every time she and Graham were alone together. It didn't matter that he'd insisted he loved her body, that he loved her skin and her curves. He could love it better in the dark. Even a man as kind and patient as Graham couldn't really love someone so padded.

The camera sat on the dresser mocking her, daring her to strip down and create evidence of her gluttony.

Jane inhaled and took off her pajama bottoms. Her white tank top clung to her midsection, showing every extra roll. Not exactly the kind of curves she wanted to show off. Slowly she undressed, turning her eyes away from the mirror as she did. The cellulite on her legs grabbed her attention and she grimaced. One look at it in the mirror and her heart sank. How could she photograph herself in this condition? She didn't care if she needed it as a benchmark, she didn't want proof she'd let herself go.

Her mind whirled back to the days spent in bed after Alex's death. Days when the ladies in their church brought them rich desserts to complement their best dinners, and Jane had indulged in every one. She'd never said no to herself because her pain told her she deserved it. She'd lost her son. Didn't she deserve to enjoy a German chocolate cake without remorse? Never mind that over the course of two days she'd eaten the entire thing.

Now, she swore she could see that cake hugging her hip bones—or at least the place where her hip bones must be.

With as few clothes on as she could stand, Jane snapped a photo of herself from the front, then the side, then quickly got dressed, wishing she'd never followed this piece of doctor's advice. She didn't need to see where she'd started—how could she ever forget this? She lived with it every day.

And it had left her feeling defeated and sad.

Jane remembered the girls had gone out the night before with the youth group. They'd brought home half of a cheesecake—for the pastor and his wife—and Graham had quickly swooped in and stashed it in the back of the fridge. But she knew right where it was. The refrigerator seemed to beckon her to it, like a magnet, and without thinking, she opened the door and located the Styrofoam takeout container.

Cheesecake wasn't even her favorite dessert, but it had been days since she'd had any sugar. And she'd exercised. Would it hurt her to have one little bite? Hadn't she earned that much with her near-death exercise experience? Surely the doctor didn't expect her to give up sugar for good.

Jane reached in and took the cheesecake container from the fridge and set it on the counter. She fished through the silverware drawer, her heart rate kicking up, until she found a fork.

One deep breath and she popped open the container. Two large pieces of thick-crusted cheesecake stared at her. She leaned in and inhaled its scent, her mouth watering for it. Without letting her brain get involved, she cut off a bite and shoved it in her mouth. She ate it so quickly she didn't even taste it, so she hurried another bite but barely chewed that one either. The next time she looked down, one entire piece had disappeared.

And she didn't remember eating it.

Jane threw the fork onto the counter and pushed the container away. Her heart dropped and she knew if gluttony needed a poster child, she'd be in the running.

A knock on the door startled her away from the counter, the evidence of her weakness mocking her. She threw the fork in the sink and shoved the cheesecake back into hiding in the fridge, wiping away any stray crumbs from her face.

Meghan's face beamed as Jane pulled open the door, but Jane's forced smile changed her friend's expression. Meghan—always beautiful without ever trying—could never understand this struggle of Jane's, and the thought of it almost angered her.

If any of them knew what she'd just done, how weak she really was, they'd be just as disgusted with her as she was with herself.

"What's wrong with you, Janie? You look upset."

Jane forced herself to pretend. "No, of course not. Come in."

"I can't believe I forgot to tell you about this," Meghan said as the screen door smacked closed behind her. "I'm making a comeback."

"Where have you been?"

"I'm talking about my career." Meghan followed Jane into the kitchen, where she hoped she'd gotten rid of all incriminating evidence of her sin.

"We're doing a big Christmas special at our cottage," Meghan continued, unfazed by the food-filled surroundings.

"Here?"

Meghan nodded. "It's called *A Down-Home Country Christmas,* and they want my family there. The way I see it, you and Lila are as much my family as Mama and Luke, so will you do it?"

Jane's mind spun, trying to calculate the number of calories she'd just eaten. How could she remedy it? By not eating dinner? By skipping the next few meals or just having a plain grilled chicken breast and a light salad with no dressing? Could she stomach salad without dressing?

"Jane?"

"What?" Jane's eyes darted to Meghan, who clearly waited for an answer to a question Jane had already forgotten.

"What's gotten into you? Are you okay?"

Jane sighed. Clearly not.

Meghan reached across the table. "Let me help. All the times you've helped me—can I return the favor?"

"I don't think so, Meg. I don't think anyone can help." Jane's eyes filled with tears and she blinked them back, begging herself to keep it together.

Meghan's face fell. "Jane, what is it?"

"Remember how you said I wasn't always heavy?"

Meghan nodded.

"I checked. You were right. So, I started thinking if I wasn't meant to be heavy, maybe I could change. I went to the doctor and found out I'm prediabetic."

"I'm so sorry, Jane."

Jane shared the rest of the details about Lori and the cheesecake and how it shouldn't be this hard to control her eating—especially when her health was on the line.

"But, Jane, we all have our issues. Otherwise, we wouldn't need God."

As the words hung in the air between them, the tears streamed down Jane's face. Meghan was right. All this time, though, she'd been trying to conquer her problem on her own. It seemed petty to beg God for weight loss when there were so many things wrong in the world.

But she'd always said God was in the details.

Meghan reached down and pulled out a familiar journal from her purse. The prayer journal Jane had given her only a few months before. "The words in this album have been my lifeline, Jane. Let them do the same for you."

Jane shook her head. "I know what these verses say, Meg. I've got them all memorized. 'I'm fearfully and wonderfully made.' 'Before I formed you in the womb I knew you.' I get it. God loves me."

Meghan's hands covered Jane's just as tears stung her eyes. "You say it like it's old news, Janie. You need to remember how powerful these words really are."

Jane wiped her cheeks dry and then finally looked away. Was Meghan giving her spiritual advice? Meghan, who'd been at rock bottom more times than anyone else Jane knew?

"Sometimes you learn things when you're in the gutter. Those words are so much more than words, Jane. They're life."

"I had no idea you felt that way."

"Thanks to you."

Jane looked away. She'd been so good at telling everyone else what God said and how it applied to their lives, but she'd failed to see it for herself.

Jane opened the little album and flipped through its familiar pages, but near the back she discovered prayers that weren't hers.

"What are these?"

Meghan stared at the book in Jane's hands. "Those are my prayers."

Jane held her gaze. "You added to it?"

Meghan nodded. "I hope that's okay."

"Are you kidding? It's better than okay." Jane stared at the pages Meghan had added to the journal. Prayers of gratitude and struggle alike came to life.

Meghan pointed to the open page. "That one is going to be a song. Those are the lyrics."

Jane shook her head. "It's amazing."

Meghan sat for a few minutes while Jane scanned the rest of the pages. "Listen, I wrote down the information about the TV special. Keep the journal for a while." Meghan stood. "I like to think that it might help you as much as it's helped me."

Since getting her family back together, Meghan seemed like a changed person. Happier, calmer, more content. What if the words God had given Jane for her friend really had helped transform her life?

Jane saw Meghan to the door, then sat down in the front room with the journal. She flipped through the pages one by one. The words on the pages jumped out at her as if she was seeing them for the first time.

Her eyes scanned the page, her handwriting messy as if hurried, which happened often when she prayed. The thoughts came to her so quickly, she couldn't write fast enough to get everything down.

*I praise you because I am fearfully and wonderfully made; your works are wonderful, I know that full well. —Psalm 139:14*

She'd meant the words when she wrote them, hadn't she? Framed in the context of Meghan's life, they made sense. God loved Meghan so much, and Jane wanted her friend to see that, to feel it deep down. Why, then, was it such a struggle to feel it for herself?

*"Come to me, all you who are weary and burdened, and I will give you rest." —Matthew 11:28*

Jane took a deep breath and reread the verse she'd written at the center of one of the pages. She'd never felt more weary, more shameful, more in need of rest.

But how did she do what God said? How did she come to Him? How did she let herself rely on Him when she'd gotten so used to relying on herself?

She wasn't a new Christian. She should know this by now.

But she didn't, and it was time to learn.

"God, I don't know what I'm doing," Jane prayed as she ran her fingers over the words. "I don't know how to run to You. I only know how to run to cheesecake."

Tears streamed down Jane's face and she let them heat her cheeks.

Just when she thought she'd figured out everything else she realized she didn't know anything at all.

NINETEEN

*Meghan*

The morning of the meeting with the television producers, Meghan awoke with a ball of nervous energy lodged in her stomach. Her hands wouldn't warm and she felt jittery and anxious.

By the time the producers arrived at the house, Meghan's emotions had come out in full force, fear of all the things that could go wrong threatening to swallow her whole. They could pull the plug on the whole thing. They could find a way to embarrass her like Shandy Shore had done. Or she could embarrass herself, without any help from anyone.

But so far, everyone she'd told had expressed nothing but giddy excitement at the prospect of being on the show, and for that reason alone, she forced herself to pull open the front door and welcome the LA team into her home.

A woman and two men stood on the porch. Meghan noted how young they seemed. The woman wore oversize sunglasses, had long blonde hair and was as skinny as a rail. "Meghan." She removed her sunglasses and flashed a smile. "I'm Liz Dayton. This is Tyler and this is Josh." She motioned toward the two men on either side of her.

"Please, come in." Meghan ushered them in and both of the men turned their attention to the house. Meghan watched as they seemed to survey every inch of her home.

"The Christmas tree will need to be moved," Tyler said.

"And we'll probably need more decorations. We can bring in Sheila," Josh said.

"Who's Sheila?" Meghan asked.

"Our set decorator," Liz said. "She's a whiz. She'll have this place looking like a winter wonderland in no time."

"I thought we wanted to stay true to our real life. Our actual traditions."

Liz smiled. "Nothing on TV is real, especially on reality TV. Can we sit?"

Meghan followed her into her own living room but kept an eye on the two men, who seemed intent on breaking down her home by camera angles.

"Now, Martin filled us in on the basics. Do you have a schedule of events we'll be covering?" Liz asked.

Meghan opened the file folder she'd put together and pulled out the Sweethaven Christmas brochure. "I went through and circled the events we'll be attending."

Liz took it and looked it over. "Looks good. We'll have a crew ready to go for at least a few of these events. The way this will work is we'll film portions live and then cut away to these prerecorded segments, you at the Christmas concert, you judging the ice-carving contest, that sort of thing. And we'll hire the cast members to come along."

Meghan frowned. "What do you mean?"

"Oh, I nearly forgot." She reached into her slick black handbag and pulled out a stack of eight-by-ten black–and-white head shots. After flipping through them, Liz set two out in front of Meghan on the table. "Which one most resembles your mother?"

"Neither of them. My mom isn't this thin." She glanced at the photos. "How old are these women?"

"They're in our 'older' category."

"Older category of what?"

"Actresses."

"Actresses? Why can't we use my real mother?"

The woman glanced at the two men behind Meghan. One man cleared his throat as the other cast his eyes downward.

"In our experience, it's best to use professionals. Especially for the live segments. We'll cast seasoned pros as your friends and family. It just eliminates so much headache."

Meghan's mind spun. How could this woman even suggest such a thing? Casting her family with people who were clearly *not* her family?

"What about our kids? They'll be in it, won't they? I mean, they've been in the tabloids. People will know if we use phony kids."

Liz shuffled through her bag, for what Meghan was sure was nothing more than an opportunity to avoid her glare.

Just then, the front door opened and Nick entered with the twins. His plan was right in the middle of backfiring and it was hard not to project her anger onto him.

"Sorry I'm late," he said. "We had to stop for the bathroom on the way home." He glanced at Nadia. "She couldn't wait five minutes."

"Liz, this is my husband Nick."

Liz stood. "So you're the brains behind our Christmas gala."

Nick glanced at Meghan, who shot him a look he could hopefully interpret. He leaned in toward the twins. "Can you guys say hi to the nice lady?"

Finn's eyes widened and he moved behind Meghan's leg.

Nadia buried her head in Nick's shoulder.

"Come on, guys, just say a quick hello."

Neither of them would budge.

Liz tossed Meghan a smile. "This is why we hire professionals," she said. "Especially with children, you just never know what you're going to get. The public understands this. We assumed you would too."

"I'm sure they just need a few minutes to warm up to you," Meghan said.

"Mrs. Rhodes, you of all people should know how unpredictable live television can be."

Meghan felt heat creep up her neck. Did she really have to bring up how Meghan had been ambushed on national television with unfortunate photos from her past?

"It's simply best to remove every variable that could become precarious."

"But these aren't variables. These are my kids," Meghan said. "I'm not sure I want to do this without them."

Liz shuffled through a file folder and produced a familiar sheet of paper. "According to the contract you signed, it's up to us to determine the cast." The contract? They'd sent it to an entertainment lawyer who'd said everything looked standard. In her excitement for her second chance, Meghan hadn't thought to read it after the lawyer, so she'd signed on the dotted line and sent it back.

It was becoming apparent that not having a seasoned manager had its drawbacks.

"We'll be back for the first event on the schedule. I've got all your contact information if we need anything further." Liz stood and hitched her bag up over her shoulder. "Thanks so much for your time."

After the three of them left, Meghan turned to Nick. "Unbelievable."

"I'm sorry, hon. I had no idea."

"They can't do this," Meghan said, motioning toward the door where the three had just left. "I've already told people about the special. They're excited, and I want them to be a part of it."

"Let me look over the contract and talk to Martin," Nick said. "If we're going to do this without Duncan, we need to read the fine print a little better."

She shot him a look.

He walked toward her. "That's not a dig at you. Just an observation. If there's nothing we can do, we'll make the best of it."

Meghan sighed. "I'm going to let them all come anyway. Once that Liz sees how wonderful our real friends and family really are, she'll have no choice but to let them be in the show."

Nick frowned. "I don't think it works that way."

"I should get to have some say in how this goes, shouldn't I? It's my Christmas special. My name's on it."

Nick stood in front of her, wide-eyed.

She didn't care if he disagreed. He wasn't going to change her mind. Her friends and family were going to be in the special one way or another.

## TWENTY

*Adele*

The computer and all the power it seemed to wield still remained something of a mystery to Adele. She woke up with a plan—decorate the house—but even as she hung the swaths of evergreen on the stairway and wrapped it with white lights, her thoughts turned to Henry and whether or not he'd written again.

Finally, after hanging a bay leaf wreath on the front door and finishing the entryway, Adele wandered toward the dining room and stared at the machine.

"Ridiculous," she said out loud and turned around. She exchanged the plain pillows for Christmas pillows in the living room, cleared a spot for the tree she'd eventually purchase from the Boy Scouts downtown and redecorated the mantel.

And all the time, she thought of Henry.

Finally, after she'd whipped the living room into proper Christmas shape, she couldn't deny that her old bones needed a break. Might as well be in front of the computer.

As she waited for the machine to spring to life, her mind rushed through the errands she needed to run, presents she wanted to buy, and through it all she reminded herself to slow down in the coming weeks—to really enjoy the holidays because they'd be over before she blinked.

The screen came on and Adele talked herself through the steps to get back to the site that promised her a connection with Henry. Once there, she began to search around, still trying to get an idea of what all could be done on this Facebook. As she did, a little box with Henry's picture popped up in the lower right-hand corner of the screen.

Adele gasped. What in the world?

She put her reading glasses on and leaned in closer and read the words "Hi there" beside Henry's name.

*Hi there?*

The box began blinking as the words "It's been too long, Adele. How are you?" appeared.

Was Henry talking to her over the computer? She stared at the cursor as the words "Are you there?" appeared.

Adele inhaled, then typed "Yes, I'm here," but the words didn't move from where she typed them into the conversation box. She studied the keyboard and then finally realized she hadn't pressed Enter. When she did, her words popped up underneath Henry's.

She was talking to Henry. Just like that. Without saying a word.

"Hi," Henry wrote.

"Hi."

The cursor blinked at her. Now what?

"How've you been?" he wrote.

"I'm good. You?" She couldn't help but think if this were a real conversation, she might be searching for a way out.

"Wonderful. Especially now that I'm back in touch with you."

Heat zipped through Adele's cheeks and she smiled. Always a charmer, that Henry. "I didn't know anything about Facebook until my kids showed me." It had been awhile since she'd typed, and her fingers barely remembered where the home row was. Little by little, it started to come back to her. She glanced up and reread what she'd written. She hadn't meant to talk about her kids. Would Henry want to avoid that topic?

"Me either," he wrote. "Actually, it was my granddaughter who showed me. She's ten."

Adele laughed out loud. For nearly an hour, she and Henry exchanged words on a little box in the right-hand corner of her computer screen. She learned that he'd been married, but his wife had passed away. They had four children and now he had eleven grandkids. None of them lived nearby.

"Remember our last summer together?"

Henry's words caught her off-guard. She did remember. She remembered what he told her on the beach that night and how it changed everything.

"I remember everything, Henry," she typed.

Sweethaven, in many ways, seemed to be in a bubble of sorts, but in those days, the condition of the country extended beyond the town's limits. Their world had been turned upside down with talk of the draft and the war in Vietnam. She and Henry had escaped it all by spending long summer nights in his father's boat, a crummy little speedboat that had been replaced by something much grander.

"Pop says this is my boat now," Henry had said as he cut the engine and they stared across the lake at the whole of Sweethaven.

"What will you do with it?" Adele asked, admiring the sun dipping below the horizon, the Sweethaven lighthouse in the foreground.

"Whatever I want, I suppose." Henry leaned his elbows on his knees. "I'd like to keep heading that way." He looked out over the lake, expanding as far as his eye could see. "Just you and me. We could get away from all this nonsense of trying to figure out what to do with the rest of our lives."

Adele hadn't started thinking about the rest of her life. Not really—not yet. But Henry was two years older.

"My dad wants me to go to med school. He's already decided I should be a doctor."

"And you don't want to?"

Henry shook his head. "I've got other ideas, but he's going to hate them."

"What are they?"

Henry started the engine again. "It doesn't matter. Let's just enjoy the night."

And while they had enjoyed the night, and many others like it, there were moments when Henry seemed burdened with a decision he had no business having to make.

Looking back on it now, Adele wished he would've talked to her about it then instead of keeping everything bottled up inside, but it wasn't his way.

The cursor blinked and Adele had to remind herself to respond to whatever Henry had just said. When she glanced up she saw his words waiting for her: "So when should we get that cup of coffee?"

Adele stared at the words, unsure of what to type next.

"Adele?"

Her hands hovered over the keyboard and her mind spun, doubting her previous decision to see him. She'd accepted that she'd never see Henry again. She'd decided his life had turned out a certain way—that he'd turned out a certain way. Could she bear it if she learned none of those things were true?

Could she bear it if she met him and that familiar old regret over a choice she'd made all those years ago twisted its way into her belly?

She started to write "Oh, next week might be hard for me . . ." but deleted it. Next, she tried, "What day were you thinking?" but was she ready to commit to a face-to-face meeting? She quickly deleted that. Back to a blinking cursor.

The sound of the back door opening startled her.

Without thinking, she clicked out of her Internet connection just in time to see Luke come into the room. "Hey, Ma."

"Luke, you scared me to death."

Luke narrowed his eyes. "What were you doing?"

"Nothin'." She stood and walked past him into the kitchen. "I'm working on my cookbook. I've got a lot to do." Never mind that she still hadn't heard back from that weasel of a man about whether or not there would actually *be* a cookbook.

"Uh-huh. Well, I just came by to make sure you're coming to Meghan's for the filming."

"You came all the way here to ask me that? Why didn't you just call?" Adele said, willing her heart to settle down.

"I would've, but on the phone, I couldn't steal one of these." He picked up a chocolate chip cookie and waved it at her.

Why was she so jumpy? What did it matter if she wanted to have coffee with an old friend? Surely her son wouldn't care one bit—so why did it feel like a secret she'd hide from her parents, like a diary stuffed under her mattress?

"Ma, are you okay?" Luke swallowed one cookie and picked up another.

"Of course. And I'll be at Meghan's. You can plan on it."

"Will you bring the cookies?"

Adele laughed, but she couldn't rid herself of the panic she felt. Henry had posed an important question and she had turned the computer off. Granted, she had hesitated, even without

Luke's intrusion, but she would've said yes eventually. Wouldn't she?

On his end, how did this look? Like she'd just abandoned their conversation at the most pivotal moment. Oh, she hated that blasted computer.

But without it, she'd never have found him again.

After Luke left, with half a dozen cookies in his pockets, Adele hurried back to the computer, but Henry had signed off.

She hadn't been this disappointed in a long time.

## TWENTY-ONE

*Lila*

Lila awoke to the smell of pancakes. She opened her eyes to find Tom setting the little table in their room at the Whitmore.

"I ordered us breakfast," he said.

She forced a smile. She didn't have the heart to tell him that her morning sickness made that pancake her enemy or that their days at the Whitmore had only increased her loneliness.

After she splashed water on her face and brushed her teeth, Lila felt a little better—good enough to sit across from Tom and at least pick at the pancakes.

"I made a few appointments to look at cottages," Tom said, inhaling a bite of his breakfast.

Lila tried to find excitement, but truth be told, she felt like she needed four more hours of sleep. Suddenly, this baby seemed to need more of everything—more food, more rest, more water. Did she really want to trudge all over town looking at cottages?

"You don't look happy." Tom frowned.

"No, it'll be great. I'm excited to find our own place." She wasn't lying—she just didn't feel like being visibly excited in that moment.

After breakfast, Lila showered and dressed, then followed Tom out to the car so they could make their appointment with the Realtor. She'd packed Saltine crackers and a large water bottle in hopes that they would ward off any ill feelings she might have.

But when they pulled into the driveway of the first cottage, she realized it would take more than bland food and proper hydration to keep the bad feelings away.

"I already hate it," she said, staring at the mustard-colored ranch behind overgrown bushes.

"You haven't even seen the inside yet."

"I don't think I need to."

"Lila, keep an open mind," Tom said. "We can always get something cheap and renovate it. I've always wanted to do that."

Lila frowned. "Well, that makes one of us."

"You're an interior designer. You could easily transform a house. Let's just see." He jumped out of the car and met Pearl Bailey standing near the edge of the driveway. Pearl was old and should've retired years ago, but she had the corner on the Sweethaven real estate market. After they exchanged hellos, he motioned for Lila to join them.

She moved slowly up the walk as Pearl fumbled with the lock. Finally, the old woman pushed the door open and they walked inside. The smell of animals and cigarettes smacked Lila in the face. Before she knew what had happened, she turned and threw up in the front bushes. She slapped her hand over her mouth, stunned, then turned to find both Tom and Pearl staring at her.

"I'm so sorry," she said. "This was a bad idea."

"I take it that's a 'no'?" Pearl's head shook involuntarily as she waited for a reply.

"Maybe we could find homes that haven't had pets?" Tom offered.

"Or cigarettes," Lila said, moving away from the stench of the house.

"Duly noted. On to the next." Pearl stuck her index finger in the air and trudged back down the walk, Tom and Lila following behind.

Back in the car, Tom still seemed shocked. "I can run through them first. If they're okay, I'll come get you. Sound okay?"

Lila sighed. "Maybe this is a dumb idea."

"What? Why?"

"My parents have the nicest house in Sweethaven. Looking for a replacement is hardly wise."

Tom took her hand. "It's not a replacement, hon. It's something completely new. Just ours without any of the baggage."

She nodded but stayed quiet. She didn't want to admit that the Christmas decorations all over town only made her sadder. Christmas, more than any other time of year, meant good memories with family—and she wasn't even speaking to hers.

Tom followed behind at Pearl's snail's pace as she rounded the corner. Pearl kept driving, but Tom slowed down in front of a little cottage set way back off the road. "What about that one?"

Lila glanced up and gasped. "Your parents' old cottage?"

He shrugged. "It seems fitting."

She stared out toward the house where Tom had grown up. Though the trees in the yard were all bare, that didn't keep her from seeing the beauty in the white two-story and its wide porch. She remembered the three-bedroom home, its huge kitchen and dining room. She could easily recall the living area where Tom's parents often spent their evenings playing gin together. Lila had always marveled at how easily the two of them got along.

She wanted that for her and Tom.

"But it's not for sale."

"Let me make a few calls." Tom grinned. "Everyone has a price."

Was Tom right? Could this be their dream home? She had to admit that she liked the idea of having a piece of Tom's childhood to share with their own child. She smiled.

"Make the calls," she said.

* * * * *

After their cottage-hunting adventure, Lila left Tom to follow up on his parents' old house so she could take a much-needed nap.

The door of the dark room popped open, but Lila barely stirred.

Tom sat on the edge of the bed and brushed her hair back away from her face. "You're still sleeping."

She took a deep breath in, her body warm under the covers. "I've been so tired."

"I know. The Luminary Walk starts in an hour. Do you still want to go?"

Lila had always loved the Luminary Walk. The few times her family had been in town for Christmas, the magic of the holiday seemed to sprinkle itself like fairy dust over the entire town.

She could use some of that magic now.

As her parents' hold on her seemed to lift, Lila felt more confused than ever. Without having their expectations to live up to, who was she supposed to be?

Tom pulled the curtains back, the dim light from the waning day pressing in. "It's cold out there, but it's going to be such a nice night."

Lila groaned. "What if Mama and Daddy are there?"

He knelt in front of her and took her hands. "Listen, I'm not going to let your parents ruin Christmas for us. We're having a baby. We're in Sweethaven."

Lila met his eyes.

"I got ahold of the owner of our old cottage."

"You did?"

He grinned. "He's arranged for us to go look at it. I think you're going to love it."

Tom had done everything in his power to make sure she knew he loved her—in spite of her changing body, in spite of her sad disposition. What Mama had said before shouldn't matter, but in the back of her mind, Lila still found herself wondering about all those trips he'd taken for work, jet-setting to countries all over the world. Without her. Had she been foolish to trust him?

Tom peeked out the window. "They're getting set up. Will you be ready in time?"

Still in pajamas and virtually makeup free, Lila was anything but ready.

"Give me half an hour."

He nodded and she hurried to make herself presentable, noting what a chore it was to put on mascara and line her lids. Perhaps this was her form of rebelling against everything Mama had taught her. Not wearing makeup certainly wasn't acceptable where Cilla Adler was concerned.

Twenty minutes later, they walked out the door and downtown where the sidewalks had been lined with luminaries. The faint flicker of the candles inside dotted sidewalks and streets everywhere they turned.

Excitement bubbled inside Lila the closer they got to the town square, where people were flocking. It always amazed her how such a small town could draw such a big crowd, but no one wanted to miss these festivities.

Among the low drone of the mingling crowd, Lila caught bits and pieces of Christmas conversations and well wishes—the kind only found in a community like this one. People seemed genuinely interested in each other, and that was something Lila wanted more than anything.

In spite of her heavy eyelids, she kept an eye out for her friends, following Tom across the street toward the center of town.

Inside the gazebo, the city council members stood, waiting to kick off this year's Christmas Celebration with the Luminary Walk, a tradition dating back to the earliest days of Sweethaven. It comforted her to know that generations before them had walked these brick roads, lined with small white bags filled with sand and a single candle to help usher in the holiday season.

Lila had been so lost in romanticizing the beauty of the luminaries, she didn't hear Campbell come up beside her.

"I've never seen anything like this," Campbell said.

Lila startled, then smiled. "It's something else, isn't it?"

Mama's words taunted her now. In light of Charlotte, was it a mistake to befriend Tom's daughter? Did it send the message she accepted what he'd done—his betrayal?

She shoved the thought aside. Mama had no business coaching anyone in the fine art of relationships. Anyone she couldn't control was cut out of her life without so much as a passing glance.

"Isn't that your father?" Campbell said.

Near the steps of the gazebo, Lila saw Daddy deep in conversation, but the person at his side stood just out of her line of sight.

"I'll be right back." Lila zigzagged through the crowd toward Daddy. As she approached, her mind raced through the dozens of times she'd caught him having hushed conversations with the mother of one of her friends, her teachers, women from his office. She'd overheard phone calls, intercepted messages, and all the time it never crossed her mind that he could have been careless—that she could have siblings out there somewhere.

How had she been so naïve?

She had no intention of speaking to her father, only letting him know that she'd caught him in the act. Who would it be this time?

As she rounded the corner, Lila waited for the crowd to part and reveal Daddy in what appeared to be deep conversation with the woman from the restaurant.

The woman saw Lila before Daddy did, and as realization spread across her face, Daddy turned, met Lila's eyes and sighed.

Lila had never felt more unwelcome.

She turned away, the pain of Daddy's lies settling in, weaving its cocoon of sadness. All these years she'd tried so hard to make Daddy proud. She'd grown up thinking if his life at home with her and Mama were a little more peaceful, a little calmer, a little happier, then maybe he wouldn't need the other women.

Why had she taken the blame for his sin?

Moments later, Daddy had moved to her side, the other woman nowhere to be seen.

"Don't stop on my account, Daddy," Lila said. "If your other family needs you, by all means . . ."

"Lila, you just don't understand." Daddy reached toward her, but she shrugged him off.

"I think it's pretty clear." Lila fought back fresh tears. Why did it hurt so much? She was a grown woman, for goodness' sake.

"There's a lot about my life that isn't clear—not to you, not even to me, I'm afraid."

"It's obvious you lied."

Daddy said nothing.

She scoffed. "All this time, I couldn't get pregnant, I kept thinking about what a disappointment I was to you."

"Lila, please—"

"But you know what, Daddy? I'm just realizing that all along, you're the one who's been the disappointment."

The mayor tapped on the microphone and called for everyone's attention.

"How could you do this to Mama? To me? Don't we matter at all?"

Daddy looked away.

"I thought that now, finally, I could give you a grandchild—a grandson, I hoped, because I knew you always wanted a boy—and you'd be so proud. So happy I was your daughter. But do you already have grandchildren? Do you already have a legacy?"

Lila stared at Daddy for a long moment and the crowd quieted.

"Right now I'd like to introduce someone very important to lead us on this year's Sweethaven Christmas Luminary Walk." The mayor's voice boomed through the speakers just feet away from where Lila stood. "This man has given more to our fair town over the years than any other single resident in Sweethaven's history. Ladies and gentlemen, please welcome Mr. Victor Adler."

Daddy held her gaze for another few seconds, then turned, smiled and bounded to the stage.

He leaned in to the microphone. "It's such an honor and a privilege to be with you folks for the start of the Christmas season," Daddy said, his drawl more pronounced than usual. "There just isn't anywhere better in the world than Sweethaven at Christmas."

Lila tuned him out, wishing she'd never left her room at the Whitmore.

She turned around, and in the distance, standing off to the side, she spotted the woman from the restaurant. The woman she guessed to be Charlotte. The woman she'd avoided out of respect for her parents.

But now it didn't seem like she owed either of them a bit of respect.

And this woman might be the only way to ever uncover the truth behind her parents' lies.

## TWENTY-TWO

*Adele*

It had been two days since Adele and Henry had connected on the computer. Despite her efforts to contact him with her explanation of why she'd suddenly disappeared, there had been no word from Henry.

She'd been checking her e-mail nonstop ever since, and, as if she had no choice, here she sat again at the computer for the third time since she woke up.

When her in-box came up empty, a sick feeling took over Adele's stomach. She couldn't sit here for one more second.

The phone rang, pulling her from her frustration.

"Hey, Ma."

Luke.

"Why don't you come down for a cup of coffee? It's kind of quiet down here, I could use the company."

"Well, that's sweet of you to think of me." And she needed to get herself away from the computer. "I'll walk over."

"You sure, Ma? It's cold."

"I'm sure."

Despite the temperature, Adele loved this time of year. Their little town, all lit up, decorated from one end to the other—it defined the word "magic."

And Adele hoped the Christmas cheer could get rid of the dark cloud that seemed to be following her around.

She wrapped her scarf around her neck twice, then pulled her long coat on, fishing her gloves from the pockets. A brisk walk in the cool air would do her good.

Outside, Adele plodded down Main Street, wondering how many more days they'd have before the town was blanketed in snow. Her toes were chilled inside her boots, but she pressed on, admiring the oversize Christmas gifts on either side of the gazebo's stairs in the town square.

The longer she was outside, the more she looked forward to the large cup of hot cocoa she'd order once she reached the Main Street Café. Sweethaven felt unusually busy this afternoon, and she found herself hoping more people had decided to spend their holidays in this place that seemed to transcend time.

Plus, they could use the business.

In spite of the flurry of activity outside, the café had an emptiness to it. Luke said he appreciated the downtime, but Adele always worried about her son, the business owner. Having an education he rarely used seemed like such a waste, especially when she knew the café caused him to lose sleep.

Her son stood at the other end of the counter chatting with a customer. He waved her over, though he had to know she much preferred to spend the afternoon prodding him about his love life.

Perhaps the customer was his buffer.

"Luke, if I don't get something hot to drink, there's a good chance I'm gonna freeze from the inside out."

"That right, Ma?" He steamed the milk for her cocoa and set the cup in front of her. "I didn't think you were serious about walking here."

If he knew the truth, she'd never live it down.

"I needed to get out of the house, I suppose. The fresh air did me good. You know how much I love Christmas."

"It always was your favorite time of year." The words weren't Luke's but rather came from the man beside her. For the first time since she sat down, she looked at him.

"Oh, I think you already know Henry Marshall, right, Ma?" Luke grinned.

He'd set her up.

"I do, Luke. I didn't realize you did."

"We go way back." He winked at her and walked away, leaving her sitting with Henry. Alone.

"Henry, about the other day . . ."

"Why don't we get a table?" He smiled at her. She remembered that smile. While he'd aged, of course, and his hair had thinned, she still saw the boy she'd loved all those years ago.

"Of course."

Henry picked up her cocoa for her and led her to a table near the back of the café. With hardly any other customers and even the wait staff hiding behind the scenes, she found herself wonderfully, horribly alone with a man whose presence still gave her butterflies.

After all these years, she'd given up ever feeling that sensation again.

"About the other night . . ."

Henry held up a hand to stop her. "It's okay. Your son explained."

Adele frowned. "What did he say?"

"Something about your being new to the computer."

Adele glanced over toward the door to the kitchen where Luke had just reappeared and smiled. He raised a brow and busied himself behind the counter. "Very new to the computer. I've only ever used it to search for antiques for my store."

Henry nodded, watching her, a soft grin on his lips. "You haven't changed at all."

Adele laughed. "Henry Marshall, you are a terrible liar."

The smile stayed securely on his face. "Sure, we're both a little worse for the wear, but you're still as beautiful as the day I saw you singing at that dance in the Commons."

Adele stilled. "You remember?"

"That memory got me through many nights in Vietnam." He looked away.

She watched him for a long moment. How many nights had she fallen asleep praying for her Henry? How many days had she spent trying not to think about the danger he was in? She'd never asked many questions about the war, but she imagined it had changed him.

But when he returned, she wasn't there to find out.

The silence between them grew awkward and Henry's expression changed. "I've got photos of my grandchildren." A smile spread across his face as he reached into his inside jacket pocket and pulled a sleeve of small photos from inside his wallet. He set them in front of Adele and pointed to each of his eleven grandchildren.

"My daughter Libby is the only one who's not married," he said. He flipped the sleeve over and revealed a photo of himself and a woman who appeared to be many years old.

Panic washed over his face, but Adele smiled and picked it up. "Is this Millie?"

Henry softened. "Yes, that's my Millie."

She stared at the picture. They'd made a handsome couple. Out of nowhere, tears sprang to her eyes. "I'm glad you've had a happy life, Henry. So very glad."

He covered her hand with his own. "It has been happy, but there's always room for old friends."

She met his eyes and set the sleeve of photos down. "I'm afraid I wasn't a very good friend to you. I never got a chance to tell you how sorry I am . . ."

"Adele, stop. You have nothing to apologize for. It's all water under the bridge." He squeezed her hand. "Why don't we start over? A clean slate?"

Could Henry really have forgotten the pain she'd caused him? Would a clean slate mean they left everything behind? Even the good?

Maybe it was what they needed in order to move forward. Maybe she had to let go of her own regret over the way things had ended between them, though she had to wonder why God had brought him back into her life now when she'd accepted that she was meant to be alone.

"A clean slate sounds good," she said.

Henry took one last drink of his now cold coffee. "Can I take you home?"

Adele smiled. "Only if you'll let me make you dinner."

"Now, there's an offer I can't refuse."

## TWENTY-THREE

*Campbell*

Every night in Sweethaven during December, Campbell learned, seemed to have a different festive event scheduled. The Luminary Walk had been pure magic, and tonight, the Christmas concert in the Square would be the same.

Her thoughts rushed back to the ring—the beautiful, too-expensive ring—and then to Luke's promise that tonight would be the most romantic night of her life.

Nerves bubbled inside her. From the window, she could see where people had started to gather in the town square. The Sweethaven Municipal Band would set up all around the gazebo, which would serve as a stage like it had for the mayor the night before. From a distance, it looked like a scene in a movie—like the perfect place to propose to someone.

Campbell's hands had turned to ice as she considered what Luke might have planned for her that night, and she willed herself to stop overanalyzing everything.

A knock on the back door told her he'd arrived, and she inhaled a slow, deep breath.

"Calm down," she said out loud to the empty room. "This could be a good thing."

It could be. Her. Luke. Marriage. That could be a great thing. But was it what she wanted? If he made his proposal into a public event, how could she possibly say "Can I think about it?" Her indecision would be their undoing.

But marriage was so final.

Luke appeared in the doorway, that lazy grin on his face. "Hey."

She forced her thoughts aside and walked into his embrace. "Hey yourself."

He took her face in his hands, leaned down and kissed her, his soft lips luring her out of reality for a brief moment. She inhaled the smell of his aftershave and tuned in to the way her stomach jumped as his thumb brushed alongside her cheek.

When he finally pulled away, Campbell met his eyes, which had a hint of mischief in them.

"You look like you're up to something," she said.

He wagged his eyebrows and smiled. "Maybe I am."

Her heart leaped, a mixture of nerves and excitement. She hadn't intended to have feelings this strong for him, but she could hardly pretend they weren't there.

Not responding to his profession of love hadn't seemed to deter Luke at all. Didn't it bother him that she hadn't been able to verbalize her feelings—any of them—to him?

"You ready?"

She nodded, switched off the lights, leaving only the one above the counter on. She had to laugh that she took security precautions in Sweethaven—a town with practically zero crime—but, better safe than sorry.

They walked out into the crisp winter and Campbell pulled on her mittens, exhaling puffs of air.

"I've got blankets," Luke said. "You'll be warm once we get over there." He wrapped an arm around her and pulled her closer.

She didn't respond but noted the way her heart jumped at the nearness of him. She'd never been in a relationship with someone so selfless and kind. And she'd never been with someone so confident. Luke had such an easiness about him that eliminated the usual awkward feelings. She loved those things about him. She loved everything about him.

There was that word again.

As they walked, Campbell stared at the town square, trying not to dive into all the reasons she hadn't said she loved him when she knew in her heart she did. Townspeople flocked toward the bustle of activity, many of them greeting Luke on the way. Lawn chairs had been set up facing the stage, and the gentle sound of the band tuning their instruments wafted out across Main Street.

"Does everyone in town come to this thing?" Campbell asked as they started across the street.

Luke put an arm out to stop her as a car rounded the corner. "Careful."

She glanced up at him and wondered if he had the ring in his pocket. In that moment, she felt sure she'd say yes.

Luke took her hand and led her across the street. "Pretty much. Christmas is such a big deal here."

"I thought summer was the big attraction here. It's awfully cold for people to want to be here, isn't it?" Campbell pulled her coat tighter around her and wished it had a heater inside it.

"People seem to brave the weather for a Sweethaven Christmas," Luke said. "The town started promoting all their Christmas events a few years ago, and now lots of people take a few weeks here in December. Last year we had a huge snowstorm and a bunch of them couldn't get out." He grinned. "Good for business."

Campbell laughed. Ahead, she saw a few lawn chairs reserved with blankets front and center. Just where someone would sit to be pulled onstage.

Adele chatted with an older woman, and Meghan's husband Nick tucked a big fleece blanket around their twins. Finn and Nadia grinned when they saw her, and for a moment Campbell imagined that one day she could be more than their art teacher—she could be their aunt.

Nick turned and shook Luke's hand. "Hey, you ready for this?"

Luke straightened. "Ready as I'll ever be."

Campbell frowned. "Ready for what?"

The two men exchanged a knowing look. "You'll see," Luke said. "Here, sit down."

Her heart raced as she looked around at the crowded Square. A wave of uncertainty washed over her, bringing with it a healthy dose of nausea. "Luke, I have to go."

He turned to her. "Why? Are you okay?"

"I feel sick."

Adele bumped her shoulder with her own. "I've got some peppermints. That always helps my stomach." She fished through her purse and pulled out two Starlight mints. "Here you go, darlin'. I'd hate for you to miss out on such a special night."

Had Luke told Adele too?

She unwrapped the peppermint and put it in her mouth as Adele squeezed her hand.

In the distance, she saw Jane and Graham weaving their way through the crowd with their youngest, Sam. Campbell could barely force a "hello" for the nerves.

Jane situated her family behind them and leaned forward. "Where's Lila?"

Adele shrugged. "Haven't seen her yet."

Campbell looked around halfheartedly, not really searching for Lila so much as searching for a way of escape. Suddenly she thought sitting right next to the stage on that particular night might be the scariest thing she'd ever done.

The music started and the queasiness began to disappear, the sound of brass instruments transporting her back to Christmases past. The Sweethaven concert band had a decidedly jazzy sound, and Campbell closed her eyes to enjoy their rendition of "Winter Wonderland," wishing her mom was sitting beside her.

All those years it had been just the two of them, but she never once felt lonely or let down. They bought a few really special gifts for each other and spent Christmas week baking, watching old movies and playing board games. It had always been one of her favorite times of the year.

"Hey, are you okay?" Luke leaned in closer, and only then did she realize she was crying.

"My mom loved Christmas." She wiped her cheeks dry as Adele shoved two tissues into her hand without looking away from the stage. Luke wrapped his arm around her and pulled her closer.

"I'm sorry, Cam."

The song ended and Campbell forced herself to stop being so emotional. It turned out she really did miss her mother. She hadn't expected her first Christmas without her mom to be this difficult, but when she wasn't wondering about the ring she'd found, she was thinking about Mom. How much she missed her. Her mother always had a way of making her feel special. Luke did that for her now, but it wasn't the same.

The mayor appeared on the stage and Adele groaned. "Always with the mayor," she said.

Campbell laughed.

"He's everywhere," Adele continued. "We can't get away from him!"

"I've got a very special surprise for you all tonight." The mayor paused. A slow grin spread across his face as he looked back and forth across the crowd. Campbell's pulse quickened.

"I'd like to welcome to the stage, someone you all know and love . . ."

Luke sat up straighter, as if he was preparing for something.

"Someone we sure are proud of around here . . ."

Murmurs passed through the crowd as people began to speculate, but the mayor remained silent in front of the microphone, allowing the anticipation to build.

Finally, he raised a hand. "Ladies and gentlemen, help me welcome to the stage Sweethaven's own Meghan Rhodes!"

Cheers erupted through the crowd, followed by whistles and shouts of "We love you, Meghan" as Luke's sister emerged from the back of the gazebo, guitar strung around her neck.

Jane leaned forward. "It's been so long since I've heard her sing."

Adele sprang to her feet. "Me too. Too long."

Campbell stood alongside Luke, applauding, because while Meghan had become something of a fixture in Sweethaven again, it wasn't every day the famous singer performed for them. For free, no less.

Meghan waited for the crowd to quiet and then cleared her throat in the microphone. "Thank you, everyone," she said. "I'm so happy to be back in Sweethaven for the holidays."

In the distance, Campbell saw the camera crew, lenses pointed at Meghan. The Christmas special. They must've wanted footage of Meghan doing what she did best—performing.

"This is the first stage I ever sang on." Meghan's words were met with more cheers and applause. "So when I found out they wanted to film a Christmas special at my house, I told the producers all about you guys and about Sweethaven and about how special it is to be here during this time of year."

Luke squeezed Campbell's hand, and just like that she didn't feel lonely anymore. Meghan spoke the truth—it was a special place to be for the holidays, and for the first time in a long time, Campbell felt like she was a part of a community, and she savored that moment.

"Before I begin, I want to ask someone to join me up here on the stage." Meghan winked in their direction and Campbell's eyes widened. "You may not know it, but I'm not the only musical one in my family." Meghan grinned. "My brother Luke—the guy who serves you your coffee—is a man of many talents, so he's agreed to sing one of our favorite Christmas songs with me tonight. Ladies and gentlemen, Luke Barber!"

The crowd erupted and Luke stood. He glanced down at Campbell and smiled and then jogged to the stage. He took his place behind a keyboard.

"I haven't heard them sing together in ages," Adele said.

"Luke sings?"

How had she not known? What else didn't she know about him? Was this what all the secrecy was about? A song?

She'd been worried about him proposing while he'd been nervous about performing in front of the entire town.

"My little brother hasn't done this in a while," Meghan said to the audience. "So, be gentle."

Luke leaned toward the microphone. "I can keep up with you, Meg."

Laughter dotted the crowd, and Campbell shook her head. How had she not known Luke was a musician? He had a piano at his place, but he'd never played it for her. He'd never even sung along with the radio.

"When we were kids," Meghan said, "we sang together as a family, but we haven't had the chance to do that in a long time. I wanted to share a little bit of my family with the town I love so much."

Luke started playing, the melody of "O Holy Night" hovering overhead, and then the band joined in as Meghan began singing, her deep, raspy voice the perfect complement to one of Campbell's favorite songs.

One of Mom's favorite songs.

When Meghan reached the second stanza, Luke joined in, his surprising baritone the perfect harmony. Together, the two of them mesmerized the entire audience—Campbell included. They sounded like they'd been singing together forever, and the power of their voices filled Campbell with so much emotion the tears sprang back to her eyes.

For a fleeting moment, she imagined her mother at her side, arm wound through hers, blinking back tears as the song moved on.

"You love him, don't you, Cam?" Mom would say. She'd come right out and say what she thought—it's the way she was. She always had a way of helping Campbell realize her emotions.

"But it hasn't been long enough to know I love him," Campbell would say, certain her feelings were something less real. Love was too scary.

Mom would shrug then and purse her lips like she did when she was deep in thought. "When you know, you know."

Campbell watched Luke as the passion of the song filled him. He seemed to forget anyone could see him at all. As they went in for their big finish, the crowd started to stand, as if the music had driven them to their feet. As the song ended, Luke opened his eyes and smiled at her.

And for the first time, she realized her own disappointment that Luke hadn't stood on that stage to propose to her.

Because what Mom would've said would've been true.

In only six months' time, Luke Barber had won the key to her heart. Campbell Jane Carter was truly, madly, deeply in love.

## TWENTY-FOUR

*Lila*

While the rest of the town sat beneath the stars enjoying the Sweethaven Christmas concert, Lila sat at a small table in the deserted Main Street Café. Only one employee worked behind the counter—a skinny kid with droopy eyes. Luke must've given everyone else the night off.

She'd replayed her conversation with her father over and over again, though she'd tried to put it out of her mind. She hadn't even realized how hurt she was over the idea of her father having other children—and grandchildren—until the moment the words spewed from her mouth. But there they were.

Last night, as she rehashed the whole scenario to Tom, she cried and told herself to get it together.

"I'm an adult, and he's been letting me down my entire life. Why is this any different?"

Tom held her as they stared up at the ceiling of their room at the Whitmore. "Hurt is hurt, hon," he'd said. "Doesn't matter how old you are."

When would her parents' grip on her ever loosen? When would she stop trying to measure up—trying to please them and be who they thought she should be?

Her thoughts turned to the way she lived her life in Macon. Junior League. Community Board. Social events where she would be seen. Even her home had been decorated to please other people. At her core, Lila had always wanted something cozy and lived in—something like Adele's house, which boasted none of the flash or wealth that she'd grown accustomed to.

The cottage she and Tom bought would be different. It would be exactly what she'd always wanted. Maybe she'd even buy something from Adele's store. And Mama would hate it and that was just fine with her.

She needed to find the courage to stand up for her own ideas—in her home and in her life.

The bell above the door chimed, pulling Lila's attention. Her breath caught in her throat as the woman she'd been avoiding—her sister—walked in, focused on Droopy Eyes behind the counter. Lila pressed her lips together and remembered how Mama had spoken to the woman in the store the other day.

If she wanted to start being the opposite of Cilla Adler, now was the perfect time.

The woman ordered as Lila enjoyed a few more moments of anonymity. Tall and thin, she did resemble Daddy, in much the same way that Lila did. They both had shoulder-length blonde hair and fair skin. Lila had never had a sister before—and for a brief moment, she wondered if the two of them had anything in common.

The woman paid for her drink, then moved down the counter toward the pickup. As she did, her eyes swung in Lila's direction and she quickly looked away.

For the first time since their conversation in the bathroom on Thanksgiving, Lila stopped wallowing in her own self-pity and wondered what this woman had been through. Assuming Daddy was her father, what had this woman's life been like without him? Had Daddy even tried to stay in touch? And did Lila have any right to defend Tom for abandoning Campbell but crucify Daddy for doing the same?

She waved the deep thoughts away and chose instead to focus on the person who stood in front of her.

Lila stood and smoothed her slacks, noting the hard knot her stomach had become. She'd started showing, and while she expected to hate getting bigger, she could only find excitement for the promise her growing stomach held.

Standing behind her sister, Lila cleared her throat and braced herself for what came next.

The woman turned toward her but didn't make eye contact. "I know. You don't want me here anymore," she said. "Your mother made that clear. Don't worry, I'm leaving." She turned away, staring at the kid making her drink, likely willing him to hurry it up already.

"Would you join me for a cup of coffee?" Lila's hands fell to her belly. "Or tea."

Her sister met her eyes, searching for an explanation, probably trying to detect a trap. Lila didn't blame her for being suspicious. After the way Mama had treated her, it made sense.

"I guess," she said, taking her drink from Droopy Eyes.

Lila returned to her table and sat down after her sister took a seat.

"You're not at the concert," the woman said.

"I didn't feel like braving the crowd."

Silence hung between them as Lila began to regret her choice to approach her in the first place.

"I'm Charlotte, by the way," the woman said.

*Charlotte. Her* sister *Charlotte.*

"I'm Lila."

"I know. It's nice to meet you." She laughed. "I guess that's not really true, is it?" There was a beat of silence between them.

"I'm sorry if my being here has hurt you. That wasn't my intention."

"What *was* your intention?" Lila winced. "I'm sorry. I didn't mean to sound angry."

"It's okay. I'm sure it's a shock to you." Charlotte sipped her drink from a disposable cup. She swallowed, then smiled through a look of sadness. She set her cup down and fished around in her purse for something.

Lila watched as Charlotte pulled a small photograph from her purse, stared at it with a wistful smile and then set it on the table, faceup. "This is my daughter."

A pang of jealousy clawed at Lila. "She's beautiful."

"She's sick."

Lila frowned.

"Aplastic anemia. The drugs aren't working. She needs a bone marrow transplant."

Lila studied Charlotte as she took the photo back and wedged it inside her billfold. When she met Lila's gaze, Charlotte's eyes had filled with tears.

"Believe me," she said. "I would never come to him unless I had no other option."

"I see." All this time, Lila had been so concerned with how this scenario made *her* feel—she hadn't considered there could be a reason for Charlotte's appearance. A horrible reason. Her thoughts turned to the day Jane lost Alex. She couldn't bear the thought that any mother would have to go through that.

"It was a bad idea," Charlotte said.

Lila shook her head. "I understand."

Charlotte swiped a tear. "My family is everything to me. I had to at least try."

"Is he a match?"

"I don't know. He hasn't been tested." Charlotte pulled a tissue from her purse and dabbed at the corners of her eyes. "I don't think she'll let him."

Lila closed her eyes and drew in a deep breath. How could Mama be so cruel? How could Daddy be so spineless?

"Did he know about you?" Lila asked. "All this time?"

Charlotte nodded.

Lila gripped her hot cup between her hands. "He lied to me," she said quietly.

Charlotte scoffed. "He wasn't the only one lying."

Lila shot her a look. "What do you mean?" Her mind raced. "Who else lied?"

Charlotte looked away.

"Charlotte, my—our—father has never been faithful to my mother. I always assumed his mistresses knew what they were getting into, sleeping with a married man, but I suppose it's different when there's a child involved."

Charlotte's brows drew together as a confused look swept across her face. "Lila, my mother wasn't the mistress."

"What do you mean?" Lila's pulse kicked up a notch.

"Your mother was."

## TWENTY-FIVE

*Lila*

The next day, Lila couldn't stop thinking about what Charlotte had told her. If it was true, Mama and Daddy hadn't only been dishonest, they'd been horrible. But how did she prove any of it?

Her phone rang and she saw Mama's picture pop up. Tom glanced at her from across their room at the Whitmore where he sat, reading a book. "Don't answer it."

She hadn't told him about Charlotte yet. He didn't understand how badly she needed to know the truth.

Lila held the phone in her hand like it was a foreign object that had cast a spell on her. Finally, she clicked it on. "Hello?"

"Where are you?" Mama sounded annoyed.

"I'm at the Whitmore with Tom. Why?"

"Did you forget the March of Dimes fund-raiser?"

Lila sighed. "I'm not coming, Mama."

Mama sighed and Lila imagined the look on her face. "When are you going to stop this nonsense?"

Lila bit the inside of her lip to keep from spewing the words that flittered through her mind. Tom stood, a look of concern on his face. "Lila, hang up the phone," he whispered.

"I'll pay you for the tickets. I have to go." She clicked the phone off. "I don't even know how to respond to her."

Tom walked over to her. "You can't carry this stress around. You're driving yourself crazy."

"There's only one way to find out the truth," Lila said. She grabbed her purse from the desk.

"Where are you going?"

"Where are *we* going?"

He frowned. "I'm not going anywhere. And you shouldn't either."

"Tom, if you want me to stop stressing about this, then help me find out the truth."

He stared at her for a few long moments and then finally stood. "Only because I'm afraid of what you're going to do if I don't chaperone."

They drove in silence to the lake house, and when they reached the end of the driveway, Lila made him slow down—just to be sure her parents really were out at the fund-raiser.

"Okay, you can park. This won't take long."

"What are we doing here?" Tom asked, turning off the ignition.

"Don't you find it strange that Mama never had the big white wedding?" Lila retrieved a spare key from underneath a statue on the front porch and shoved it in the lock, letting herself in.

Tom followed her, a baffled look on his face. "I can honestly say the thought has never crossed my mind."

Lila went straight for her father's study and moved the computer mouse around until the screen sprang to life.

"This is crazy. What are you looking for?"

Lila stopped and looked at him. "Charlotte said—"

"Charlotte?"

"My sister."

Tom's eyebrows shot up.

"Haven't you heard? I have a sister now."

"Of course I know about your sister, but when did you talk to her?"

"At Luke's café. She said that her mother was married to my father and he cheated on her with *my mother*."

Tom frowned. "Your parents have been together forever. Was your father married right out of high school?"

Lila clicked around on the computer, looking through Daddy's files. "What if he was? What if the other woman was his childhood sweetheart and my mother, the one who's been playing the victim all these years, the one who said she had no knowledge of Charlotte, was the real home wrecker?"

Tom sighed and sat on the couch. "I suppose it all makes sense. Your parents' marriage has always been a wreck."

"I can't prove anything unless I can find the marriage license. I know there's a way to find all of this online, but I'm going straight to the source."

"What are you trying to prove?"

Lila slumped on the ground. "That they've been lying. That they need to own up to all of it and tell the truth—and try to make it right." She sighed. "Tom, I've spent years trying to live up to Mama's standards, only to find out that everything she harped on me not to be—she was. She's a fraud."

"Why do you think she harps on it so much? She doesn't want you to make the same mistakes she made."

But Tom didn't know Mama like Lila did. Mama had always been critical and controlling. She'd made Lila feel like she'd never measure up.

"Now you can stop trying to be who she wants you to be and start being who you are."

Lila frowned. "What's that supposed to mean?"

"You weigh every decision by her standards. Even the nursery back home. When you said you wanted to do brown and light green, she talked you into finding out if we were having a girl or boy. For decorating purposes."

Lila stilled. It was true. She said she wanted to be surprised and Mama convinced her it was ridiculous. She should find out so they could get everything they needed ahead of time. After all, Lila wouldn't want to be seen in public for at least a couple of months after the baby was born. Maybe longer, depending on when she got her body back.

"Lila, the woman still controls your life." Tom moved from the couch to the chair across from where she sat. "Maybe it's good for you to see that she's not the standard by which to measure yourself."

He watched her from across the room and she wondered how pitiful she looked to him in that moment.

"Charlotte has a daughter who needs a bone marrow transplant."

Tom's brows knit together. "She does?"

Lila nodded. "I think Mama is keeping Daddy from giving it to her—just to protect her lies."

After several seconds, Tom finally said, "I'm sorry, hon. I didn't know."

Lila stared at her own fingers hovering above the keyboard. "I want to help her if I can. No mother should lose her own child."

Tom leaned forward and took her hand. "You're right."

Did he conjure every single miscarriage she'd had the way she did? Did he remember with startling clarity the fallen faces of nurses delivering bad news? Some filled with empathy; others detached as if they'd simply recited the menu items at a restaurant, as if the words hadn't broken their hearts.

She took a deep breath and forced herself not to think about the babies she'd never meet and turned her attention back to the computer. "Daddy had all of their important documents—birth certificates, marriage license, titles, deeds, will—everything, digitized a few years ago. Something his lawyer suggested. If I'm right, then there's proof right here that they've been lying."

"And if you can prove it . . ."

"I can convince Daddy to give Charlotte what she came here for."

She found a file labeled "Important docs" and clicked on it.

Tom walked around behind her so he could see the screen. "Are you sure you want to know, Lila?"

She ignored him.

"In all my years I've never heard stories of a big, beautiful wedding. I never thought that was odd until now." Mama wasn't the small-affair type. She'd relish the opportunity to be the center of attention—unless she had something to hide.

Lila scrolled through the various documents, clicking open her birth certificate, scans of social security cards and titles to their vehicles.

"Look, this one is a marriage license," she said.

Tom leaned in closer. "It says they were married at the courthouse."

Lila nodded. She had thought a bombshell would shatter her, but instead, she felt her resolve to uncover the truth strengthening. "Yes. It also says they were married three months before I was born." She leaned back in the chair and stared at the scanned license on the screen.

"So Charlotte was telling the truth," Tom said.

Lila met his eyes. "Yes. And my mother's been living a lie."

TWENTY-SIX

*Adele*

Ever since their not-so-chance meeting at the café, Adele and Henry had been spending their evenings together. Adele couldn't deny she loved the company—and she loved having such a voracious eater to cook for.

"I'm still waitin' to find out about this cookbook, but you're going to have to help me narrow down my recipes, just in case," she'd told him the night before.

Henry had shoveled a bite of her down-home meat loaf into his mouth and shaken his head. "I'm not going to be a bit of help to you."

"Why not?"

"There is no way I can pick a favorite. You're just too good." He waggled his eyebrows at her. "Delicious."

She smiled at the memory as she put the finishing touches on her fried chicken. She had a feeling Henry was going to lick the plate clean on this meal too.

The knock at the door startled her. She glanced at the clock and saw that time had gotten away from her. Through the door, she saw Henry standing on the front porch, and her mind raced back to simpler times when he'd come to the door of this very same cottage, knock and wait to face her father's grave stare.

Henry had never been intimidated by her dad, and after a while, he even won the old guy over with a mutual love for the Chicago Cubs and a solid work ethic.

Adele pulled the door open and wiped her hands on the blue-and-white-checkered apron around her waist.

Henry smiled at the sight of her and she noted a strange fluttering in her belly. He handed her a brightly colored bouquet of flowers and stepped inside. Adele brought the flowers to her nose and inhaled. It had been years since anyone had brought her flowers. Henry leaned toward her and kissed her cheek. At the nearness of him, Adele suddenly felt sixteen again.

Henry stepped back and took his coat off. "It smells wonderful in here."

"You've said that every night this week." She took his coat and hung it in the front closet.

"Then it must be true."

Adele served their dinner in the dining room, surrounded by a wall of windows. They sat across from each other, the fading light of the sun casting a yellowish hue to the room. Adele dished up the fried chicken and collard greens for Henry and then did the same for herself. When she set the platter down, she met his eyes and found him smiling at her.

"What are you lookin' at, Mr. Marshall?" she said, stifling a smile of her own.

"A very beautiful woman."

Adele's face heated and she imagined how red her cheeks must be. "Stop that now."

He reached across the table and took her hand. "I mean it, Adele. You're every bit as beautiful as I remember."

"Well, thank you. You're not so bad yourself."

As the night waned, she let herself relax, and somewhere along the way realized how very much she enjoyed Henry's company.

He gave the fried chicken a thumbs-up and told her the cookbook would be incomplete without that in it, which was exactly what he'd said about each of the other meals. For dessert, she served coffee and apple crisp, one that had the perfect balance of apples and crumble. She didn't much care for a crisp without any crumble.

After they ate, Adele sat while Henry insisted on cleaning up. "You cooked. I'll clean."

She had to admit, she'd worn herself out preparing the meal, so she welcomed the rest. How she'd loved having someone to cook for again. Made her feel important, like she mattered to someone. When Henry finished with the dishes, they sat in the living room where the old book with all their memories sat on the coffee table.

"Am I in this?" Henry asked as he picked it up.

"More than once."

He smiled and started flipping through the pages. When he got to the photo of the two of them outside one of the Sweethaven dances, he held it up with a grin. "Look at how beautiful you are."

Adele waved him off. "I was just a kid."

"And you're every bit as feisty and full of life today as you were then. Millie was a lot like that right up until the end." Sadness filled his eyes and Adele could see Millie had been to Henry like Teddy had been to her. They'd already had the loves of their lives; wasn't it selfish to hope to have that again?

"I wish I could've met her," Adele said, her voice quiet.

Henry laughed. "Oh, the two of you together, I can just imagine. I'd be a goner for sure."

Adele took the book and flipped to the back. "Look at you here."

Henry's eyes fell to the image of a boy dressed as a soldier. He stilled.

"Remember you sent that to me from Vietnam. You and your buddies. I bet you got into a lot of trouble over there."

Henry nodded but didn't look away from the photo. "This guy, Vince, he was from Brooklyn." He leaned over and pointed to a dark-headed young man with a wide gap-toothed smile.

"And you were friends?"

"The best." Henry ran a hand over his whiskered chin.

"Do you still keep in touch? Maybe on Facebook?"

He shook his head. "He died right in front of me. If it had been ten seconds later, it would've been me. He saved my life."

Adele took the book and closed it, then covered his hands with her own. "I'm sorry, Henry."

"It was a long time ago." His smile had lost its luster.

"How is it that you seem to have forgotten all about the way you and I parted?"

Henry lifted his chin and looked her squarely in the eye. "I haven't forgotten, but I don't blame you for the way things happened."

"I should've waited."

Henry wiped a tear from her cheek. "You don't mean that. Think of the life you wouldn't have had."

She took his hand and held it in her own. "I know. And the life you wouldn't have had."

"We were so young—it just wasn't meant to be."

Adele nodded as their eyes met. She and Henry were mismatched right from the start. So why had this ache in her heart returned at the thought of losing him all over again?

"I've been thinking, Adele. We're not so young anymore."

She laughed. "That may be in the running for understatement of the year."

Henry flashed a smile. "Maybe now our timing is good." He punctuated the sentence with a shrug, a question in his voice.

She folded her hands in her lap and stared at him. "What are you sayin', Henry?"

"What if we did something crazy? What if you came to see how you like Grand Falls? We could find you a nice little place near mine. Or we could . . ."

She frowned. "We could what?"

His eyes were wide like a boy who'd been caught spying on the girls' locker room. "Get married?"

"Henry Marshall, as I live and breathe, that's crazy talk." She leaned back on the couch and waited for him to start laughing with her.

But he didn't. Instead, he got down on a knee in front of her and took her hand in his. "I asked you once, Adele, and I know it didn't work out, but I'd be honored if you spent the rest of your life with me."

Adele's jaw went slack and she fumbled over her words. "Henry, I don't know what to say. Don't you think it's a little soon to be talking marriage? You haven't even kissed me yet."

He raised a brow. "Do you want me to?"

She blinked, suddenly as unsure as she was the first time he kissed her.

He leaned toward her, eyes intent on hers. When he reached her lips, he closed her eyes and kissed her sweetly. "I never forgot your kisses."

Everything in her head told her it was crazy. She couldn't leave Sweethaven. She couldn't up and move to Grand Falls—not when her family had finally reunited, when she finally had people to cook for on holidays. But then she let herself get a little lost in Henry's mocha-colored eyes and she knew a part of her had never stopped loving him.

But married?

"Just think about it. I'm here for another day, and maybe you can come visit me in Grand Falls and that will help you decide?"

She nodded but stayed silent.

Henry brushed his thumb across her cheek. "I know it's all of a sudden, but there was a time you knew me better than anyone. We're not so different now, are we?"

Adele studied his expression. All those feelings she'd buried or forgotten were still there. She looked away.

Henry squeezed her hand. "Besides, at our age, we can't afford to date for any length of time."

Adele smiled. "Oh, Henry, you do make me laugh."

She saw him out and welcomed another kiss from this man she never thought she'd see again—and she wondered how on earth she'd managed to get herself proposed to. Again.

As she closed the door behind him, Adele waited for the sound of his car driving away before she burst into giggles that would rival any junior high schooler's. Henry Marshall wanted to marry her.

And while it defied all reason, she thought, as she trudged up the stairs for bed, that she might be inclined to say yes.

## TWENTY-SEVEN

*Jane*

Jane sat in her car drumming her thumbs on the steering wheel, try-ing to work up the courage to venture into unfamiliar territory. The gym at the Sweethaven Community Center had never been a place she wanted to go, but the weather wasn't cooperating with her plan to exercise outdoors. At least not until she'd built up some strength. How could she take off in the opposite direction of her house with no indication of how far she could go—especially with these frigid temperatures?

But sitting there, watching people come and go, looking like born athletes, Jane suddenly lost her nerve.

A knock on her car window startled her out of her self-pity.

She looked up and saw Meghan standing beside her window. "What are you doing out here?"

Jane sighed. "Trying to work up the nerve to go in."

Meghan glanced at the door of the community center. "Come on. I'll show you around."

"Really?"

"Of course." Meghan opened the car door and Jane got out. "You already look like you've lost some weight."

Jane shrank at the compliment. "I've been too scared to get on the scale."

They walked toward the front door of the community center. "I'm proud of you, Janie. You're taking care of yourself. It's nice to see."

Jane smiled as they approached the front desk, but the good feelings vanished when they were met by a twentysomething Barbie doll in very tight clothes.

Heat rushed up to her cheeks and suddenly Jane realized how very much she didn't belong there. Meghan must've sensed her apprehension because she grabbed her arm and pulled her closer to the counter. "You just sign your name here and pay Morgan."

Jane glanced up at Morgan and forced a smile. The Barbie doll smiled back. "It's your first time?"

Jane nodded and scribbled her name on the line below where Meghan had signed.

"I'd offer to take you on a tour, but you're in good hands. Ms. Rhodes is one of our most faithful clients." Jane could swear she heard a little bell ring at the sparkle of Morgan's flashy smile.

Jane followed Meghan through the locker rooms and then out to the pool where her nostrils filled with the smell of chlorine.

"The lap pool is open all day, so you could try that if you want. And they have water aerobics classes." Meghan motioned toward a row of old ladies bobbing up and down in the water following the lead of a fully clothed woman teaching them from the side of the pool.

"I think maybe a treadmill or something," Jane said. She couldn't imagine getting into a swimsuit every day.

Meghan laughed. "Water aerobics isn't for everybody."

They walked upstairs through the weight room and into the cardio room where a row of treadmills and other similar machines stared at her.

"Why don't we try the elliptical?" Meghan grabbed a magazine and Jane did the same.

Two sweat-tinged women on stair-stepping machines watched as Jane followed behind Meghan. Probably wondering what such a big person was doing at the gym. Again, she had to force herself not to run for the door.

Meghan hopped up on one of the elliptical machines—a cross between a stair stepper and a treadmill and far more intimidating than either.

Jane stood beside her machine and stared at it. "I don't know about this, Meg."

"Look, it's easy." Meghan flipped on the machine, clicked around on its digital face, adjusting the settings until finally she had thirty minutes on the timer. Meghan's legs started moving in a gliding motion, like she was running without lifting her feet off the ground.

Jane set her bottle of water in the drink holder and climbed up onto the machine. Scared to mess up the settings, she concentrated on the timer and started moving her legs.

After five minutes, she was dripping sweat. On one side of her, Meghan was coasting along, and on the other side, a muscular guy ran four-minute miles on the treadmill. Jane caught a glimpse of herself in the mirror and met the eyes of a woman across the room on a stationary bike.

*She's probably timing me to see how long I last.*

*She's probably waiting for me to have a heart attack.*

"Jane?" Meghan's voice pulled her from her self-deprecation.

"Yeah?"

"You've got it on the highest resistance."

"What?" Jane looked down at the settings. "I don't know what that means."

"Ten is the hardest." Meghan reached over and clicked a downward facing arrow to the number two. "Try that for a little while."

Suddenly, Jane's legs felt like Jell-O, but the ease of resistance made a huge difference. She still didn't last the entire thirty minutes, but at least it was a start.

"I'm going into the weight room," Meghan said when their half hour was up.

"I think I'm done for the day," Jane said, wiping sweat from her forehead.

"You did so well today, Janie. Really," Meghan said with a smile. "Just coming here is half the battle."

Jane responded with a weak smile. She looked at the woman across the gym. Would she ever stop feeling so inadequate?

## TWENTY-EIGHT

*Adele*

The day after Henry's proposal, Adele got the call from Kathy.

"We love your ideas and your food," the editor told her. "We'd love for the cookbook to be a go. We're sending over a contract for you to look over."

Adele held in a squeal until she hung up the phone, but seconds later, panic set in. It set in so fast, she didn't even think to call the Circle with the news. She had hundreds of recipes, all attached to some of her favorite stories, how would she ever narrow them down?

Then there was the little matter of Henry's proposal. If she accepted, it meant a move and a tough conversation with her family and the girls. If she declined, she risked breaking his heart. Again. The decision weighed heavy on her, so she did what she knew to do—she baked.

For two days straight, all she did was bake. She told herself it was research for the dessert portion of the cookbook, but the truth was, she needed the distraction, and baking helped her clear her head.

Now, though, looking over a table overflowing with delectable dishes, Adele began to think a new method of processing her emotions might be in order.

She called Meghan and told her to get the girls over to her house. "I need help with something."

"Is everything okay, Mama?" Meghan had asked.

She wouldn't tell her any more than that. If she told her slender daughter she needed help eating the mountain of sweets she'd accumulated, none of them would come.

"Oh, it's fine. I just have a few things to, uh, share with you. And I thought maybe we'd get a jump start on our scrapbook. No sense waiting till summer when we have Thanksgiving photos to scrap."

She hung up the phone and began pacing the house. She'd tried to bake away the reality that Henry had asked her to marry him, but even that hadn't worked. All it had done was get her even more worked up.

Why couldn't she simply hand this situation over to God? He'd take care of it like He'd done a thousand times before, but she hadn't given Him the chance. Instead of going to her knees with it, she'd gone to the cupboards—and she couldn't hide that fact unless she wanted to dump everything in the garbage.

The sound of footsteps on the front porch interrupted Adele's introspection, and then she heard the door opening.

"Mama? We're all here." Meghan's voice was a welcome addition to the quiet house. Adele greeted them in the entryway.

"It smells so good in here." Campbell took her coat off and inhaled a deep breath.

"Are you trying to kill me?" Jane had a terrified look in her eyes.

"Oh, girls, I'm so glad you're all here. Come on in." She ushered everyone into the dining room, where she'd laid out all the treats.

"I'm going to need some help narrowing things down." Adele set a Texas sheet cake on the table and glanced up to find four pairs of wide eyes staring at her, confused.

"Mama, what is all this?" Meghan asked.

"Dessert."

"For an army?"

"I got word a couple days ago," Adele said. "The cookbook is a go."

"That's wonderful, Adele," Campbell said.

"You must be so excited." Jane stared across the table full of off-limits food.

"You really didn't need to go to all this trouble, Adele," Lila said. "I think I've had that lemon cake with the cream-cheese frosting at least ten times. You already know it's delicious."

"I can't be here." Jane turned around, panicked. "Just smelling it is going to make me gain ten pounds."

"No, darlin'. I made you a sugar-free apple compote. It's in the kitchen."

"Mama, *what* is going on?" Meghan put a hand on her hip like she did when she was a teenager.

"It's nothin', just a little baking is all."

"This isn't either. This is stress baking. You do this when you're upset." Meghan raised an eyebrow, waiting for an answer.

"Fine. Yes, I might be a little bit stressed."

"Because of the cookbook?" Campbell asked.

"No. Well, yes, I am a little worked up over that, but—" How did she say it out loud? Telling them would break her heart. "Let's go in the living room, girls. I've got some news." Adele followed them all into the coziest room in the house and waited until everyone was comfortable. Their exchange of confused glances didn't escape her. "Do y'all want some dessert?"

"Mama! Spill it. What on earth is going on?" Meghan stood, arms crossed, and stared at her. Clearly her daughter was not in the mood for Adele's stalling.

Adele sat on the edge of her rocking chair, remembering how Henry had proposed right there in that very room. It was the second time he'd proposed to her. The first time, she'd been too young.

"Let me tell you a story," Adele said. "To give you some background." Her mind moseyed back and in an instant, she was sixteen again, standing under the night sky with Henry at her side. He'd been quieter than usual their last few dates, and tonight had done nothing to change that. Adele had started to wonder if he didn't want to see her anymore. Had his feelings for her changed?

They walked out on the dock and sat down, where they both put their feet in the lake, letting the water lap over their skin. The moon shone brighter than usual, illuminating Henry's troubled expression.

"Thanks for taking me out tonight," she said.

He glanced down at her and smiled. "Are you kidding? There was nowhere else I'd rather be."

"Really?" Hopefulness resounded in her voice.

"Of course." His face fell. "I love spending time with you." He stilled for a long moment, then said, "That's why this is so hard."

Adele frowned. "Why what is so hard?"

"What I'm about to tell you."

Her heart sank. He needed to break up with her. He'd most likely romanticized it for her sake, but she braced herself for her first heartbreak. "What is it, Henry?"

"I enlisted in the army."

Adele's mind spun, trying to understand the words he'd just spoken. Tears sprang to her eyes. Just yesterday she'd heard about another boy from Sweethaven who'd been killed in action in Vietnam. She'd said a prayer of thanks that her Henry didn't have to go over there and fight. "Thank You, Lord, for keeping him safe," she'd said.

And he was purposely putting himself in harm's way?

"Henry . . . why?"

"I want to serve my country." He shook his head. "I've been thinking about this all summer, Adele, ever since I turned eighteen, and I know it's the right thing to do."

Adele pulled her feet out of the water and stood up. "No, it's not the right thing, Henry. The right thing is for you to be here. With me."

He stood and moved toward her, but she held up a hand that told him not to come any closer. "Adele, please."

"I won't sleep a single hour when you're gone. How will I survive?" Her breath caught in her throat and she swatted the images of him with a gun out of her mind. "People die over there. Ronnie died over there. We knew him, Henry. This isn't a game."

He wrapped his arms around her and held her, the nearness of him drawing the tears from her very core. "I'm going to be all right," he said.

"You can't possibly promise that." Her voice caught and tears stained his shirt. "I can't lose you, Henry."

"You'll never lose me. I love you." Henry pulled back and took her face in his hands. "I need to know that you're going to be here when I get back." He reached into his pocket and pulled out a small silver band. "I want you to marry me, Adele. I want to spend the rest of my life with you."

Through her tears, she gasped. "I'm only sixteen."

"I know. But I know I love you, and I want us to be together."

She took the ring from him. No diamonds, and it still sparkled in the moonlight.

"I'll get you a real one when I get back," Henry said. "But I wanted you to have something for when I'm away. It'll keep the other guys away."

Adele met his eyes. "There are no other guys."

He leaned down and kissed her, holding her face, his thumb moving softly across her tear-stained cheek. After a long moment, Henry took a step back. "Will you wait for me?"

She nodded. "Yes, Henry. Of course I will."

They sat on the dock for at least an hour past her curfew, and a few days later, she said good-bye to him at the Sweethaven Train Depot.

Adele looked up at her captive audience, all four of the women wide-eyed and waiting.

"So, what happened?" Meghan asked.

Adele looked away. "Henry kept his promise. He was fine. But I didn't keep mine."

Silence washed over them and it seemed for several seconds they were all afraid to take a breath. She knew why. She'd made a promise and she'd broken it. She'd walked away from love because it had gotten too hard.

"I thought if I moved on and put Henry out of my mind I'd stop worrying about him. By the time he came back, I was engaged to someone else." She glanced at Meghan. She'd leave the part out about that someone being her biological daddy.

He'd never been anything close to a father to Meghan.

"I think we need to dive into the sheet cake," Lila said.

Adele's laugh sounded nervous in her own ears. "I tell you all this to tell you that thanks to you girls, Henry and I have reconnected."

Jane let out a squeal and the others started chattering. "When can we meet him?" Campbell asked.

"Soon, I hope." Adele met their eyes, one by one. "He's asked me to marry him and move to Grand Falls."

More squeals and chattering.

"You're getting *married*?" Jane covered her mouth with her hands and shook her head.

"Adele, that's wonderful news!" Campbell smiled.

"I hope you're having four bridesmaids," Lila said. "One with a big old belly."

Adele laughed. The girls' excitement had sparked something in her, and the stress of her decision melted away. Then she met Meghan's eyes. Her daughter had been oddly quiet.

"Meg?"

She put on a smile, but Adele saw right through it.

"What's wrong?"

Meghan shook her head. "No, Mama, I'm happy for you, of course." She pressed her lips together. "It's just all so sudden."

"I've known him all my life, darlin'," Adele said.

"No, Mama. You *knew* him. You don't know him now. You don't know what he's become."

Adele stared at her. "You girls are the ones who found Henry for me. Don't go changing things around on me now that it's workin' out."

"I'm not trying to rain on your parade, Mama, and I'm sure not trying to tell you what to do. I just want you to be careful—make sure you know what you're getting into. There are all kinds of stories about men conning women and taking their money. Teddy left you in decent shape."

"But I'm not wealthy by any means. Besides, Henry has his own money. He doesn't need mine." Adele held Meghan's gaze. "For the first time in years I feel like someone needs me again." Adele willed herself not to cry. "And girls, you may all take that for granted, but it's an important thing—being needed."

"But is it a reason to jump right into marriage? Why don't you date him for a while?" Meghan asked. "At least let us meet him."

Adele nodded. "Of course I want you to meet him."

"Good. Let's set something up," Lila said. "I can't wait."

"But you need to understand something, darlin'," Adele said. "I'm making this decision for myself. I turned my back on Henry once before because I was too afraid to keep my promise, and I'm not going to do that again."

Meghan leaned forward and held Adele's gaze. "Mama, you can't change the past. I understand that better than anyone. Don't make another mistake trying to right an old wrong." She reached out for Adele's hand. "I'm just watching out for you, same like you'd do for me."

Adele took her hand and smiled. "I know you are, hon." She looked around the room. "I'm so lucky I have you girls back in my life."

"Yeah, who else would eat all that sugar?" Campbell said, laughing.

"Speaking of, you can't put chocolate in front of a pregnant woman and expect her not to eat it," Lila said. "Where are the forks?"

"Plates and forks on the table," Adele said.

"Who said anything about a plate? Just give me the pan." Lila followed Campbell and Jane into the dining room, leaving her face-to-face with Meghan.

"I don't want to upset you, Mama," Meghan said. "I just don't want you to get hurt."

"I know, Meg, and I appreciate that." Adele smiled, thankful to have Meghan back, worrying about her for a change. "But I'm a big girl now. I promise."

"Just think about it. You don't have to rush. I just can't imagine you being happy anywhere but right here in this house." She pulled Adele into a hug, and Adele drank in the moment. All those wasted years she and Meghan weren't speaking—and here they were, just like old times.

But now, the tables had turned and it was Meghan speaking common sense and Adele acting rash.

After the girls ate too many desserts, they pulled out their scrapbooking supplies and Thanksgiving photos.

"If we're not careful, we're not going to have anything to work on over the summer," Meghan said.

"Excuse me," Lila said. "I will have a baby to scrapbook." She beamed and they all began trimming photos and placing embellishments, each creating one layout for the album on their Thanksgiving experience.

"Don't give me any pictures with food in them," Jane said. "That apple compote was good, Adele, but it sure wasn't Texas sheet cake."

Meghan put a hand on Jane's. "It gets easier." She smiled at her old friend and seeing them all there like that warmed Adele to the core.

She did love Sweethaven, and she loved having the girls right there with her, working on pages like they did as kids. Maybe there was some truth in what Meghan said.

After everyone left, Adele turned to face the quiet of the old cottage. The house she'd grown to love.

And suddenly everything she thought she'd decided hung in the balance, and Adele was more confused than ever. A part of her had always loved Henry, but all of her had always loved Sweethaven.

And leaving this old place behind would be a different kind of grief.

## TWENTY-NINE

*Meghan*

Meghan had been going through her days as if everything was fine, but at the back of her mind, the Christmas special—and the fact that the producers wanted to oust her own family—had her worried.

"Maybe we should just cancel it," she told Nick the morning of the rehearsal.

"Don't be crazy. The worst thing that could happen is that your real family doesn't get to be a part of it, and you know they'll understand. It's not like it was your decision."

It was true, and that's why it bothered her. For years, her career had been mishandled by a self-serving manager. It was time for Meghan to be in control of her own future, but that meant standing up to pushy television executives.

And she didn't want a reputation of being a diva.

A housekeeper had been in the day before, but Meghan still had the duster out when the doorbell rang. She stashed the filthy rag in a drawer and wondered out loud why she hadn't just told her family there was a chance they wouldn't be in the special after all, but the only reply was dead air.

Meghan opened the door to find Liz and her entourage shivering on the front porch.

"This is the most frigid, coldest place," Liz said. "How can you stand to live here when you could be anywhere else?" She came into the entryway and peeled off a too-thin jacket to reveal a wisp of a blouse. No wonder she was freezing.

"I made coffee for you guys. It'll warm you right up." Meghan watched as the group of them pushed inside, chattering about camera angles and lighting challenges.

"We could've filmed a Hawaiian Christmas special, you know," Liz said. "You *are* a famous musician."

Meghan smiled. "I like it here."

Liz shook her head. "That's something I don't think I could ever understand." She walked into the living room and watched the others moving furniture and setting up shots. Before long, Meghan's quaint cottage looked more like a television set.

"I thought this was just a rehearsal," Meghan said as they removed a large family photo from over the fireplace and replaced it with a wreath.

"It is, but we need to map everything out. Once we do, we'll need to keep the set just as we leave it until after the show. And we'll most likely be filming some filler today just in case the timing is off somehow. It's always better to have more to work with than to be scrambling around." Liz turned her attention to her iPad.

"Liz, I wonder if I could talk with you before we get started?"

The woman glanced up and met Meghan's eyes. "Of course."

"I want you to reconsider using my real family and my Sweethaven friends. I don't feel right about using actors—it seems like a lie."

Liz hugged the iPad to her chest. "Why don't we see how it goes today and then we can revisit this afterward? If, after you meet everyone, you still feel the same, we'll discuss it, but with the time crunch we may not be able to do much to change anything."

"They're all coming today. Just meet them. My mom and brother, my friends." Meghan hated how desperate she sounded, begging like a preschooler for her own way. She was Meghan Rhodes, for crying out loud. Shouldn't *they* be asking *her* what to do?

But the sad fact was, she needed this Christmas special more than they needed her.

Liz held her gaze for a long, condescending moment and then pursed her lips. "Fine. We'll consider it. Do any of them sing?"

Meghan nodded. "My mom and brother can both sing. In fact, they filmed Luke singing with me at the Christmas concert."

"Fine. Bring them to me when they get here."

The front door swung open and Luke walked in, followed by Campbell. Liz raised a brow. "Who's that?"

"That's Luke, my little brother."

"All right, Meghan. He's in. I can't promise anything about the rest of them." She tossed another glance in Luke's direction, as if she were sizing up her prey. "But he is definitely in."

Meghan tossed up her arms and walked away.

\* \* \* \* \*

*Campbell*

Campbell's realization that she had let herself fall in love with Luke didn't come at the best time. Now, she found herself anticipating his proposal every time she saw him. Earlier, as she put on her makeup, she imagined what it would be like for him to get down on one knee during the filming. Sure, the special was about Meghan's small-town Christmas, but a proposal would make for good television, wouldn't it?

She'd patted gloss over her lips as she studied her closet, trying to decide what she'd want to wear on the day her boyfriend asked her to marry him.

On the way over, Campbell glanced down at her bare left hand and envisioned the ring on her fourth finger. Although the ring was a bit much for someone unassuming like her, she'd decided not to complain. How could she even consider such a thing when Luke had obviously spent way more money than she would ever expect picking out the perfect ring to symbolize his love?

Now, standing in Meghan's dining room, Campbell found herself fidgeting and nervous.

Was the ring in his coat pocket? Or perhaps he'd taken it to Meghan's earlier? She reminded herself to slow down. Luke might have other plans for proposing. Like a candlelit dinner for the two of them. If it didn't happen today, she knew it would happen soon.

But the anticipation was driving her crazy.

"You okay?" Luke glanced down at her.

"Sure. Just a little nervous. I've never been on TV before."

*And I've never been proposed to before.*

"You'll be fine. Just sit there and look beautiful." He kissed the top of her head.

She smiled. "I'm only going to be in the background."

"Singing Christmas carols," Luke said. "You can handle that, right?"

"I don't sing," Campbell said.

"Just mouth along with the words."

"Lip-synching. Nice." Campbell laughed. "By the way, I didn't know you sing."

"I don't anymore."

"You should. You were really good at the concert." She faced him and smiled.

"How about I reserve my musical talents for you? I only did that because Meghan begged me."

Campbell looked around Meghan's cottage. She wondered what it had looked like before Nick renovated it as a gift to Meghan. She knew Luke had helped transform the old place, but she had no way to measure his talent.

Judging by the way the house looked, though, she could see he was a talented architect. But he'd traded all that for the simple life and now only consulted with his old firm.

In the front room, cameras were being set up, the cords and equipment cluttering the perimeter of the entire space.

The crew worked together to transform the room, talking through the details of the filming, but most of it didn't make much sense to Campbell.

Lila and Tom arrived next, followed by Jane and then Adele, dressed in a Christmas sweater with actual ornaments on it.

"Ma, you came in costume," Luke said.

"Getting into the Christmas spirit." Adele winked at him. "Do you think it's too much?"

Luke started to respond and then closed his mouth. Thankfully, before Adele could chide him, Meghan appeared in the doorway.

"So, there are a few things we're still working out," Meghan said. "This is Liz and she's going to help us muddle through this rehearsal."

Liz stepped forward, iPad in hand, and cast a look across the room. "Where's your brother, Meghan? Oh, there you are." Her eyes twinkled as they settled on Luke. "We want you front and center, right over there on the couch next to Tasha." She pulled Luke by the arm into the living room, where he was greeted by a petite brunette with almond-shaped eyes and perfect skin.

"Scoot in real close, like you're a couple," Liz said. "We really want that cozy feeling."

"Then why don't you let him be cozy with his real-life girlfriend?" Adele asked with a glance in Campbell's direction.

"Mama, please."

"I'm just confused is all, darlin'. Why would you need anyone to pretend to be cozy with Luke when Campbell is right here?"

Meghan sighed. "I'm sorry, you guys. I didn't know it, but they have to use actors to play my friends and family."

"Luke's not an actor," Adele said.

"Except for Luke. You can all be in the background, but the foreground will be trained singers and actors."

Luke shot Campbell a look from the other room, and she didn't know whether to laugh at how uncomfortable he seemed or cry at how much she hated seeing another woman by his side.

What about the proposal?

"So who's playing your mother?" Adele asked, her arms crossed over her chest.

"No one. They've decided to keep the crowd . . . younger," Meghan said.

Adele tossed her an annoyed look.

"I know, Mama. Believe me, I'm not happy about this at all. But with the music, they need singers."

Adele's chin notched upward. "I *am* a singer, darlin'."

"It's okay, Meghan," Lila said. "I'm so bloated today they probably couldn't fit all of me in one frame anyway."

"Can we stay and watch though?" Jane asked. "I've never been around a real TV crew."

Meghan's smile was weak. "Of course. And I'll treat you all to dinner as soon as this charade is over."

"Do you at least get your real husband?" Adele quipped.

Meghan sighed, then looked at Campbell. "I'm sorry, hon," she said. "I know it's weird to see Luke with a pretend girlfriend."

"It's okay," Campbell said, waving her hand, even as a lump of disappointment formed in her stomach. To think she'd actually concocted another whole proposal.

"Thanks for understanding, you guys."

"Meghan!" Liz called her from the other room. "We're about ready."

Meghan turned back and looked at the rest of them. "Duty calls."

She walked into the living room, leaving the rest of them staring, unsure of what to do next.

"I feel weird," Lila said. "Maybe we should go."

"I'm not goin' anywhere," Adele said. "I'm sure if those fuddy-dud producers would look up from their phones for one second they'd see they are making a terrible mistake. Who is that girl with her arm around Luke?"

"I guess this is how the girlfriends of movie stars feel, huh?" Jane said.

"Yeah, and now you know why the divorce rate in Hollywood is so high." Lila shook her head, then glanced at Campbell. "Not that you have anything to worry about, of course."

"At this point," Liz said, her attention on Luke, "we're going to have you sing a little bit with Meghan, but when everyone joins in the chorus, I want you and Tasha to have a moment."

"A moment?" Luke looked confused.

"Like a little something special just between the two of you. A glance, a smile. Make us think you're in love."

Campbell could feel Jane and Lila's eyes on her.

She pressed her lips together and pretended she was fine, but Campbell didn't like this one bit—feeling like an outsider with her own boyfriend.

"If she tells that girl to kiss him, I'm going to come unglued," Adele said. "Campbell, honey, why don't we go into the kitchen?"

"No," Campbell said. "It's fine. Luke's obviously even more uncomfortable than I am."

No sooner had she said the words than the pretend girlfriend whispered something that made Luke laugh. Really laugh—not a fake one, for the camera.

They all stared for another long moment. The producer walked over to Luke and the brunette. "You two make a great-looking couple. Luke, when you and Meghan sing the duet, would you mind singing right to Tasha here? We want to convey the feeling of a romantic Christmas."

"On second thought, maybe you're right," Campbell said. "Would one of you take me home?"

Without hesitation, and perfectly on cue, all three of the other women said in unison, "I will."

# THIRTY

*Meghan*

Rehearsing for the Christmas special under Mama's watchful glare was unnerving, especially knowing how upset Mama was. Meghan couldn't blame her. What mother wouldn't want to be a part of her daughter's success? Especially when she'd been cut out of it for so many years.

"Meghan, are you listening?" Liz's stern tone cut through Meghan's thoughts.

"What?"

"What Christmas carol did you want to do at this point in the show?"

Meghan glanced at Luke, who sat on a couch next to a girl who'd been instructed to act like she was in love with him.

She was very convincing. So convincing Campbell had left.

Nick put a hand on Meghan's shoulder. "I think we were thinking something fun here, weren't we, Meg?"

Meghan wanted to get up and leave, but she knew that would do nothing to restore her career. Why wouldn't they just give her what she wanted—the family she'd fought so hard for?

"Yeah, I think so. 'Jingle Bells,' I think?"

Liz wrinkled her nose. "Maybe we could do something a little less cheesy. How about 'Angels We Have Heard on High'?"

"Isn't this the segment where the kids come in?"

"Yes."

"I thought the kids would enjoy 'Jingle Bells.' My own kids love that one."

Liz cleared her throat, then pressed her lips together. "We'll make a note of that. For now, let's do 'Angels We Have Heard on High.'" She turned around and searched the entryway for her assistant, Kristy, a girl in her twenties with dishwater hair and pale white skin. "We're ready for the kids."

Off in the distance, Meghan could see her own kids, playing Memory with a member of the crew. Would it hurt their feelings if they overheard one of these other children call her Mom?

Kristy returned with two small kids trailing behind. The girl had screaming red hair, much like Meghan's before she'd added lowlights. The boy's hair was a lighter brown, a trail of freckles running across his face.

"Meghan, these are your kids."

Meghan smiled at them. It wasn't their fault, she reminded herself.

"Now, kids," Liz said, her voice firm. "You're going to sit beside Mrs. Rhodes. You're going to smile the entire time and it's important that you perform from the second we start filming."

Meghan shot Nick a look. Nothing about this would be natural. Nothing would be real. The entire thing would be staged. He looked away, probably thinking the exact same thing.

"Why don't we do a test?" Liz said. "You're both going to look right here." Liz held her hand above the camera, her eyes wide.

Meghan glanced at the kids. The girl seemed poised and ready for action, but the little boy stared at his hands in his lap.

"You, boy—" Liz turned to Kristy. "What's his name?"

Kristy looked down at her clipboard. "Dylan."

"Dylan, look up this way at the camera."

Dylan's eyes widened. "I have to go to the bathroom."

"I'm ready," the little girl said. "My mom said professionals take care of these things before they're on set."

Liz avoided Meghan's eyes. "Kristy, why don't you take him to the bathroom? Crew, we'll take five."

Everyone dispersed and Meghan made a beeline for Liz. "My kids would be more natural at this. And so would my own family."

Liz turned to her.

"I don't want to do this unless it's genuine, and nothing about this is genuine."

Liz sighed. "I'll call Martin."

Meghan didn't want to be difficult, and she didn't want to ruin this opportunity, but she couldn't stand the hurt in Mama's eyes, the discomfort on Luke's face or the disappointment Campbell must've felt watching Tasha whisper in her boyfriend's ear. She wouldn't be the reason for any more pain among the people she loved. If she was going to do this, then she'd do it without any pretension and on her terms.

Otherwise, she supposed, her days in the limelight would be over.

## THIRTY-ONE

*Lila*

After Meghan finished rehearsing for the Christmas special, she invited all of them for dinner at The Grotto.

"I need to make it up to all of you," she said on the phone.

"I'm craving pizza," Lila said, knowing that The Grotto's roasted chicken and shrimp would not suffice.

Meghan sounded surprised. "You?"

"It's the baby," Lila said with a laugh. "But I'm a changed woman. I'm going to stop bein' so fussy all the time."

"All right," Meghan told her. "I'll let the others know."

An hour later, they were enjoying Frado's deep-dish Chicago-style pizza.

"I gotta tell ya, Mrs. Olsen, I didn't think I'd ever see you back here again," Angelo said as he brought their pizzas to the table.

"Angelo, you were so charming the last time I was here, you must've known I'd be back," Lila said.

Angelo grinned. "Feel free to come back anytime. Especially if you're going to bring so many beautiful women."

They all laughed as he walked back to the kitchen.

Then the table quieted. "Lila," Jane said, glancing toward the door. "Your mom."

Lila followed her gaze to the door of the restaurant where her mother, wearing a long black coat with fur at the top, dress pants and a pair of heels, breezed in. She spotted Lila and the others and waved, a smile lighting her face.

"Not now," Lila said under her breath. How did Mama find her? Had she followed her here?

"Hello, ladies," Mama said, scanning them.

A chorus of hellos rang out, but Lila chose to stay silent.

"Lila, may I have a word with you?"

Mama had decided to pretend everything was just fine between them, but she didn't know Lila knew about her little secret. Lila could count on one hand the number of times she'd stood up to her mother. How many times had Mama pulled her out of an event, an appointment with a client, a dinner? What she needed always came first. But what about what Lila needed?

What about the truth?

"Mama, how did you know where to find me?"

Mama lifted her chin. "If you must know, I followed you from The Whitmore."

Concerned glances ping-ponged across the table.

"I'm having dinner with my friends. If you want to say something to me, you can say it now or call me in the morning."

Mama stiffened. "I would call, dear, but you don't seem to answer the phone lately."

Lila looked away. Mama had left several messages when she got word that she and Tom were serious about buying their own cottage. She'd called to talk her out of it, Lila was sure. She hadn't responded.

"Can we talk later, Mama?" Lila glanced around the table. Her friends all seemed overly interested in their menus and place settings.

"I simply need to know when you're going back to Macon. We're right in the middle of decorating the nursery, and your father and I leave tomorrow."

"I'll handle the nursery, Mama. I've decided to go with the brown and green like I originally planned."

Mama drew in a slow breath. She leaned in closer, as if that could keep the others from hearing. "What has gotten into you, Lila? You're not wearing a stitch of makeup. You're eating in this hole-in-the-wall restaurant that probably isn't even up to code, you're buying a ramshackle cottage of your own and you're changing all your plans with the nursery?"

"Your plans."

"What?"

"Those were your plans, Mama. I wanted the green and brown."

Her friends shifted in their seats, and Lila hated how uncomfortable this was making them, but when she felt Jane's hand on her own, underneath the table, something told her to be thankful she wasn't alone.

"The crib is being delivered at the end of the week. Will you be there?"

Lila shook her head. "I think I'm going to do the nursery alone, but thank you for offering to help."

Mama's eyebrow arched ever so slightly—hardly detectable to the naked eye. "Fine, if you insist on being stubborn."

"I appreciate that," Lila said.

Mama stared at her. In that moment, Lila felt bolder than ever.

"For years I've done what I thought you wanted me to. I've been who you told me to be. But I'm not going to do it anymore—and I'm not going to let you make my child feel inadequate like you've always done to me."

Never mind Mama's cruelty toward Charlotte. The woman's daughter was dying and all Mama cared about was her own reputation.

Her mother blinked several times in quick succession and then lifted her chin. "What are you saying?"

"I'm saying that I'm going to be different from now on. It's time for me to grow up. And if you don't like that, I'm sorry. But I know the truth about you and Daddy and all the lies you told me—and I don't want my child around someone who has no use for the truth."

Mama gasped. The look on her face would forever be seared in Lila's memory—one of hurt, anger and embarrassment. Mama quickly composed herself, turned and walked out.

As quickly as Lila's anger had come, it left, replaced instead with regret and the horrible knowledge that she would rue the day she crossed Cilla Adler.

"You all right, darlin'?" Adele's eyes looked sad.

Lila stared at her own hands in her lap. "I have a sister." She glanced up and found she had everyone's attention. "Turns out my father was married when he and Mama met. The truth is, my mother was Daddy's first mistress."

Lila explained every detail she knew, right down to the reason Charlotte had come to Sweethaven.

"I'm the reason Charlotte grew up without a father," Lila said. "It's my fault."

"How is this your fault?" Meghan said. "Your parents were grown-ups. You didn't make them act like teenagers."

"Still, if Mama hadn't gotten pregnant, maybe Daddy never would've left that woman and Charlotte's daughter would have the transplant she needs."

Adele leveled her gaze, eyes set on Lila. "Listen to me about one thing. I pride myself in not meddling in any of your business—"

Meghan let out a laugh and Adele whacked her across the arm. "Stop it, missy," she said. "I do pride myself. I don't want to be bossy or tell you what I know. But I'm gonna tell you what I know."

Lila nodded. She'd listen to what Adele knew any time.

"What I see when I look at your mama is a woman tryin' to keep it together when she's built her whole life on a house of cards."

Lila's eyes stung and she reached for a napkin.

"Lie stacked on top of lie. It's bound to come apart sometime. She's so worried about what other people will think of her, she's lived with this horrendous secret her whole life. And now it's all smackin' her straight in the face."

"Adele, I appreciate what you're saying, but my mother is the most prideful person I know." Lila wiped her eyes.

Adele smiled. "Trust me, hon. Your mama is just as insecure as the rest of us. And I believe she wants nothing more than for her daughter to love and respect her. That's why she didn't want you to know the truth about her mistakes."

Lila looked away. She wanted to nurse her anger. She didn't want to feel sorry for her mother—the woman had made her doubt herself at every turn. Cilla Adler certainly didn't deserve anyone's pity.

But as she drove back to the Whitmore that night, a part of her had softened. What if Adele was right? What if her shame had kept Mama from living an honest life?

Could Lila find it in her heart to forgive the woman she so desperately wanted to put in her place?

## THIRTY-TWO

*Campbell*

It had taken a bit of convincing, but Campbell agreed to join the others for Meghan's apology dinner. Sitting through another Adler family drama had her wondering why she hadn't stayed home in her yoga pants and big sweatshirt.

As they were about to leave, Campbell's phone rang. Luke's name popped up on the caller ID and she excused herself from the table.

"Hey," she said into the cell.

"I'm calling to apologize," he said. "I didn't get a chance to see you before you left."

"It's okay."

Luke sighed. "No, it wasn't okay. I should've said something. Or bowed out myself."

*Yeah, you should've.*

"Let me make it up to you?" Luke's voice sounded hopeful. "I'm thinking dinner, just the two of us. I feel like we've been around other people for three weeks straight."

Dinner alone. Just the two of them. Her pulse quickened, but she kept her voice steady. "Sounds good. When?"

"Tomorrow night. I'll pick you up at seven. I want to take you somewhere nice—Rosatti's or The Grotto. You deserve a nice dinner out. Especially after today."

She'd let him grovel a little, though she'd made peace with his pretend girlfriend over the course of dinner. Campbell hung up the phone and found Jane waiting just a few feet away. "Everyone's by the front door. I thought I'd wait for you." She handed Campbell her purse.

"Thanks."

"I wanted to make sure you were okay."

Campbell ran a hand through her hair. "I'm fine. It was just annoying is all."

"Was that Luke?" Jane then shook her head. "I'm sorry. How nosy of me."

"No, it's not nosy. It's kind of nice to have someone getting in my business. My mom was great at that."

Jane put a hand on Campbell's shoulder. "I am always here for you when you need someone to butt into your business."

"Well, yes, since you asked. That was Luke. He wants to take me to dinner to apologize."

Jane tilted her head and let out a slight sigh. "He's so sweet."

Campbell looked away.

Jane leaned in a little closer. "He is sweet, isn't he?"

After a deep breath, Campbell closed her eyes. "I found something I wasn't supposed to. Talk about nosy."

"What was it?" Jane looked alarmed.

"A ring."

She clapped her hands over her mouth to conceal what Campbell was sure would've been an ear-piercing scream. "A *ring*?"

Campbell glanced around the restaurant, thankful no one seemed to be paying attention to them.

"Yes. An altogether too expensive ring."

"He's going to propose." She clapped her hands over her mouth again.

Campbell shook her head. "I don't know. That was a couple of weeks ago, and to be honest, I kind of wonder if he changed his mind."

"Or if he's going to do it tomorrow night at dinner. Where's he taking you?"

"To The Grotto. Or Rosatti's. He said he's not sure."

Jane gasped. "He's going to propose."

But Campbell reminded herself that she'd expected his proposal twice now and been disappointed both times. After today, she wondered if it would ever happen.

"What are you going to say?"

"I don't know," Campbell said. "I thought for a while I didn't want him to ask, but now I'm not sure anymore."

Jane smiled. "I think whatever happens, you're just going to know. In that moment, you're going to know if it's right."

The others stood beside Angelo at the cash register, and as they approached, Campbell said a silent prayer of thanks that the man's voice drowned out her conversation with Jane. "Do you think I should marry him?" she whispered.

The smile on Jane's face faded and she stopped walking. "Honey, I think if you love him you absolutely should marry him. But only you can make that decision." Then, as if she'd read Campbell's mind, Jane said, "And if your mom were still here, I think she'd say the same thing."

Campbell looked away, her eyes scanning the old tables and red chairs in the restaurant. "She always had a way of helping me make the right decisions."

"And she raised you to learn to make them for yourself. Trust me, hon. You're going to be okay. Tomorrow night, you get yourself all dolled up and enjoy every second because this is one of the most exciting times in your whole life."

"I just wish she were here for it."

Jane pulled Campbell into a tight hug. "I do too, Cam. I really do."

## THIRTY-THREE

*Jane*

Jane turned the key in the front door, her stomach still growling. She'd ordered a salad with light vinaigrette dressing, but it hadn't filled her up. It hadn't even made a dent. While everyone ordered dessert, Jane sipped her ice water with lemon and pretended her mouth wasn't watering at the sight of chocolate cake.

Now in the kitchen—the most dangerous room in the house— she wished she had cookies or ice cream or something sweet. Just a bite. It would take care of the craving.

But one bite would lead to two, which would lead to three . . . and pretty soon she'd have inhaled two thousand calories.

She knew because she'd looked up her favorite treats, hoping the numbers would deter her from bingeing. So far, it had worked.

Jane stared into the refrigerator. She'd purposely thrown away everything tempting, buying only fresh fruits and natural foods. At the checkout, though, she realized the sad truth that eating healthy might be great for her waistline, but it sure wouldn't be great for her bank account. She spent almost two hundred dollars on food that was supposed to last a week.

So unfair.

Now, she regretted it. Would anything take away this craving?

The back door opened and the girls walked in, chattering until they saw her standing in the dark, refrigerator door wide open. They were in Sweethaven for a long weekend before finals started.

Jane had been gone all day and she forgot they'd come back for the weekend.

"Mom?" Emily flipped the light on.

"What are you doing?" Jenna stared at her.

Caught like a cat with a bird in its mouth, Jane shut the door and turned away.

"Just eat, Mom. What's the big deal?" Emily went to the freezer and pulled out a carton of ice cream.

"Where'd that come from?" Jane stared at it.

"You can't expect *us* to give up everything you're giving up." Emily opened the carton and scooped the fudge ripple into a bowl. "Want some, Jen?"

Jenna glanced at Jane and shook her head. "No. I'm not hungry."

How did she do that? How did she turn down ice cream like it was the easiest thing in the world? Like it had no hold over her whatsoever?

*God, please let me get to that point.*

"But you probably shouldn't eat it in front of Mom," Jenna said.

"Mom, if you want some, have some." Emily held it up to Jane.

Jane looked away.

Jenna grabbed the container, closed it and put it away at the back of the freezer. "Emily, what is wrong with you?"

"We don't need to lose weight, so why can't we eat like we always do?"

Jane's heart sank. Her family hadn't been as receptive to these changes as she'd hoped, and suddenly she realized that she couldn't live in this bubble alone forever. "I'm sorry, Em. If you want to eat junk food, you're going to have to make it for yourself."

"But since when is pasta junk food?" Emily ate a bite of her ice cream. "I mean, you won't buy anything good anymore. It's lame."

"Someday maybe you will appreciate it. Someday when you go to your doctor and you don't have any cause for concern, you can look back on this time as the time your mother finally taught you about nourishing your body. And that junk food"—Jane glanced at the bowl of ice cream—"isn't going to do it."

Emily shrugged. "It's just totally unfair that you're making this big decision for all of us. Like, we have no say in it at all. It's not our fault you're fat."

Jane gasped. The words sliced into her and her mind whirled back to junior high school. Jane walked toward the lunch table carrying her hot lunch tray when one of the girls stuck a foot into the aisle. Jane crashed to the floor, her chicken nuggets and french fries flying across the cafeteria. The crash of her silverware hitting the tiled floor silenced the entire cafeteria, before the room erupted in laughter.

Tears stung Jane's eyes.

"No reason to cry about it. Trust me, you can stand to skip a meal," one of the girls said.

Jane ran to the bathroom, ketchup smeared across her shirt. She burst through the door and came face-to-face with Emma O'Dell.

"It's your turn, huh?" Emma sat on the radiator, feet propped up on the sink.

"What do you mean?" Jane wiped her cheeks, then wet a paper towel, trying—and failing—to rid herself of the red stain on the front of her shirt.

"They sent notes around this morning and told everyone not to talk to you. Said if any of the girls hung out with you they'd regret it."

Jane sniffed. "But why?"

The girl shrugged. "I was on the list last month. That's why I bring my lunch now and eat in here."

"In the bathroom?"

"It beats out there." She held up half her sandwich. "Want some?"

Jane stared at the offering through clouded eyes. She took the sandwich. "Thanks."

She spent the rest of the year hiding from those girls and determined to never say a mean thing about anyone—because she knew how it felt to be the butt of everyone else's jokes.

Now, standing in front of her daughters, Jane fought back new tears and wondered if she'd raised a daughter who thought it was okay to call people names. Was Emily the kid who tripped the less popular girls and made them cry?

"Emily, I think you should go to your room," Jane said, in the calmest voice possible.

"Mom, I'm sorry. I didn't mean for it to come out that way." But Emily's tone told the truth—her daughter wasn't sorry, at least not for saying something hurtful. Sorry that Jane had decided to send her to her room.

"Emily. Go to your room."

Her daughter stared at her. "This is so stupid." She walked out, leaving Jane standing in the kitchen.

Jenna took a step toward her. "I'm sorry, Mom. I'll talk to her."

"It's okay," Jane said.

But as Jenna left the kitchen, loneliness swept through Jane. She'd wished she had someone to do this with her, but she knew she couldn't rely on anyone else to make her lose weight. Her success rested solely in her hands, in her choices.

And in that moment, she wanted to choose ice cream. She wanted to douse it in hot fudge, curl up in her bed and forget about her worries.

Her thoughts turned to tomorrow. How would she feel if she woke up with the memory of her own weakness clawing at her? How would she digest the truth that she'd allowed a weak moment to undo her hard work in an instant?

With a hand on the freezer door, Jane took a breath. "Help me, God," she said. "I want the ice cream, but I know it's not good for me. I know I'll be miserable tomorrow if I give in."

She stood for a few moments waiting for some magical heaping of self-control to fall on top of her, but nothing happened.

Emily had left the hot fudge on the counter, and Jane stared at it as the seconds ticked by. She actually considered turning the bottle over and squeezing the chocolate straight into her mouth.

Her thoughts turned to the hours she'd logged at the gym.

"Not this time," she said, finally mustering the courage with every last ounce of willpower. She capped the bottle, stuck the chocolate back in the fridge and walked out of the room, shutting off the light as she did.

"Not this time."

She knew she was doing the right thing, and she had heard countless times that it would get easier, but in that moment, nothing felt further from the truth.

## THIRTY-FOUR

*Lila*

Lila felt like she'd just stepped back in time as she walked up to the cottage where Tom had grown up. "It's kind of surreal," he said, jiggling the doorknob on the front door. "Huh. Still loose."

She smiled. He'd gotten in touch with the owner, who, it turned out, rarely made it to Sweethaven anymore and had been thinking of listing the house. He'd sent a key to Pearl, who waited for them inside.

Lila stood on the front porch and surveyed the front lawn. Several mature oak trees dotted the expansive yard, and Lila loved that it seemed so private. For a brief moment, she could almost see their little boy or girl riding a tricycle up and down the long driveway.

"You coming?" Tom's voice from inside reminded Lila there was more to a house than memories. She walked inside and found Pearl standing in the kitchen.

"Tom, it's so much more open than I remember it," Lila said. From the entryway, Lila could see an oversize family room, a formal dining room and a kitchen that opened up to a large deck off the back of the house.

"It's so much smaller than I remember," Tom said.

"We'd have to paint. And replace the floors." Lila imagined white woodwork and cabinets with gray walls and rich curtains.

"But that's all cosmetic," Tom said. "We could do that easily. Might even be fun."

"The new owners have kept the house in pristine shape." Pearl flipped through a stack of papers inside a manila folder. "Looks like they don't even rent it out for the summers."

Tom looked over the paperwork, then met Lila's eyes. "Hon, we can work with this."

She went upstairs and peeked in on the three bedrooms and two bathrooms. The master had a large walk-in closet, its own bathroom and plenty of space. Lila pulled the curtains back and nearly gasped. The view of the lake all but took her breath away.

"This is it," she said.

"What'd you say, hon?" Tom stood in the hallway, checking out the linen closet.

"This is our house." She turned and faced him.

He smiled. "Then let's buy it."

Tom and Pearl headed back to her office to write up the offer, but Lila needed to rest. She drove back to the Whitmore already assembling a mental mood board to start decorating their new cottage. Mama always thought Tom's parents weren't good enough to associate with—what would she say when she found out Lila planned to buy their old cottage?

It didn't matter. Lila had a good feeling about this place. About this new life.

She parked the Mercedes in a parking space around the back and used her room key to let herself into the bed-and-breakfast. Sweethaven welcomed many tourists every summer, but the need for hotels was scarce, giving the Whitmore a monopoly on out-of-town lodging. She walked into the foyer and glanced into the common area, where she saw Charlotte reading on the chaise longue in the corner.

Her stomach flip-flopped at the sight of her, and Lila couldn't rid herself of the idea that if the woman had simply stayed put, her life wouldn't be such a mess right now.

Sometimes she welcomed blissful ignorance.

But the idea shamed her. Charlotte hadn't come here to turn Lila's world upside down. She'd come in search of a cure for her ailing child. How could Lila—or anyone else—fault her for that?

She started up the stairs, but Charlotte hurried toward her.

"Lila, wait."

Lila turned and faced her.

"I hoped we could talk. I've been waiting for you."

"How'd you know I was here?" Lila came down a step.

Charlotte shifted. "Your father told me."

Lila looked away. Had she and Daddy been getting reacquainted?

"I know you're probably exhausted. Could I just have a few moments of your time?" Charlotte wore jeans and a lightweight sweater and looked laid-back, yet put together. She had an easiness about her. One Lila envied. Everything about her had gotten uptight and critical.

Like Mama.

Lila followed Charlotte into the empty sitting room, and they sat in two wingback chairs in front of the fireplace.

"I can see why you'd want to come back here every year," Charlotte said, drawing her legs up underneath her.

"It does have its charm," Lila said.

A strange silence fell between them.

"I wanted to apologize to you, Lila. I didn't think through my coming here." Charlotte wrung her hands. "I wasn't exactly honest with you before."

"What do you mean?"

"I'd do anything to save my daughter," Charlotte said, her eyes glassy. "But I have to admit that a part of me wanted to confront him too. I finally had a reason to find him—to look him up and make him feel guilty for what he did to us."

Lila cleared her throat.

"Maybe I should've looked for other options. If I had, your world would still be intact."

Lila looked away. It would certainly be nice not to have the inner turmoil of the truth. Part of her thought so anyway.

"I know it's hard to imagine, but I want you to know, I don't blame you for anything." Charlotte's lips turned up in a slight smile.

Lila pressed her lips together and tried not to feel sorry for her sister. But if Lila hadn't been conceived, none of this would be happening, and everyone would be happier.

It occurred to her that Campbell probably felt the same way.

"The truth is, I never really knew him. I spent a lot of years mad about that. Really, really angry that he'd chosen her over my mother and you over me."

"I don't think it was like that, Charlotte."

"That's how it felt." She stared at her hands, folded now in her lap. "Do you know I wasn't even a year old when he left us?"

Lila's heart sank. How had her father justified his actions for so many years?

Charlotte looked away. "They were high school sweethearts, my mom and our dad."

Lila found herself wanting to know more. "What happened?"

A sad look crossed Charlotte's face. "Your mom happened."

"I'm sorry."

"Don't be. I've always felt like it was my fault she lost him. If she hadn't been pregnant, I wonder if he would've strayed."

Was Daddy really that shallow?

"Anyway, I never meant to hurt you in all of this."

Lila took a breath. "It's not your fault. I think it was just time for me to know the truth. I have to admit, it's helped me take a closer look at the kind of person I want to be. The kind of mother I want to be. That's gotta count for something, right?"

Charlotte smiled. "I was lying in bed last night and I started thinking about how something good might come out of this after all."

"Such as?" Lila couldn't imagine anything good coming out of this. Mama swore Charlotte came for Daddy's money. Charlotte told a different story. How would any of them ever see eye to eye?

Charlotte rummaged through her purse until she finally pulled out a small book of photos. She handed the book to Lila. "These are my kids."

Lila stared at the book. Her sister's kids. Daddy's grandkids. His legacy.

Her thoughts turned to the baby growing inside her. She'd longed for the day she'd hold her own child in her arms—not just for herself, but for her parents. Daddy had always wanted a son. If Lila could give him a grandson, somehow she thought he'd be proud of her. Finally accept her exactly as she was.

Charlotte cleared her throat. "I was just thinking I may never have the kind of relationship with my father that I want, but I have a sister right here in front of me."

The lights from the Christmas tree in the lobby twinkled in the dim light.

A sister.

She'd always imagined having someone to play house with, someone's hair to braid, someone to confide in.

Lila opened the book and saw three little faces smiling back at her. Two blonde-haired girls and a boy. She ran her finger over their smiles and blinked back tears. "They're beautiful."

Charlotte leaned forward. "This is Drew, he's the oldest. And the girls, Julia and Maddie."

Lila met Charlotte's eyes and found hopefulness waiting for her there. "Which one is . . . ?" Lila glanced back at the photo.

"Maddie. My youngest."

Maddie's braided hair boasted a perfectly tied ribbon at the end, and her big brown eyes were so full of life. From the image, Lila never would've guessed the girl was sick.

Charlotte had the life she'd always wanted without any of the bells and whistles. Just the normal, everyday things like soccer practice and dance lessons. Did she know how lucky she was?

"Lila, I know it's a lot to ask, but I wondered—"

The front door opened and sent a gusty chill through the living room, cutting Charlotte off midsentence. The fire flickered as the wind swept through.

Lila watched until the door closed and found Daddy standing, looking lost and broken, in the lobby. He turned and looked back and forth between them. His face fell.

"Oh no," Charlotte said, her voice barely audible.

Daddy took his hat off and clutched it at his chest, as if it could somehow give him supernatural strength to face them.

Lila straightened as he walked toward them and wondered if Charlotte would leave or if Daddy would grovel in front of his *other* daughter.

"Hello," Daddy said. "I didn't expect . . ."

Lila felt Charlotte's eyes on her, but she kept her gaze on Daddy. No matter how pathetic he seemed in that moment, she wouldn't feel sorry for him. He'd done this to himself.

Her mind wandered back to the last time she'd seen him—how they'd left things unfinished at the concert. It had been humiliating to admit her true feelings to Daddy. And he hadn't even responded. He'd simply jaunted on the stage like nothing had happened—like her feelings didn't matter.

Just like he always had.

What could he possibly say to her now that would change anything between them? Her eyes had been opened.

"I'm sorry, I can go." Charlotte stood.

Daddy put a hand on her shoulder. "Actually, Charlotte, I came to talk to you."

Lila's jaw went slack and she stared at her father, his eyes intent on the other woman. Always the other woman.

## THIRTY-FIVE

*Campbell*

Campbell stared at her reflection in the mirror. After running her lipstick over her lips, she'd finally completed her look—if only her nerves would calm down.

Her thoughts fluttered back to the ring, and she glanced down at the empty spot on her left hand.

She'd imagined Luke's proposal a hundred times since he asked her to dinner, and while she was trying to remain calm, she wasn't having much luck.

The knock on the door startled her. She checked her teeth, then ran her hands through her hair. "It's time," she said to herself.

When she opened the door, Luke's eyes widened. "Wow. You look amazing."

Campbell smoothed the black dress she saved for special occasions. "Thanks. You do too."

Luke rarely dressed up, but a fitted suit coat and nice jeans worked for him. He took a step closer, eyes fully on her, without a hint of awkwardness. "You're beautiful."

Campbell tried to respond, but her breath had caught in her throat.

He smiled, then took his time kissing her. She'd never been treated like something so precious. When he pulled away, he frowned. "Are you okay?"

Tears had filled her eyes, and even she didn't realize it until that moment. She nodded. "I'm sorry. Moments I want to remember forever remind me of my mom." She pulled the door closed and locked it, trying to push away thoughts of how frightened she was to allow herself to love him. Would that fear ever go away?

Luke opened the door to The Grotto for her, and Campbell walked past him, thankful for the warmth of the indoors. December had brought with it a bitter cold, and she seemed to shiver through most days. The lobby of the restaurant was decorated for Christmas with swaths of evergreen and twinkling white lights. If the fireplace hadn't warmed her, the holiday certainly would have.

Except for the part about missing her mom. She hadn't expected to feel it so deeply, but as she considered starting a real, grown-up life with Luke, she found herself wishing for Mom's advice every day.

The hostess ushered them to a table right in the center of the restaurant, but before they sat, Luke turned to her.

"I'm sorry, Shellie, do you mind moving us somewhere a little more private?"

Shellie smiled. "Only because you have the best lattes in town."

"Next one's on me," Luke said.

Their table in the corner boasted an exquisite view of the lighthouse and all the privacy they could want. Especially for a special night.

Campbell hadn't been the kind of girl to imagine her wedding day. She didn't watch the royal wedding or spend any money on bridal magazines. But lately, she had been staring at her bare left hand more often than she cared to admit and had tried out her name with Luke's last name.

Campbell Barber.

She could get used to it.

After they ordered their dinner, Campbell met Luke's eyes. Nervous energy bubbled inside and she found herself searching for chatter to fill the silence.

"Are you excited for the Christmas special?" she asked, instantly wishing she hadn't brought it up.

"Not if you're not there with me."

She sipped her water. "Well, we both know I'm not a singer, so you'll have to tough it out."

"Campbell, I—"

"It can't be all bad having a beautiful girl pretend she's in love with you."

His expression changed. "It is bad if it's not you."

She laughed nervously and the waiter brought their dinner.

"It looks wonderful," Campbell said, eyes focused on her plate.

"I hope you like it." Luke smiled and they started eating.

"Meghan's cottage looks beautiful. How much of that did you do?"

Campbell listened as Luke explained the various changes he and Nick had made in the old house. She loved hearing him talk about architecture.

"Someday I want to design and build my own house."

Campbell swallowed a bite of chicken. "You do?"

He nodded. "I've already got the perfect place for it."

"In Sweethaven?"

"Just outside of town." Luke set his napkin on top of his empty plate. "I bought the land a few years ago. Almost have it paid off, then I'm going to build." He reached into his pocket and Campbell held her breath. He produced a small napkin, but not before he caught her reaction. "You okay?"

"Yes, of course," she said, begging herself to get it together.

Luke handed her the napkin, plain white with the outline of a house drawn on it in black ink.

"If you flip it over, you can see the floor plan."

She did, marveling at how he'd created this home from nothing but his own imagination. "It's beautiful."

"Thanks. I already talked to Nick about what it would take to get it built. I think we might start on it this summer."

She set the napkin down and stared at him. "This is really amazing, Luke. You're really good at this."

He grinned. "Don't tell anyone. I kind of like being 'just the coffee guy.'"

"You sell yourself short."

He smiled before his expression turned serious. "Cam, I wanted to tell you something."

Her heart pounded. "Okay."

"At the end of every year, I always look back on the last twelve months and try to figure out how I can make the next twelve better."

"Sounds like a smart thing to do." Campbell heard the words, but they hardly registered.

"But this year . . ." He looked away. "It's been, well, amazing. I'm freelancing with my old firm and running the café. It's the best of both worlds." He met her eyes. "And you and me."

She held his gaze, her breath shallow.

"I meant it when I told you I loved you." He took a breath. "And if that makes you uncomfortable, I'm sorry, but it's how I feel."

"No, it doesn't make me uncomfortable . . ."

He smiled. "Yes, it does."

She smiled but looked away. "Maybe a little, but not because I don't feel the same way."

His eyes widened. "You do?"

She hadn't prepared herself for this. Not really. All the imagining in the world couldn't have prepared her for this.

The waiter reappeared beside their table. Great timing. Luke leaned back, letting go of her hands.

"Can I interest you in coffee or dessert?"

Luke shook his head. Campbell smiled at the man and asked for a cup of coffee. He nodded and hurried off.

"What is it, Cam? Why are you scared?"

"I'm not scared," she said.

The waiter returned with her coffee, turned her cup over and poured a cup.

"Thank you."

With a slight bow, the waiter left.

"Then what is it?"

Campbell stirred cream into her coffee. When she set down the spoon, he reached across the table and took her hand, watching her.

"Luke, it's just . . ." She met his eyes, waiting for her response.

"It's just what?"

Campbell looked away. "Maybe I am scared."

Images of her mom's face flashed through her head. The last person she really loved had left her, and that pain—she couldn't go through that again.

"Scared of what?"

Campbell tried to swallow the lump in her throat. When she failed, Luke scooted into the chair next to her and took her hands.

"I'm not going anywhere," he said.

Campbell looked at him, tears clouding her eyes. "My mom didn't think she was going anywhere either." She looked down. "People leave, Luke. Whether they want to or not."

She quickly swiped away the tears that escaped down her cheeks.

"If I have anything to say about it, I'm not going anywhere," Luke said, holding her face in his hands. "Just let me love you."

Campbell nodded. "I'll try."

And more than anything, she wanted to.

THIRTY-SIX

*Lila*

Lila stood at the door of her parents' lake house. She knocked again. The pain of Daddy's words at the Whitmore rushed back fresh, and she wished she could force it all aside and pretend it didn't hurt her. But it did. His only objective seemed to be making things right with Charlotte, but his actions begged the question "What about me?" like they had so many times before.

The door opened and Mama stood, perfectly poised, in the entryway. Her eyebrow sprang upward. "Lila?"

"May I come in—just for a minute?"

Mama stared at her for a few long seconds and then stepped aside.

"Would you like to sit down?"

"No, Mama, I'm meeting Tom in a few minutes, but I wanted to come here and set the record straight."

Mama frowned. "I don't understand."

"Charlotte told me you knew about her a long time ago."

Mama's lips tightened. "That woman is delusional. And now she's got your father thinking he's got to give her his whole life savings or something. That's your inheritance, by the way. You'd do well to stay away from her yourself."

"Stop it, Mama. Don't you see what you've done?"

"Lila, I'm the one whose husband has another child." Mama paused. "But that's the same role you've been playing, isn't it? Tell me, how do you pretend so well?" Her eyes narrowed, but this time Lila saw what she was doing. Judging her so she didn't have to turn the attention on herself.

"You were pregnant when you married Daddy."

Mama's eyes widened. "I was not."

"I found your marriage certificate. You were six months pregnant." Lila forced herself not to cry. "Is that why you hate me so much, Mama?"

Mama looked away.

"You blame me for your sham of a life. You have all the money and designer dresses and fancy parties, but you're married to a man who doesn't love you. And you think it's my fault."

"You don't know what you're talking about." Mama turned away.

Lila drew in a deep breath. "Tell me it's not true. If you'd never gotten pregnant, you wouldn't have gotten married. You think it's my fault. Why else would you be so cold to me all these years?"

She spun around and faced Lila. "Because you never turned into who you were supposed to be, Lila. You were my daughter. You were supposed to be"—she looked her over—"more."

Lila closed her eyes to keep tears from falling. "I know I'm a disappointment to you, Mama, but you don't have to worry about that anymore. I don't want you to be a part of my life. It's too painful."

Mama's expression changed. "You don't mean that. You're carrying my grandchild."

"I've spent my entire life trying to become who you want me to be, and if that's not good enough for you, there's nothing more I can do." Lila thought back to all the times her mother had made her feel like a failure. If she won second place at a pageant, Mama wanted to know why it wasn't first. She'd been high school salu-tatorian and Mama wanted a valedictorian. Even as an adult, Lila had wasted so much time being the person she thought Mama wanted her to be.

Mama met her eyes, and for a moment, Lila thought she looked sad. But Mama's usual glare quickly returned.

"You have no idea what it's been like for me—being married to a liar, raising his daughter."

The words struck like a slap across the face. "I'm your daughter too."

Mama looked away.

"All these years, if you've been so miserable, why didn't you just leave?"

"I made a promise to be married to your father." Mama met her eyes. "But at least I have no delusions about who he really is."

"You did, though, didn't you?" Lila watched her mother for a long moment. Suddenly it started to make sense.

"Never."

"You fell in love with him." Lila took a step closer. "You thought you could change him, but when you realized you couldn't, it turned you mean and bitter."

Mama crossed her arms. "Of course I thought I loved him. I was young and foolish and he was rich and charming." She looked away. "And married."

For the first time she could remember, Lila felt sorry for Mama. She'd been a prisoner in her failed marriage, whether anyone was talking about it or not. Mama had tried to give herself to Daddy and Daddy hadn't wanted her.

"Don't look at me like that, Lila." Mama leveled her gaze.

Lila blinked away the tears. "I'm sorry, Mama."

"Just go." Mama walked to the door and opened it, staring off in the distance.

Lila pulled a photo from her coat pocket and handed it to her mother.

"Who's this?"

"That's Maddie," Lila said. "Charlotte's daughter. You're so caught up in your own life that you don't even have the heart to let Daddy get tested to see if he can help save this girl's life."

Mama tried to hand the photo back to Lila.

"No, Mama. You keep that. You look at it and remember that this is your chance to do something good."

Without another word, Lila walked outside. The door slammed shut behind her.

## THIRTY-SEVEN

*Jane*

Jane sat at the kitchen table with the little prayer journal open in front of her. Somehow, it had become a lifeline for her again.

For this page, she'd decided to journal her feelings on a sheet of paper and tuck it inside an envelope she'd affixed to the page.

She stared at the blank page in front of her.

*Lord,*

*While I still have some of my old insecurities, something inside me has changed. I don't even know if I've lost a single pound, but I've never tried so hard for so long. Every time I finish a workout or turn down dessert, I feel so strong—like somehow the chains that have kept me bound up are starting to loosen.*

*I feel like, for the first time, I might actually be successful. I think I can do anything.*

Jane smiled as she reread the words. What a difference it made to take care of herself.

After she folded the paper and slid it inside the envelope, Jane walked outside. She had a date with an elliptical.

But before she got in the car, she looked up and saw the long stretch of road in front of her. What if she didn't go to the gym today?

What if she exercised outside? A walk wouldn't be too bad, even though the sun hid behind the clouds and the temperature chilled her to the bone.

Jane stood on the road, bundled in a fleece sweatshirt, scarf, gloves and stocking cap. To any passersby, she most likely looked ridiculous, and it would be even more ridiculous for her to try to run.

But in her mind, she pictured herself jogging down to the corner. *But it's so cold.*

Excuses. She had plenty of them. Running was something she'd always told herself she could never do.

Was God challenging her perception of her strength?

She started trudging down the hill of their neighborhood and out onto Peony Place. She'd walk out toward the edge of town to avoid the watchful eyes of anyone who might be out and about. What she didn't need were comments on the fact that the fat lady who broke the chair in the church was huffing and puffing up the hill.

She could practically hear what they'd say. *It's about time she did something about her weight.* Or *I hope she doesn't keel over and die right here on Main Street.* Or, worse, *Oh, I can't watch her bouncing up the hill like that. I'm so embarrassed for her.*

She shoved the imaginary insults out of her mind and listened to the sound of her feet hitting the pavement.

Before long, the chill went away and Jane started to sweat. She inhaled the crisp winter air and it coated her lungs with a coolness that made her cough. Behind her, the blocks she'd already traveled seemed like nothing. She was so out of shape she wouldn't even make it a mile. As she walked, she thought about all she'd been through in the last six years. Every tragedy—big or small—had driven her to the kitchen. She ran straight for the comfort of the food. She ate at night when everyone was sleeping, hiding the chocolate and the cookies to uncover later when she was alone.

*Run.*

The word came at her like a fly buzzing around her head. She slowed her pace to catch her breath. She knew God's voice. She'd learned to listen to it, but He never talked to her about food or exercise. Or had He? Had she simply chosen not to listen?

"I can't run."

*Run.*

She laughed. It had to be God because she'd never tell herself to do something so ludicrous. But why would He want her to run? Why did it matter? She looked up ahead. About three blocks of highway away was a Speed Limit sign. She could run to that, couldn't she?

"This is insane."

She could barely walk a distance, and here she was, thinking about running.

Jane stopped and stared in front of her. "Run. Okay, God. Here goes nothing."

She started with a brisk walk and then, without thinking, she picked up the pace until finally she jogged toward the Speed Limit sign. Her feet pounded on the pavement and she could feel her body protesting. The fat parts of her legs and stomach were displaced and then put back together in such a way that she imagined tomorrow she'd be bruised. The pain of it struck her with extreme force, but she kept going.

"I hate this," she said out loud.

*Run.*

She wouldn't quit. She couldn't. But she'd never become a marathon runner or someone who enjoyed exercise so what was the point? As she neared her intended finish line, Jane started to slow down.

*You're not done yet.*

"No, I am. I'm done."

*Don't quit.*

Jane couldn't be certain it was God speaking to her anymore. At this point, she imagined it could be her own delusions from the lack of oxygen to her brain. But she listened and she forced herself to keep going. One more foot in front of the other. As she ran, she thought about how hard it would be to make the decision every single day to eat healthy foods. To move her body. She didn't drink or smoke or do the things other people did. So she liked food. Was that so bad?

But look what she'd done to herself. Her breaths grew shorter and shorter as she struggled, but she kept putting one foot in front of the other.

"What . . . am I . . . running for?" She struggled to speak, though she wanted to yell at God with everything she had left. Why did she have to run?

Jane forced her feet to move. They felt like cement blocks by now and her breath stung her throat, cold and weak. Her body ached and she didn't want to go one more step.

But she kept moving forward, sacrificing comfort, giving this struggle as an offering.

The run was a physical expression of what she felt inside. She'd never pushed herself like this before. And all these years, she'd been running to the refrigerator when she should've been running to God.

Like pictures on a movie screen, Jane saw those moments of crisis playing in front of her as she pressed forward. The months following Alex's death, she spent on the couch with ice cream. The months after Sam's birth, she spent hidden away with cookies from the bakery down the street. As recently as a few weeks ago, when she broke the chair on the stage in front of Lori and the rest of the congregation, she'd comforted herself with a bag of potato chips and French onion dip.

And she'd eaten the entire thing.

Hot tears stung her cold cheeks and clouded her eyes as she pushed herself to take just a few more steps. And then a few more. And a few more.

She'd done this to herself because every time something bad happened, or something good—she ran to the food.

*Run to Me.*

The words echoed in her mind.

She'd chosen the food over God every time. Every single time she needed comfort. And look what it had done to her.

Food was not a faithful friend.

The tears came quicker now and Jane's light cry turned into a deep sob, straight from the gut. She finally slowed her pace and bent over, struggling for air. And in that moment, she knew what she had to do—and she finally had the courage to go for it.

She'd proven to herself that her body wasn't the problem—the battle was in her mind.

If she failed tomorrow, she'd try again the next day.

She'd been running toward the wrong things, and that had to stop.

Finally, she understood. Her life depended on it.

THIRTY-EIGHT

*Meghan*

Meghan knew better than to believe in fate. When she awoke the morning of the Christmas special and saw what it looked like outside, she could only smile.

"I think maybe God wanted them to use our family too," Nick said, standing at the bedroom window. "No way anyone can fly in from LA today."

The Hollywood family was supposed to arrive in an hour, but judging by the blizzard outside, no one was getting in or out of Sweethaven—maybe for several days.

Nick's phone buzzed on the side table. "It's Martin."

"Put him on speaker."

Nick answered.

"It's a mess out there. I don't even know if I can get out of the driveway," Martin said. "I just heard from Liz and she and the others didn't make it out of California. I'm not sure what to do about the show tonight, but I'm making some calls."

"Martin, if you can handle the crew, we can handle the cast," Nick said.

"You sure?"

"Absolutely. I'll go pick up everyone myself if I have to. By tonight, we'll have a full house ready to film."

"All right. And I'll stand in Liz's place."

Meghan bit her tongue but thanked God silently.

When Nick hung up, he turned to her and smiled. "See, all that worrying for nothing."

Meghan grinned, picked up the phone.

"Hello?"

"Mama, have you looked outside?"

"'Course I have, darlin'. It's a good thing I stocked up at the store yesterday. I'm gonna stay home and bake all day long."

"Actually, I have a better idea. Why don't you let Nick pick you up? I need some really good singers—and someone to play my mom—in my Christmas special."

"Is that right?"

"I know you're still a little sore about the faux family, but this is just how I wanted it all along. Please?"

The line went silent.

"Mama?"

"I'm here."

"So, what do you say?"

"Which one of my Christmas sweaters do you want me to wear?"

\* \* \* \* \*

*Campbell*

Campbell stood in front of the mirror in Meghan's foyer, fresh makeup on her face. Meghan had invited them all back over for a second chance at filming the Christmas special. Only this time, the cameras would actually be rolling.

"I think the blizzard is God's way of smiling down on us today," Meghan said. "Oh, and I told them you could all sing. Can you sing?"

Campbell shook her head. "But I can lip-synch."

Megan's jaw went slack, and then she smiled. "It'll do."

A few of the crew members had stayed in Sweethaven, but Liz and most of the actors were planning to fly in that morning. Now they had what seemed to be a more intimate feel, and Campbell had to think the show would be better for it.

Jane and Lila sat in chairs having their makeup done, a flurry of activity filling the house. Campbell spotted Luke in deep conversation with Nick in the corner of the living room.

Would Luke go to Nick for advice? He took something out of his pocket and shielded it from the rest of the room. Nick smiled, patted Luke on the back and then walked away. Luke put whatever it was back in his pocket.

Before he could catch her, Campbell disappeared into the makeup room.

"What's wrong with you? You're white as a sheet," Lila said.

Jane met her eyes. "How was dinner the other night?"

Campbell shook her head.

"Hon, I'm so sorry."

"Let's talk about something else." Campbell tried to catch her breath. What if this new filming was all a sham—a way to catch her by surprise? Men always seemed to think proposals had to be big, grand gestures. How could she begrudge him that?

"Sorry for what? What's going on?" Lila swatted at the hand trying to apply powder to her T-zone.

"Nothing. Drop it."

Lila looked surprised.

"I'm sorry. I just don't want to talk about it right now," Campbell said.

"Talk about what?" Luke appeared in the doorway and Campbell forced a smile.

"Nothing."

"Okay." Luke surveyed the three of them, then turned his attention back to Campbell. "Hey, can I talk to you for a second?"

Campbell nodded. He turned toward the porch, and she glanced back at Jane, whose smile and eyes both widened. She took a deep breath and followed him into the kitchen. Snow had begun piling up on the deck, and Campbell wondered if any of them would make it out of the driveway.

"It's crazy in there," Luke said.

She nodded.

"You okay? You seem nervous."

"I'm not a big fan of cameras."

"You're a photographer." He laughed.

"Cameras pointed on me." She smiled.

"Well, you're going to be great in there. I'm the one who has to sing." When he met her eyes, his smile faded. "You sure you're okay?"

She nodded. "Fine."

A woman with a headset and clipboard appeared in the doorway. "Luke, we need you in here."

"Be right there." He brushed Campbell's hair away from her face. "I'll see you inside, okay?"

"Sounds good."

She watched as he walked into the living room, where he met the new producer.

"I love you, Luke," Campbell whispered.

Once they were all gathered in the living room, Campbell did her best to follow the lead of the people who actually knew what they were doing. As long as she didn't say anything, she should be fine.

But the nagging idea that Luke might end up on one knee in front of her wouldn't go away.

As they went to their first commercial break, the director clapped his hands. "Just need everyone to look a little more relaxed." He met Campbell's eyes. "Okay?"

Her eyes widened and she nodded. Relaxed. She could do that. She scanned the room until she found Jane's eyes on her. Jane frowned and mouthed the words "Are you okay?"

Campbell nodded. She'd worked herself up into a panic over what she was sure would be nothing. Just like the concert. And dinner. Luke would've proposed by now if he was going to.

"We're back in ten-nine-eight." The director began holding up fingers. When he reached three, Meghan smiled, telling a story about one of her earliest Christmas memories. Luke wound his hand around Campbell's shoulder and leaned closer.

"This is about to get really good."

Campbell shot him a look. When she looked back, Meghan had paused, the end of a segment, but before the music began, Nick leaned forward and looked into the camera.

"I can still remember the first time I heard Meghan sing," he said.

Meghan looked at the director, who seemed unfazed by Nick's going off-book.

"We were in high school and she used to walk home with her guitar slung over her shoulder. She looked like an angel."

Their little crowd began to murmur.

"Anyway, we've had our ups and our downs and just a few months ago, we decided to get married again. Like a dummy, I gave my beautiful wife the same old ring I bought her when we were just kids."

Nick reached inside his jacket pocket and pulled out a little black box. "I thought it was about time you had a real wedding ring."

Campbell's heart dropped as Meghan opened the box, revealing the same ring she'd found in Luke's apartment. The same ring that had caused her to panic like a frightened schoolgirl every time she was with him.

Campbell watched as Meghan slipped the ring on her finger and threw her arms around Nick. "I love it. Thank you."

The music started and the director pointed at Luke. A second camera focused on the two of them, and Luke began singing "Grown-Up Christmas List." Campbell's mind spun and humiliation settled on her shoulders.

How could she have been so stupid?

The director started motioning for her to smile, but Campbell couldn't muster the strength.

The ring had never been for her. There was no ring. No proposal.

And that left Campbell with an ache in her stomach the size of the Grand Canyon.

# THIRTY-NINE

*Adele*

The filming at Meghan's house went well, and Adele left feeling like she'd shown those producers not to stick her behind the scenes. She'd even led them all in her rendition of "Away in a Manger." But on her way to meet Henry, all she could think of was Campbell.

She saw the girl's face when Nick gave Meghan that beautiful ring. She saw the disappointment behind her eyes and, frankly, Campbell wasn't a very good actress. She hadn't hidden her pain very well, much to the director's dismay. For a moment, she felt Campbell's pain as if it were her own.

And that pain had brought with it a startling clarity.

Adele pulled in the driveway and found Henry's car parked out front. From the looks of it, he'd let himself in.

She hurried in the back door and was met with the smell of food cooking in her kitchen.

Henry stood at the stove with his back to her, but as she closed the back door, he turned around.

She laughed at the sight of him in her frilly pink apron. "I'm not sure that's your best look."

He grinned. "I couldn't risk getting spaghetti sauce on my shirt. I have to be presentable for my lady." He took a step toward her and kissed her on the cheek. "You look beautiful."

She waved him off. "They put all kinds of extra makeup on me for this Christmas special."

"Well, it suits you." Henry pulled a chair out away from the table. "Have a seat. Tonight, I am going to cook one of my specialties for you for a change."

"It smells heavenly. Can I steal your recipe for my cookbook?"

Henry laughed. "Not a chance. This is my grandmother's recipe. Spaghetti and meatballs and they'll make you cry they're so good."

She watched him as he maneuvered his way around her kitchen, well acquainted with everything and careful not to make too big a mess. She liked the thought of spending her days and nights with Henry. Maybe it was crazy and maybe it was too soon, but now that she'd found him, she couldn't let him go again.

The image of Luke and Campbell at the filming rushed back to her.

"You look like there's something on your mind," Henry said, glancing at her over his shoulder. "You wanna talk about it?"

Adele looked away. "It's nothing."

He set the wooden spoon down and turned to face her. "You forget how well I know you."

How could she forget? How could she forget that day when she finally saw him again—wounded, but safe and back on American soil? She hadn't waited for him and, yet, here he stood now, making spaghetti and meatballs in her kitchen, waiting for her to decide if she wanted to be with him.

"You've been thinking about my proposal," Henry said, sitting across from her.

"I have."

"And?"

She met his eyes. "Today I realized my son is going to propose to his girlfriend. Not yet, but soon. She's the sweetest girl, and I love her like my own daughter."

Henry smiled. "I'm sure she feels the same about you."

"They'll get married and have children and their children will run the streets with my other grandchildren, and that's all going to happen right here, in Sweethaven."

He nodded. "I understand."

Adele took a deep breath. "Henry, when you were in the war—"

"Let's not go back to that, Adele. It was a long time ago."

Adele put a hand over his. "Let me say this."

He inhaled and then nodded as if to tell her she had the floor.

Before even beginning, her mind wandered back to the day she said good-bye to him, standing in the airport watching him board the plane. She wouldn't see him again for two years, and by then, she'd worried herself sick too many times to count.

Henry had returned from the war the day before. He'd sent word that he'd be arriving at the Sweethaven bus depot, but Adele hadn't responded. Or gone to meet him. Or looked him up later that night. Instead, she had hidden herself away, pretending not to know he was back—pretending she didn't care, that it didn't tear her heart in two.

He found her home alone, and when she heard the knock at the door, she knew it was him, coming for her like he said he would. Unlike her, Henry kept his word.

She answered the door, and as soon as she met his eyes, she couldn't see through the tears. He pulled her into a hug, where she cried, the stress of the past two years spilling out of her.

"Hey, it's okay," he said. "I'm home."

She pulled back and looked at him. He looked older, like a man. Like a man who'd seen images he'd never forget—fought a battle that would stay with him forever.

"I didn't think you were ever coming home."

"I told you I would." He smiled. "It's so good to see you." Henry grabbed her hand, but before she could respond, a car pulled in front of the house and distracted them both.

"Oh no," Adele said.

Henry turned just in time to see Greg Faley exit the car and head up the walk. He reached the two of them and then stood on the bottom step, staring.

Adele pulled her hand away. "Greg, I didn't think you were coming over so early today."

"Obviously." Greg took out a cigarette and lit it up, then blew the smoke in Henry's direction. "Who's the soldier?"

Adele glanced at Henry, who had obviously started to realize the truth—that the girl he'd waited for had moved on. He'd been off fighting in a war and she'd stayed behind, breaking his heart.

"Greg, can you give us a minute?"

"Yeah, but hurry up. We've got a date." He walked inside, leaving Adele and her guilt standing in front of Henry.

He shook his head. "I can't believe . . ."

"Henry, I'm sorry. It's . . . I can explain."

But he didn't give her a chance. He didn't want to stick around for her excuses. She said she would wait and she didn't.

Now, sitting across from him, a second chance in her lap, Adele could hardly speak the words.

"When you were gone, I thought about you every night. I slept with your photo under my pillow."

Henry smiled. "Yours was taped to my bedpost."

"But I guess I don't handle stress very well because I stopped eating. I didn't go out with my friends anymore. All I did was sit at home and worry about you. I prayed for you all the time. And every time we got word that another soldier had died, we mourned and grieved, but I felt relieved that it wasn't you."

He frowned. "You didn't tell me that."

"I didn't tell anyone. It all made me feel terrible about myself." Adele looked away. "One day, I met that guy—Greg—down on the Boardwalk. He was rebellious and didn't care about anything, and for some reason, I thought that was what I needed."

"You really don't have to explain." Henry looked away.

"No, Henry, I've lived with the guilt of what I did to you for all these years. I do have to explain." She pressed her lips together. "I guess Greg got the better of me because he convinced me I didn't have to follow anyone's rules. And I didn't. I was rebellious and stupid and I did things—many things I regret."

Henry's face fell. "You were pregnant."

Adele looked away. "I was so ashamed. I was too young, but we got married and Greg moved us to Nashville. It didn't take long before I realized he was not cut out for any of it. Poor Meghan—she never really did get over not having a relationship with her father."

"I'm sorry, Adele."

"No, Henry. *I'm* sorry. I can't help but think if I'd just waited—if I'd been braver and trusted God to take care of you, well, none of that painful stuff would've happened." Adele wiped away a tear.

She'd wrestled through this with God on more than one occasion. Sometimes she still struggled to trust Him.

"But you also wouldn't have had Meghan. And you wouldn't have been so understanding when one of her friends turned up pregnant. And you wouldn't have appreciated those wonderful years with Teddy."

Adele let the words fill her up. How did he know her so well already?

"But all that wasted time . . ."

He took her hands. "We've found each other now, haven't we? We have the rest of our lives to spend together."

Adele stilled. She met Henry's eyes and watched that same look of recognition wash over his face.

"You're not going to marry me, are you?" he said.

"I think I'm just crazy enough to go ahead and marry you, Henry." She paused. "But I can't leave Sweethaven."

He took a deep breath. "I understand."

"And you can't leave Grand Falls?"

He shook his head. "Not sure I can."

Her eyes fell to their hands, inches apart on the table. "Then, I suppose we're at a crossroads."

"Seems like we are." He held her eyes for too long a moment, and sadness washed over her. Then Henry stood and went back to stirring his sauce. "But at least we can have a good meal tonight."

Adele's heart sank. She would enjoy every second of their night together, but when she said good-bye to him, she knew she would never be the same.

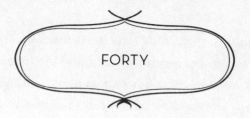

FORTY

*Jane*

Jane awoke to the sound of an empty house. Graham, always an early riser, planned to take Sam out for breakfast, and the girls were probably still sound asleep. While she needed the time alone to get herself healthy, she loved falling asleep next to her husband. She missed them all so much when they were apart.

She walked into the bathroom and stared at the scale. She hadn't dared to get back on it since visiting the doctor's office, but she felt like she'd lost at least a little bit of weight. With the exception of the cheesecake incident, she'd stayed on her diet, exercised every day—she had to be lighter.

A nagging question loomed in the back of her mind.

What if she wasn't? What if she shed her clothes, stood on that scale and discovered none of this suffering paid off? What if she hadn't lost a pound? Worse, what if she'd gained?

Jane turned away from the scale and hurried through her morning routine. Contacts in, teeth brushed, workout clothes on. But when she turned around, there it was again, enticing her with the promise of a smaller number than she had in her head.

"There's only one way to find out," she said, shutting the door to hide her act of rebellion. Her heart raced as she tried to keep from imagining how much she might have lost since she started this journey. If she didn't envision a number, she wouldn't be disappointed.

Stripped down to nothing, Jane turned away from the mirror and stood with her toes touching the edge of the scale.

"God, I know You've got much more important things to attend to, but if there's any way You can take this number down a little bit, I'd be really grateful."

Jane took a deep breath and closed her eyes. She stepped up on the scale, careful to put her bare feet directly in the center of her cold metal enemy.

Before looking at the numbers, she stared at the ceiling, inhaled and then let out her breath slowly. Once she'd worked up enough courage, she glanced down and allowed the numbers to register. Numbers that tattled on her, that represented a measure of her self-control.

Jane stared at the three green numbers illuminated on the digital scale.

It couldn't be right. She couldn't have . . .

She hopped off, let the scale reset itself and then stepped back on—cautious so as to not disrupt anything inside the inner workings of the machine.

There it was again. The same number waited for her.

She'd lost eight pounds. Eight. Just like that.

Well, not just like that. She'd worked hard for every one of those pounds. Every one of Adele's desserts she'd passed up, every long walk she'd trudged through, every grilled chicken breast she'd eaten—had paid off.

She was really doing it.

And while she was terrified to find out what it would be like to try to continue with the distractions of real life looming, for now, she would choose to be thankful for the weeks without anything else to do but focus on getting healthy.

Jane stared at the number until the scale went black again. If she could lose eight pounds, she could lose twenty. And if she could lose twenty, she could lose fifty.

A feeling of elation whirled up within her and she stood in front of the mirror.

"Jane Atkins, you can do this," she said. A smile lit her face as she hurried back into her workout clothes, a newfound energy welling inside her.

She couldn't wait to tell Graham.

In the kitchen, Emily sat at the table, eating a cup of Jane's Greek yogurt.

"What are you doing up at seven thirty?" Jane asked, eyeing the yogurt. "And what are you doing with that? I thought you hated health food."

Emily looked down at the empty cup. "It's not so bad."

Jane smiled. "I put fresh fruit in mine. You can try that tomorrow if you want."

Emily turned the spoon around in the hollow yogurt cup. "Are you going to the gym?"

Jane nodded and grabbed her water bottle from inside the fridge. She'd learned to chill it overnight so it was just the way she liked it during her workout. So many of her habits had already begun to change in such a short time. Clearly part of the battle was making time to prepare everything. To always have healthy snacks ready. To set out the workout clothes and shoes the night before.

She'd been doing these little things and it had made all the difference.

Emily stood and threw away the yogurt cup. Black yoga pants and a long-sleeved T-shirt covered her skinny frame. "Can I go with you?"

Jane closed the door to the fridge and stared at her daughter. "You want to come walk with me?"

Emily smiled. "You look like you're losing weight."

Jane beamed. "Eight pounds as of this morning."

"Mom, that's awesome." Emily's grin warmed Jane's heart.

"But you hated everything about this, Em. Why the change of heart?"

Emily shrugged. She'd never had a weight problem, she was built like Graham. Jane had prayed with every pregnancy that if she had a girl she'd be built like Graham, and God had listened, giving her two beautiful, athletic girls who didn't have to think about what they ate. At least not yet. "It's changed you, I think," Emily said.

"What has?"

"Your taking care of yourself—you seem—" Emily shrugged. "Happier."

Jane let the words settle. She *was* happier. And her daughter had noticed. For the first time in a long time, she felt like perhaps she'd taught Emily something worthwhile. Something she could carry with her well into adulthood.

"It's easy to get caught up in what I have to do for everyone else," Jane said. "I am the mom."

"And the mom does everything," Emily said.

Jane laughed. "Well, not everything—but the mom does a lot. And you're right, Em. Making time for myself has changed more than just the numbers on the scale. It's changed me from the inside."

Emily took a step closer. "I'm sorry I was such a brat about all this. When Jenna told me about the doctor I . . ." Emily's eyes filled with tears. "I just don't want to lose you, Mom." She threw her arms around Jane and squeezed her.

"Em?"

Emily buried her face in Jane's shoulder like she hadn't since she was a little girl. "We already lost Alex. We can't lose you too."

Jane clung to her daughter and let her sob until finally her body stilled and she pulled away. It made sense now. Emily had always lashed out when she was afraid or confused. Why hadn't Jane seen it earlier? Her anger wasn't directed at Jane; she was just a little girl who didn't want to lose her mom.

"I'm taking care of it, Em."

Emily grabbed a tissue and wiped her face dry. "I'm really proud of you, Mom."

Tears sprang to Jane's eyes. "I'm proud of me too."

Emily straightened, as if to let Jane know she was done with her breakdown. "So are we going to exercise or what?"

"You can come with me, but you better be prepared to work. I'm not slowing my pace for you."

Emily laughed. "I'm ready for you, old lady."

Jane grabbed her water bottle, the car keys and a sweatshirt and thanked God that somehow Emily had come around—somehow Jane's journey had made a difference to her daughter, and that was reason to celebrate.

Only this time, she'd do it trying to break her record at the gym rather than diving headfirst into a pan of brownies.

FORTY-ONE

*Lila*

Lila hurried to the car, her breath visible in the crisp, winter air. She'd forgotten how much she hated the cold. Winters spent in Sweethaven were rare growing up, though she had experienced a few. Now she remembered why she lived in Georgia.

Her coat felt taut around her midsection, her belly a reminder that life as she knew it was about to change. After a few minutes' drive, she reached the church parking lot. Hers was the only car in the lot. Sweethaven was the only place on earth where the church doors were never locked. And for whatever reason, that morning, the church had called her name.

Lila walked inside, thankful for the warmth of the small chapel. She sat down in the last pew. She didn't consider herself a religious person—that had always been Jane's place—but now, with a baby growing inside her, and everything she thought she knew unraveling, Lila wanted some answers. Trouble was, she had no idea how to go about conversing with a God who, she was sure, had bigger things to worry about.

"Lila?"

Jane's voice startled her. She hadn't heard the door behind her.

"What are you doing here?" Lila asked. With puffy red cheeks and damp hair matted to her head, Jane looked like she'd just run a marathon.

"What are you doing out in public like that?" Lila laughed. "I'm sorry—I didn't mean—I'm sorry." Her and her big mouth.

"It's okay. I was at the gym with Emily. We were driving by and I saw your car, though I just realized this second maybe you came here to be alone."

Lila scooted over in the pew. "No, please, sit."

Jane sat down next to her but didn't say anything.

"I guess I'm just feeling a little lost is all," Lila said. "I'm scared I'm going to turn out just like my mom. That I'll have a child who feels like I'm never satisfied—that he or she can't ever be good enough."

"You're going to be a great mom, Lila. It's good you're seeing all of this now—before you have the baby—because it's going to change you."

A tear fell onto Lila's hand.

"I know you're upset about your parents, but I don't think you're seeing the truth by accident."

Lila frowned. "What do you mean?"

"You've grown up thinking they were better than you—that you weren't good enough. But look at them, Lila, they're just as messed up as the rest of us. They need Jesus just like we do."

Lila smiled. "You're going to go all pastor's wife on me, aren't you?"

Jane scrunched her nose. "Sometimes I forget. Too much?"

Lila shook her head. "No. I believe you when you talk about God. You're one of the only people who seems genuine about it."

"That's because I know it's the truth." Jane put a hand on her shoulder and smiled. "I have to go—Emily's in the car, and obviously I need a shower—but if you need anything, just call me, okay?"

"Thanks, Jane."

Her friend stood. "You know, Lila, you can talk to God about all this stuff. I mean, He'll listen."

Lila nodded and watched Jane leave. But in the quiet of the sanctuary, with its high ceilings and pictures of Jesus, she felt overwhelmed again at the idea of asking the air for help.

A deep breath in and Lila tried to find words—words that sounded worthy of a conversation with God—but she came up with nothing.

"I'm a mess," she said out loud. The quiet suddenly comforted rather than taunted, and Lila found the strength to continue. "I'm a mess, God, but I guess You already know that."

Lila tossed a look over her shoulder to make sure she really was alone.

"I don't know what else to do, but I'm mad at Mama and I'm mad at Daddy and I'm mad at Charlotte and if I really thought about it, I'd be mad at Tom all over again."

Her anger writhed inside her, balled up in a knot the way she'd been taught to carry it. Hidden away so no one could see. "Nobody wants to see the ugly side of you, Lila," Mama had told her. "That's the part you save for yourself unless you want to end up old and alone."

Lila sat for a long moment and then finally stood. How ridiculous. What did she think—a booming voice would speak back to her? Why had she even come here? How did she expect to find answers in an empty building?

She rushed to the car, embarrassed. A paper tucked underneath the windshield wiper of her car flapped in the cold wind.

Lila pulled it out, got in the car.

She opened the folded sheet and saw Jane's handwritten words scrawled on the page.

*Lila, I thought of this when I got in the car. It's helped me through so much. I thought it might do the same for you.*

*Love, Jane*

Lila glanced underneath Jane's note and saw a Bible verse written—no doubt from memory.

*"Therefore, as God's chosen people, holy and dearly loved, clothe yourselves with compassion, kindness, humility, gentleness and patience. Bear with each other and forgive one another if any of you has a grievance against someone. Forgive as the Lord forgave you."*
—*Colossians 3:12–13*

The words leaped off the page. *Forgive as the Lord forgave you.*

Lila shook her head. How could she forgive them? Any of them? Jane was a fool to think she ever could. Or maybe Lila was the fool. Maybe she'd fooled herself into believing she'd forgiven Tom, but maybe she hadn't. Mama had managed to open old wounds, and Lila had to admit—his betrayal still hurt.

And discovering the truth about Mama, about her father, about Charlotte . . .

No, Lila didn't want to forgive them. Any of them.

She read the verses again and as she did, her mind thought about the same part. It said the Lord forgave her, but what had she done? She'd never hurt anyone the way other people had hurt her.

As soon as the thought popped into her head, Lila remembered Patton Gallagher—the man who'd caught her eye when she thought she was getting divorced.

Not putting an end to his flirtation had surely caused Tom pain. And Suzanne—the friend she'd claimed to love. Rather than embracing her when she turned up pregnant at seventeen, Lila had turned her back on her. She'd never spoken to her again after that, and while she claimed to be hurt by Suzanne's leaving, the truth was, Lila had been in shock that one of her friends had gotten pregnant when she was still in high school. She'd been so judgmental, so critical. Not just of Suzanne—of everyone. She'd been mean and unkind.

Had God forgiven her those sins?

She'd never asked.

Her mouth went dry and Lila forced herself to swallow. "I'm sorry," she said to the empty car. "I'm so sorry."

And for the first time in her life, she meant it.

And she wanted to be forgiven.

And she wanted to forgive. The only question was—how?

FORTY-TWO

*Adele*

Adele rolled out the sugar cookie dough, and for the first time in as long as she could remember, she didn't find any joy in it. She missed Henry already. She hadn't seen him in a few days, and he'd made no attempt to reach her. Without thinking, Adele grabbed a kitchen towel and walked toward the blasted computer only to find out that, as she suspected, he hadn't written.

It didn't seem fair, really. Why should she find him after all these years only to lose him again?

But just because they couldn't get married, did that mean they couldn't still be friends? That was all they'd been doing, really—keeping each other company. Adele didn't see why that had to end simply because she refused to move to Grand Falls.

She returned to her cookie cutters, cutting out bells and stars and holly leaves one by one.

As she worked, she heard the front door open. She wasn't expecting company.

"Hello?" Adele wiped her hands on her apron and walked into the entryway, where she found Henry standing there, looking a little surprised himself.

"I'm sorry," he said. "I should've knocked."

Adele's breath caught in her throat. "What are you doing here?"

Henry closed the door, a chill whipping through the house. He stood for a moment, staring at her. "I went back to Grand Falls, to my house and my old friends, but . . ." He looked away.

"But . . ."

"I had to come back." He met her eyes.

The oven beeped. "I've got to get my cookies."

He nodded. "Of course."

She didn't want to leave, but the buzzer wouldn't quit until she turned it off. "My grandkids are coming over later to decorate them with me."

Henry followed her into the kitchen. She opened the oven, aware of how her heart raced. Why couldn't this man leave her in peace? How many times would she have to let him go?

"These aren't ready," Adele sighed, sticking the cookies back in and resetting the timer. "They just need another minute."

Henry stood across the room from her, holding his hat in front of him with both hands. His expression alternated between panic and sadness. It nearly broke Adele's heart.

"I've been thinking. It wasn't fair for me to ask you to move to Grand Falls and not to offer to move here."

She met his eyes.

"I could sell my house."

Adele shook her head. "What if you hate it here?"

He took a step closer.

"I won't hate it here. How could I? I'll be with you."

She held his gaze for a long moment.

"Adele, we're good together, you and me."

"I know, but we're old and set in our ways."

"Yes, and you're stubborn."

She eyed him. "As are you."

"But I'm handsome." He grinned. "If you don't have to leave Sweethaven, don't you want to be with me?"

She did—more than anything—but she'd given up being impulsive years ago.

"I love you, Adele."

Her heart warmed. Maybe she was that same girl from years ago.

"And I think you love me."

She nodded.

"So let's do this. Let's get married."

Adele took a deep breath, willing her wobbly stomach to settle down. "This is crazy."

He grinned and pulled her closer to him. "This is love."

## FORTY-THREE

*Jane*

Jane trudged out to her car in the grocery store parking lot, her body temperature still elevated from the gym, loving the way the cool air felt on her face. She put her groceries in the backseat, and as she glanced up, she noticed Graham's car parked at the café. She loaded the groceries into the back of the van and walked across the street, but as she approached, she spotted her husband through the window—and he wasn't alone.

Jane gasped when she realized Lori stood beside his table with a wide, flirty smile on her face. In spite of the cold, Lori's shirt dipped down to reveal ample cleavage, and her jeans were tighter than shrink-wrap.

"Jane, I thought that was you." Campbell's cheerful voice pulled Jane's attention, but her stomach turned. What was Graham doing talking to that woman?

Campbell frowned. "Are you okay? You look pale as a ghost."

Jane shook her head. "I'm sure it's nothing."

Campbell peeked into the café window, then moved back out of sight. "Who is she?"

"My worst nightmare. She used to make fun of me when I was a kid. She's the one who told me my butt was as big as the Empire State Building."

"That doesn't even make sense."

"I didn't say she was smart." She looked away. "But she *is* skinny. And pretty."

"Don't be too generous. There's a difference between the two."

"What do you mean?" Jane met her eyes.

"Just because someone's skinny doesn't mean she's pretty. Especially when she's ugly on the inside. If this woman is flirting with Graham, then she's ugly."

Jane sighed. "I appreciate the sentiment." She remembered the way Lori had looked at Graham back at the church service. She'd probably been waiting for her chance to pounce on him ever since. In Lori's mind, someone like Jane didn't deserve someone like Graham.

And maybe she was right.

"Come with me," Campbell said, linking her arm through Jane's.

"Where?"

"Are you going to just stand out here, hiding around the corner? This isn't high school, Jane. You're the wife."

Jane hadn't thought of it that way. She rushed around the back with Campbell and they went into the café by way of the kitchen. Everyone waved hello to them as they passed through as if it were perfectly normal for them to be there.

"Why'd we come in this way?" Jane asked as they reached the door to the restaurant.

"Don't you want to know what she's saying?"

Jane's heart kicked up. Maybe not. Worse, she didn't know if she wanted to hear what Graham was saying. Her husband was the epitome of loyal, but he was still a man. And if a woman practically offered herself to him, how would he refuse? How would any man?

They peeked through the windows at the top of the swinging doors that separated the main floor from the kitchen. "I don't know about this," Jane said.

Campbell stared out the window. "What nerve."

Jane glanced back just as Lori reached down and touched Graham's shoulder. She waited for a split second as he said something to her. Before Lori could respond, Jane pushed open the door and marched toward the table where she stood between them, forcing Lori to take a few steps away.

"Lori, I know what you're doing and it's not going to work."

The woman tossed her hair over her shoulder. "I don't know what you're talking about, Jane."

Jane narrowed her eyes and forced her voice to steady, reminding herself people could see her. "I'm talking about your thinking you can waltz in here in your tight jeans and your tiny shirt and flaunt yourself in front of my husband. I know what you are, Lori, a miserable woman who makes herself feel better by taking things from other people."

Lori gasped.

Jane stayed calm. "And you do it in such a way that you can deny it later. It's time to grow up and get a life of your own."

Lori set her jaw and squared her shoulders. "You don't know what you're talking about."

"Just stay away from my husband. In our world, marriage means something."

It was harsh, and she'd have to repent for it, but it was a confrontation that was years in the making, and it had come out of a strong need to protect her marriage—she couldn't apologize for being passionate about that. She'd almost lost Graham after Alex died. She swore she'd never put her marriage in jeopardy again.

Lori turned and stormed off, apparently dumbfounded, and Jane sat down across from her husband, suddenly embarrassed. "I'm sorry," she said.

Graham raised an eyebrow. "Bet that felt good."

She leaned forward. "Better than it should've. I *am* a pastor's wife."

"So that means you can't speak your mind?"

Another reason she loved him. He never put labels or stereotypes on her. "It wasn't the most Christian thing to say."

"Especially since she was talking to me about the coffee here." He took a drink.

"Today it's the coffee, tomorrow it'll be how beautiful your eyes are and what strong hands you have."

He smiled. "My eyes are beautiful?"

Jane laughed. "Everyone loves your eyes, Graham."

"Yeah, well, my eyes love you, so you have nothing to worry about."

Jane studied him.

"What is it?"

Jane could feel her cheeks heat. "I'm not as thin or as beautiful as Lori. I can't help but think that if someone like that wants to be with you, then why on earth do you stay with me?" She stared at her folded hands.

When she looked up, she saw Graham staring at her with a knowing look and the hint of a smile on his lips. "Don't look at me like that."

"Jane. If you think I would ever be interested in someone like Lori, you don't know me as well as I thought you did."

"But she's so skinny. Her hair is all long and flowing."

Graham laughed. "I didn't even notice."

She eyed him.

"I saw someone who was insecure and looking for validation from a married man. Before you burst in here, I was about to tell her that I was just leaving because I had to find my beautiful wife who I hadn't seen yet this morning." He took her hands. "Because I missed her and I'm still crazy in love with her after all these years."

Jane swallowed the lump in her throat. "You were not."

"I might've made it sound more manly than that, but yeah, I was." He squeezed her hand. "You know I've learned all the ways to handle women like her."

"Women who flirt."

"Yes. And who are lonely and want the stability that you have. She's jealous of you, hon."

Jane scoffed. "Well, that's a first." She'd spent her whole life wishing she had the things Lori had.

"Jane, I promise you, I'll never do anything to hurt you. I don't care who else comes along. You're the one I want."

Jane met her husband's eyes and saw no judgment there—only unconditional love—no matter how much she weighed or what her hair looked like.

"So, I'm not a disappointment to you?"

"You're my best friend." Graham stood. "Why don't you let me take you home?"

She glanced up at him and knew exactly what ran through his mind. He was a man, after all. The kids were all gone at a church event for the day and they had the house to themselves. Her husband wanted to show her how much he loved her.

And she was inclined to let him.

## FORTY-FOUR

*Lila*

After talking to the owner of the house, Tom had worked out a rental agreement until their closing was final. They'd set that date for January, so in the meantime, they could move in—they just couldn't make any major changes until the house was officially theirs.

At this point, anything was better than living at the Whitmore. If she had any sense, Lila would've gone back to Macon, but something kept her in Sweethaven. The magic of the holidays, maybe. Or the promise of being with her best friends.

Or the nagging thought that somehow she had to help Charlotte.

Tom pulled into the driveway of their new home and turned off the engine. "It's almost ours."

Lila admired the simplicity of the home. After the snowfall, it looked even more beautiful, and the views of the lake were spectacular.

"I may never go back to Georgia," Lila said.

Tom laughed. "This cold isn't getting to you?"

"I'm getting used to it."

Tom led the way up the front walk and stopped when he reached the porch. "I'm glad we're doing this," he said. "It's the perfect way to start a new chapter."

"Definitely." Lila smiled. She needed a new chapter.

Later that night, after they'd somewhat settled in, Lila watched Tom pack for his trip. He'd taken a couple of weeks off and wanted another one at Christmas, so Lila understood he had to go, but that didn't make his leaving any easier.

"Maybe you should go stay with Adele while I'm gone," Tom said, zipping his small suitcase closed.

She studied him in his pilot's uniform and smiled. "Are you worried about me, Captain?"

He met her eyes. "I just hate that I have to leave you right now."

Lila waved him off. "Are you kidding? You'd just be in the way. I'm going to have this place redecorated by the time you get back."

Tom sat on the bed beside her. "Lila, I know you, and I know that as soon as I walk out that door you're going to start moving furniture and hanging curtains and removing wallpaper."

"Well, not in that order."

"I'm serious. You need to be careful. You're under enough stress as it is."

She forced a smile. The truth was she wanted something to occupy her mind more than anything else. She didn't want to question whether or not that day was the day she'd finally find it in her heart to forgive her parents for their phony life.

"Can I at least put up the Christmas tree?"

Tom stared at her. "Will you get someone to help you?"

"You worry too much."

He kissed her and said good-bye, leaving her alone with the waning sunlight.

Hours later, Lila had finally gotten the prickly tree she and Tom had picked out the night before to stand upright in the stand. She'd strung lights and added ornaments, most of them new purchases from the Gingerbread House. She had brought a few of her favorites with her from home. She removed them from their careful packaging one by one, each with its own story, memories attached like a price tag to a new dress.

At the very bottom of the box, Lila found one more ornament, wrapped in white tissue paper. As she pulled off the paper, she uncovered her oldest ornament. Her father had given it to her when she was five. Unlike most parents who bought cartoon-inspired ornaments, her parents chose a Swarovski crystal heart with the words "Daddy's Little Girl" etched inside.

Lila turned over the ornament in her hand as her mind drifted back to the happier times she'd had with her family. She had been so fortunate to grow up in a home where she wanted for nothing. And while Mama had been unbearable at times, Lila decided not to let that turn her cold. In this new chapter she'd purpose to treat other people the opposite of the way Mama did.

She hung the crystal on the tree, the weight of it bending the branch.

Her mind jumped to Charlotte. She sighed. Treating Charlotte the opposite of the way Mama would treat her meant treating her like her sister.

If she was serious about changing, then it was time to put the theory to the test.

Lila grabbed her purse, pulled on her coat and headed toward the car.

As she drove toward town, Lila called Charlotte to make sure she was still staying at the Whitmore.

"I'm still here."

Lila could hear the sadness in her sister's voice. "Have you been home at all?"

After a pause, Charlotte said, "No, but I'm packing up to head out tomorrow."

Why did that make Lila sad?

"Can I stop by? I wanted to talk to you about something."

"Of course, I'll come down."

Poor Charlotte. Hanging around hoping that Daddy would change his mind. That Mama would loosen her grip.

Did Charlotte hope she'd finally get through to Daddy? Would Lila be that dedicated in fighting for her own child? Lila pulled in front of the Whitmore and parked the car. She walked up the icy walk just as the front door opened and Charlotte appeared in the doorway. "Lila?"

Before Lila could respond, her foot caught on a slick patch of ice. Like a kid falling down on the ice rink, Lila tumbled to the ground, crashing to the pavement, the cold, wet snow chilling her hands.

"Lila!" Charlotte rushed to her side. "Are you okay?"

Lila looked up at Charlotte, whose face looked pale even in the moonlight. "The baby."

Charlotte gasped.

Lila let her head rest on the cold pavement, afraid to move. Afraid to find out that she'd lost another baby.

"It's going to be okay." Charlotte grabbed her phone and dialed 911. "Yes, I need an ambulance at the Whitmore Bed-and-Breakfast. It's for—my sister—she's pregnant and she just slipped on the ice."

Charlotte listened to the voice on the other end of the line. "How far along are you?"

Lila could feel tears trickling down her cheeks. "Sixteen weeks."

"She's sixteen weeks." Charlotte's face fell. "Okay. We'll keep her still." She hung up and turned her attention to Lila. "I'm going to get you a blanket. Don't move."

Lila nodded. When Charlotte returned, she covered Lila with the comforter from her room. "Just stay still."

"I can't lose another baby," Lila said.

Charlotte's face went pale, then, as if she were putting on her brave face, she smiled. "You won't. It's going to be fine."

But Lila knew her baby was at risk. She wasn't far enough along to have the proper insulation to withstand a fall like the one she'd just taken. Already, she could tell her tailbone had been bruised.

After what seemed like an eternity, an ambulance—the only one in town—roared down the block, stopping in front of the bed-and-breakfast.

"I'm fine, I'm sure I'm fine," Lila said. Charlotte had insisted she not move. She tucked the blankets around Lila and did her best to keep her warm. Now, two paramedics rushed toward them with a stretcher.

"Are you in pain?"

Lila nodded. "Just from where I fell. My backside."

"Okay, we're going to get you to the hospital," one of the paramedics said. He pulled the blankets back. "They said you're pregnant."

Lila blinked back her tears, remembering the other babies she'd lost. So many times she'd almost been a mother. She thought this time would be different. This time, she'd told herself, it was okay to hope.

But as they lifted her into the ambulance, panic swept through her. She glanced at Charlotte, who stood under the streetlamp, hands clasped in front of her like she was praying.

"Can she come with us?" Lila asked the paramedic.

"If she hurries." He glanced at Charlotte and motioned for her to get in the ambulance. She rushed in and sat beside Lila.

Lila closed her eyes. "I'm scared," she said.

Charlotte took her hand. "It's going to be okay."

The siren sounded and they sped toward the hospital one town over. When they arrived, Lila was rushed inside where doctors and nurses threw around words like "miscarriage" as if they were part of their normal vocabulary.

"Can you call my husband? My friends?" Lila asked Charlotte as the doctor asked her to leave the room.

Charlotte nodded, took Lila's phone and disappeared into the hallway, leaving Lila alone with her doctor, Dr. Simpson. She welcomed the familiar face. He'd taken over her care while she was in Sweethaven.

"Tell me what happened."

A knot formed in her throat. "I slipped on the ice."

"It's pretty slick out there." He lifted her shirt just above her belly and hooked her up to a fetal heart monitor.

"Is the baby okay?" she asked, swiping away a tear.

"I'm going to do an ultrasound and check the heart rate." He gave her a reassuring smile.

The jelly he squirted on her belly came as a shock of cold, but in moments, she saw her baby's face on the screen of the ultrasound. Emotion clogged her throat.

"Is it . . . ?" She closed her eyes, unable to imagine what would come next.

Then, like the sound of a bass drum, Lila heard the baby's heartbeat, and it sounded strong.

She glanced at Dr. Simpson. He smiled at her.

"You've got a fighter in here. The heart rate sounds good."

Relief washed over her as tears sprang to her eyes.

"I'm going to want to keep you overnight, but yes, it seems like the baby is doing fine. No need to panic."

"Oh, thank God."

*Thank You, God.*

"You need to wear better shoes if you're going to go out in this weather," Dr. Simpson said, looking at her heels. "Would you like to know what you're having?"

Lila's eyes shot to the screen, but she couldn't make out where to look or what to look for. She saw a perfect head in profile, with the most beautiful nose and a hand up by the little face, but she couldn't tell if she would soon hold a boy or a girl.

A knock on the door drew her attention away from the screen and Charlotte walked in. "I'm so sorry to interrupt, but Tom's on the phone. He insisted I find out what was going on."

Dr. Simpson smiled. "He's out of town?"

Lila nodded. "Can I take the call?"

"Of course."

"Honey?" She heard the panic in his voice.

"It's okay. We're fine." Lila smiled through fresh tears and saw a look of relief wash over Charlotte's face. "Listen to the heartbeat." Lila held up the phone, so he could hear. "Dr. Simpson wants to know if we want to find out what we're having."

Lila glanced at Charlotte, who started to walk out. "No, Charlotte. Stay. Please."

Her sister's eyes widened and she closed the door, then moved closer to Lila.

"Tom, I'm going to put you on speaker."

Dr. Simpson moved the ultrasound around until a new image popped up on the screen. "You sure you want to know?"

Lila smiled, then wiped away another tear. "Yes. Please."

Charlotte took her hand and squeezed.

"Looks like you two are having . . . a boy," the doctor said.

"A boy?"

Lila's heart jumped. She thought it was a boy.

"Did you hear that, Tom? We're going to have a son."

She took the phone off speaker. "Tom?"

"I'm here," he said, his voice cracking. "I'm just really happy."

Lila closed her eyes and smiled. "We're going to have a son." Tears escaped her closed eyes. She opened them and saw Charlotte beaming at her side.

"I'm glad you're here, Charlotte," Lila said. "Thank you."

Charlotte's expression changed and she nodded. "Me too."

Lila let her head rest on the stiff hospital pillow. If this was what it meant to have a sister, Lila thought she could get used to it.

## FORTY-FIVE

*Lila*

When Lila awoke the next morning, it took her a minute to remember where she was. Charlotte sat in the chair next to her, eyes closed, and in the hallway, quiet voices murmured.

Lila glanced at the monitor, staring at the pulsing beat of her son's heart. "Thank You, God," she whispered, her heart full to bursting.

Charlotte stirred. Her eyes flickered open. "You're awake."

Lila smiled. "You didn't have to sleep here."

"I had to leave messages for everyone—I didn't know when they would arrive. I think everyone's here now, in the hallway."

"Who's everyone?"

Charlotte sat up. "All of your friends."

"Tom?"

"Do you really think he'd be in the hallway if he was here?" She smiled. "He should be here"—she glanced at her watch—"in about an hour." Charlotte paused, then looked down. "Your parents are here though."

Lila pulled up the covers around her, a chill washing over her. "You called them?"

Charlotte looked away. "I felt like I should. I'm sorry."

"No, it's fine."

Her sister pressed her lips together and took a deep breath. "I'm mad at them too."

Lila's mind spun back to the verse Jane had written out for her. Would it really be better if she forgave them?

Movement in the hallway caught Lila's eye. "How long have they been here?"

Charlotte followed her gaze to the nurses' station just outside the door where Daddy stood, alone, a cup of coffee in his hands. "For a while now. They got here in the middle of the night."

"He looks sad."

"I think he is."

How was it that she could still be so angry with both her parents and yet feel so sorry for them at the same time? Their whole life had been built on lies. And now, with everything unraveling, they stood to lose the only family they had. "Do they know it's a boy?"

Charlotte shook her head. "I wouldn't dream of sharing your good news. That's for you to tell—when you want to."

"I'm sorry I was so mean to you before."

"Don't apologize. I'm the one who should be sorry—for turning your world upside-down."

"No, I think I should thank you."

Charlotte raised an eyebrow.

"If you hadn't come here, I'd never have known the truth. I'd still be living my life trying to make everyone else happy and proud of me. I feel so free now—like I can finally just be myself." Lila smiled. "I may stop wearing makeup altogether."

"Let's not get crazy," Charlotte said. "We're no spring chickens."

Lila smiled. "And I don't know if it'll help, but I want them to test me to see if I'm a match for Maddie."

Charlotte perked up at Lila's words. "You do?"

"I do. And I pray I'm a match because I'd really love to do something special for my niece."

A knock on the door drew their attention away. Mama stood in the doorway, but she didn't walk into the room. Instead, she stood there, almost asking permission to enter.

"I just wanted to check on you," she said, avoiding Charlotte's eyes.

Charlotte stared at the floor. "I'll check in with you later."

Lila nodded. "Thank you, Charlotte. For everything."

Without another word, Charlotte gathered her things and walked out. Mama stiffened as she passed, her chin higher than usual.

"What was she doing here, Lila?" Now Mama moved toward her.

"She was the one who called the ambulance for me."

"But why were you with her in the first place? Don't tell me you plan to let that woman into your life."

Lila stared at Mama for a long moment. "That woman is my sister. And like it or not, yes, I want to get to know her. She has children. I'm an aunt. And since Daddy won't get tested to see if he can save her daughter's life, I'm going to do it."

Mama scoffed. "This is ludicrous."

"Mama, I know you don't understand it. I know you're content to spend the rest of your life nursing your bitterness, but I'm not going to let myself become a younger version of you. Besides, she's not the one who did anything wrong."

"Listen here—"

But before Mama could finish, Tom rushed in, eyes intent on Lila. He still wore his uniform, along with a look of fear. "You're okay?"

Lila turned away from Mama and gave Tom her full attention. "I am now."

He hugged her, then rested a hand on her stomach. "And the doctor said the baby's okay?"

She nodded.

Tom glanced at Mama, who watched them, her fingers working her pearl necklace.

"I've got to run," Mama said. "Now that I know you're both okay. We'll check in on you later."

Lila didn't respond but watched Mama walk out.

Forgiving someone who admitted no wrongdoing would prove to be much more difficult than she originally thought.

\* \* \* \* \*

Lila had been assigned to several days of bed rest, though the doctor assured her she'd be well enough to go to Adele's big Christmas celebration. She'd been looking forward to Christmas week since she arrived in Sweethaven for Thanksgiving, and she had no intention of missing it. She'd spend the holidays with her friends eating too much and laughing for too many hours. And with the Christmas Eve service—by candlelight—she couldn't think of a better way to celebrate.

She had a feeling this year would be a very special Christmas.

Her eyes fell on the tree she'd decorated. At home in Georgia, her tree had been cream and gold—elegant and vintage. This year, she'd opted for something more fun—a color scheme of turquoise and red. She couldn't love it more.

With time on her hands, Lila took out a blank scrapbook she'd been stashing away for something special. Finally, she figured out what it was she wanted to do with it.

She didn't have much with her, but there was enough to make a title page. She rummaged through her box of papers, adhesives, stickers and embellishments, laying everything out on the first page of the album. The photo, one of her and Tom on Thanksgiving, would be nice for an introductory layout.

Once she had everything in place, Lila took out her adhesive and secured the pieces down, adding a cluster of small flowers to the lower left-hand corner of the photo. Then she took out her pen and journaled on a decorative card she would tuck in beside the photo.

While she didn't consider herself a scrapbooker necessarily, Lila had realized it was a scrapbook that had brought her friends back to her after too many years apart. That scrapbook reminded her of what had always been most important—the people in her life. Not the things, not a big fancy house or beauty pageant sashes.

She couldn't help it if she wanted that to continue.

That prayer book Jane had made for Meghan had also made its rounds, and while Lila might not be the first to sing its praises, it had spoken to her in a way she couldn't explain. Somehow, there was something about securing these truths or memories down into an album.

Now, standing outside room number three at the Whitmore, Lila held the little book she'd made to her chest. She knocked and waited until Charlotte opened the door.

Her sister smiled. "It's good to see you up."

"I was hoping you'd come back to the hospital. I don't feel like I got to properly thank you."

"Come in." Charlotte moved aside so Lila could step into the room. "I thought you might need some time with your family."

Lila met her eyes. "You are my family."

Charlotte looked away.

On the bed, Lila saw an open suitcase. "You're packing?"

Charlotte nodded. "I've been gone too long already."

Lila scanned the room. "I thought maybe you'd bring the kids up here."

"I think it's time for me to go back home."

Lila nodded. Her family missed her, of course, but Lila was surprised at the depth of her own disappointment to learn Charlotte wasn't staying.

"I brought you something. To say thank you." Lila held the small, tissue-paper-filled gift bag out to her sister.

Charlotte took the bag. "You don't owe me any thanks." She waited a few long seconds and then opened the bag, pulling out the small scrapbook.

"Lila, this is really beautiful." Charlotte turned the book over in her hands.

"I don't know if you know this, but my friends and I get together and make scrapbook albums after each summer in Sweethaven. It's something of a tradition—and now that we've found each other again, we're carrying it on."

"I'm not very artistic." Charlotte opened to the opening page and read the short paragraph Lila had written about herself. Just the facts, really, but the things that sisters should know about each other.

"I know you have your life and I have mine, but I was thinking it might be fun to share stories in this little book. I'll do a page and send it to you, you'll do a page and send it back. It's a way for us to keep tabs on each other."

Charlotte ran her hand across the layout.

"And then, years from now, we'll have it to share with our kids." Lila waited for a moment, clinging to the idea that she would have someone to pass her memories down to. She'd given up the idea so many times, to have a real person growing inside her nearly took her breath away.

Would she ever get used to the idea of being a mother?

"I think it's a great idea," Charlotte said. "Thank you for being nice to me."

Lila smiled. "I always wanted a sister."

Lila hoisted her purse over her shoulder. "One more thing. I understand if you need to leave, but I wanted to invite you to spend Christmas here, in Sweethaven. We're all going over to Adele's, and her philosophy is, the more the merrier. I already asked if I could invite your family."

"My kids too?"

"Of course. I'd love to meet them. Especially Maddie." Lila watched as Charlotte dabbed at the corners of her eyes with a tissue.

"I'll talk to my husband."

"You won't ever experience anything like Christmas in Sweethaven," Lila said. "We're going to go to the candlelight service at the Chapel on Christmas Eve and then straight over to Adele's for a meal you'll never forget."

Charlotte held the book to her chest and smiled. "You know, Lila, you're not anything like I thought you'd be."

Lila studied her for a moment. "What do you mean?"

She looked away. "I thought you'd be just like your mom, but you're nothing like her."

A warm feeling washed over Lila. "Thanks for that." Lila looked away. "I don't think she means to come across the way she does." She knew Mama was abrasive. Even her own friends back home tip-toed around her. One time Lila overheard two of them talking about Mama's "holier than thou" attitude at a dinner party. When they realized Lila had heard everything, both of the women begged her not to say a word to her mother.

How sad that without the intimidation factor, Mama wouldn't have a single friend. She probably wouldn't even have a husband.

Lila met Charlotte's eyes. "I feel sorry for her."

Charlotte sighed. "Me too, and I really didn't want to. I wanted her to feel so guilty for what she'd done—for making me hunt down my own father in hopes of saving my daughter's life. I think I kind of wanted them both to suffer for what they've done."

"I think it worked."

"But I was wrong. It didn't make me feel better, and it hurt you in the process. Lila, if you can, try to forgive both of them."

There was that word again.

Lila looked away. "Think about Christmas. We would love to have you. The Christmas Eve service is beautiful." She handed Charlotte the church bulletin where she'd circled the information on when and where.

"I'll let you know."

"Thank you, Charlotte." Lila pulled her sister into a hug.

She took her time leaving, watching every step, eyes focused on her sensible shoes. As she walked out of the Whitmore, Lila said a silent prayer of thanks for Charlotte. While she might not have liked the idea at first, Lila had realized having a sister could turn out to be one of her greatest blessings.

The door opened behind her and Lila turned and saw Charlotte, coatless, rushing out.

"They're going to come, Lila!" she called out the door. "We'll be there for Christmas Eve."

"Wonderful!" Lila grinned, surprised how genuinely happy she felt.

How was that for a Christmas miracle?

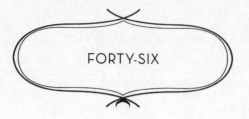

## FORTY-SIX

*Adele*

Adele looked over her checklist. Her guests would arrive in just a couple hours and she still had so much to do. She'd baked three different desserts and taken the Christmas cookies out of the freezer, creating a lovely dessert table in the dining room. Now, to move on to the savory side of the menu.

The ham was in the oven, potatoes boiling and appetizers started. She could do this, even though she was starting to slow down. Having so many guests over had gotten more difficult as she'd gotten older.

But she moved forward, fueled by sheer excitement.

Outside, the day was gray and overcast, giving more sparkle to the white lights on Adele's tree. The entryway shone with the swaths of greenery wrapped through the banister, and she lit candles to fill the little cottage with the scent of evergreen.

Ready or not, Christmas had come.

The back door opened and Luke poked his head in.

"Are you here to pick through the food before dinner actually starts?" Adele stuck a fork in the potatoes. Still too firm to mash.

Luke scoffed. "Would I ruin my appetite before your famous ham and potatoes?"

"I should hope not."

"Came to find out more about this Henry guy. Meghan said he asked you to marry him." Luke sat down at the kitchen table and waited for her to respond. Why was it so hard to talk to him about Henry?

Because she still felt like she was stepping out on his father.

"I read that scrapbook you've got from when you were a kid."

Adele stared at him. "When did you do that?"

"It's been on the shelf for years. Finally opened it one day and started reading. Sounds like you had it bad for that guy."

"That was a long time ago."

Luke shrugged. "Seems like a nice guy to me."

She held his gaze for a few long seconds.

"I've gotta go pick up Campbell. We'll be back early in case you need help."

Adele's thoughts wandered back to that moment at Meghan's when Nick pulled out that beautiful ring for his wife. She could see disappointment on Campbell's face, though Luke had obviously been expecting the surprise. Was Campbell hoping for her own ring this Christmas?

"Luke, how are you and Campbell?"

Luke frowned. "What do you mean?"

"Is it serious?"

He laughed. "You're not going to start analyzing my love life now, are you?"

Adele studied his eyes and made the rash decision to shut her mouth for once. She didn't need to stick her nose in their business, even though she feared he might lose Campbell if he wasn't careful. "I'll see you in a little while."

He watched her for a minute, as surprised as she was that she'd chosen not to dole out romantic advice, and then headed out the door.

For the rest of the morning and early afternoon, Adele worked at a frantic pace to get everything done. By now, she should have had entertaining down to a science—but she still wanted everything to be perfect.

Especially on the day Henry would meet the rest of her family.

Adele could hardly concentrate for the nerves that threatened to take over.

She'd already burned a pan of brownies and left the pot of potatoes on the stove so long they turned to inedible mush. What next? Setting fire to the kitchen?

They all began to trickle in, most bringing food to share. Lila arrived with Tom and later welcomed her new sister and her sister's family. Adele smiled to see Lila finally becoming the person she always knew she was meant to be. Cilla Adler had certainly done her best to turn her daughter into a snobby socialite, but from the looks of things, Lila had realized that didn't suit her anymore.

Jane, visibly slimmer, hurried in with her family and instantly starting helping in the kitchen.

"I need something to keep me busy so I don't drown myself in Texas sheet cake."

Adele opened the door to the refrigerator. "I made you a few special goodies—sugar-free and low in calories. I didn't want you to miss out."

"You did that for me?"

"Honey, you're an inspiration. I might have to start an exercise program of my own."

"Really?"

"Sure." Adele closed the fridge. "*After* Christmas."

Jane laughed and left the kitchen with a cheese tray.

Adele's nerves kicked up and she willed herself to calm down. She had people to take care of, people who were relying on her for a magical Christmas experience.

She kept one eye on dinner and another on the front porch. When Henry finally arrived, her heart jumped. She must've looked nervous because Meghan met her in the entryway and put an arm around her.

"We're all going to love him, Mama."

Adele drew in a deep breath. "I hope so, darlin'."

Henry walked up the stairs and met her eyes through the window. He smiled as Adele opened the door and welcomed him with a hug. She stepped back and motioned toward Meghan. "Henry, this is my daughter Meghan."

Henry extended a hand toward Meghan. "I'm a huge fan."

Meghan laughed. "You like country music?"

"I like all music. Your voice reminds me of your mom's when she was young."

Meghan tossed Adele a look. "Is that right? You'll have to fill me in on what my mother was like when she was a teenager." She led Henry into the dining room and introduced him to her family. Moments later, Adele heard Meghan laugh, and her heart stopped fluttering. Why had she been so worried? Of course Henry would fit right it.

That's what he did.

As Adele put the finishing touches on dinner, Henry sat in the next room telling stories about Sweethaven when they were growing up. As he talked, Adele's mind wandered back, remembering how different things were back then. She wouldn't say simpler, because Henry had to go fight in a war, but the climate was different. And as he spoke, Adele imagined him here, in her home—not just as a visitor but as a permanent resident.

Something about it fit.

As she finished loading all the food onto the table, Meghan walked into the kitchen. "I like him," she whispered.

Adele smiled. "You do, huh? Does that mean I have your blessing to run off with him?"

Meghan popped an olive into her mouth. "I don't want you leaving Sweethaven or anything, but I think I'd feel better knowing Henry was around to keep you company."

Adele handed her the relish tray. "Do something useful, would you? We have guests to feed."

Meghan grinned. "Mama, it's good to see you happy again."

Adele looked away. All those years she'd accepted she'd be alone—and now, Henry. She hadn't gotten used to it yet.

"I mean it. You deserve it."

"Don't go gettin' all sappy on me, Meg."

Meghan turned and walked out. Adele glanced into the living room where Luke and Henry sat at the little card table against the wall, each with his own fan of playing cards splayed out in front of him.

Seeing the two of them like that reminded Adele of all the years Luke hadn't had with his own father, and while she knew Henry wasn't a replacement for Teddy, he could be a nice addition—to all their lives.

Luke laughed at something Henry said, and Adele admired his easygoing way. He glanced at Adele and winked. One by one, he'd win them all over.

Adele called them all to the dining room, where they admired the spread she'd put together.

"Now, these are all dishes that will be in my cookbook, so I want to know if anything doesn't taste good." Henry stood at her side, a full foot taller than her, and she glanced around the circle—friends who were more like family, and family who'd become good friends.

"I just want to take a minute to thank you all for being here today. It's been a long time since I've had everyone I love together under the same roof, and I can't think of anyone I'd rather share it with."

"She's gonna cry," Luke said.

A laugh rushed out just as a tear trickled down Adele's cheek. She swiped it away and scanned the circle again. "I'm thankful this year to have new friends with us"—she glanced across the room at Charlotte—"but also for the return of old friends as well."

Henry slid his hand in hers.

Adele glanced at him, then cleared her throat. "And I'm happy to announce that Henry and I are gettin' married."

Contagious gasps moved through the room like dominoes, but the shocked expressions quickly turned to smiles and congratulations.

She turned to Henry, whose shock hadn't quite worn off.

"I assume the offer is still good?"

Henry laughed. "Always." He pulled her into a tight hug. "That's the best Christmas present I've ever gotten."

FORTY-SEVEN

*Campbell*

Campbell sat at the dining room table, her plate empty in front of her, while Luke chatted with Nick about the logistics of a new job he'd just started. Her mind wandered back to the joy she'd seen on Adele's face when she announced her engagement to Henry, and again, humiliation wormed its way in.

She wished she'd never told Jane she thought Meghan's ring was for her.

A glance across the table at Meghan's bejeweled left hand sliced through her, cutting her embarrassment in tiny little pieces that seemed to fill her up from the inside.

At midnight, they'd all head over to the Sweethaven Chapel for the candlelight Christmas Eve service, but in that moment, the only thing Campbell wanted was solitude. After dinner had been cleaned up, the dishes put away, Campbell waited at Luke's side for his conversation to lull. He finished his sentence and wrapped his arm around her waist.

"You okay?"

She nodded. "I think I'm going to head home for a bit before the service tonight."

He stood.

"No, you don't have to drive me. I'm fine walking. It's just a few blocks."

"Cam, it's freezing outside. I'm not letting you walk." He turned to Nick. "Thanks for the help, bro."

Nick nodded and took a bite of pie. "Anytime."

Luke turned to Campbell and smiled. He had no idea how humiliated she felt—or even why she felt humiliated. It wasn't fair to punish him for something he had no way of knowing.

And wasn't she the one who'd balked at the idea of marriage only a few short weeks ago when she found the ring in the first place?

In his truck, Campbell struggled to get warm. Luke reached behind the seat and pulled out a blanket and handed it to her. "I keep it with me in case of emergencies."

"We're only going to be in the truck for a couple minutes." She laughed.

"Yeah, but why should you be freezing during those two minutes?"

She spread the blanket over her lap.

"Better?"

Campbell nodded and they pulled away. When they reached the gallery, she turned to him. "Thanks for the ride. And for including me in your family's Christmas. It meant a lot to me."

"Can I come up?"

Her heart jumped. She risked saying something stupid if he didn't leave right that second. But she nodded and before she knew it, they were walking into her apartment.

"Do you want something to drink?"

Luke shook his head. "No, I just want to make sure you're okay."

She looked away. "I'm fine."

"I know you miss your mom—especially this time of year."

Campbell scolded herself. She hadn't even been thinking about her mom. She'd been thinking about how stupid she felt for allowing herself to believe Luke wanted to marry her. She'd been wallowing. Not grieving.

After a long pause, she sat down on the couch. "I do miss her."

"I thought so."

"But that's not why I've been so distant."

He sat down beside her. "Is something else bothering you?"

She cleared her throat. "I found that ring in your apartment. Weeks ago."

Luke's eyes widened.

"I thought . . ." The words got stuck in her throat. She stared at her hands, clasped together in her lap.

"You thought what?"

"I thought you bought it. For me." She stared out the window, aware of his eyes on her. "The truth is, Luke, I do love you."

As the words hung between them, Campbell's eyes found his.

"I love you and it scares me how much. I fall asleep thinking about you. When I wake up, I stare across the street hoping to catch a glimpse of you. I told myself I'd never let myself get this attached to another person ever again, but I can't think of a single thing in my life I want to do without you."

His eyes left hers and found her lips. He reached behind her head and pulled her to him and kissed her, a kiss that told her he felt exactly the same way.

"I'm sorry I was snooping around your apartment," she said, abandoning his lips.

"I don't mind. I think it's kind of cute."

"This isn't cute at all. Nothing about this is cute. I feel so embarrassed." She glanced up and found him watching her, a semi-amused look on his face.

"I'm never going to live this down, am I?"

He shrugged. "Maybe not."

"You think this is funny."

He laughed. "No, I promise I don't, it's just . . . didn't you think that ring was kind of gaudy?"

Campbell laughed. "I would never say that about Meghan's ring."

"But you did, didn't you?"

"She can pull it off being a famous singer and all." Campbell sighed, mind floating back to the moment she found that ring in Luke's apartment. She had been surprised by how big it was. It didn't seem like his style. Or hers.

Now, it made sense.

Luke leaned closer to her. "Yeah, when I think of you I think of something more like this."

She glanced down at his hand, now resting on her knees and holding a small black ring box, not unlike the one that held Meghan's oversize diamond.

"What's this?"

"Open it."

She stared at him, the same hint of amusement dancing in his eyes. He held up the box and she took it, her heart racing. As she pulled open the box, a small gasp escaped.

A laugh lodged itself in Campbell's throat, where it was met by an inexplicable sob, which she quickly stifled in an effort to regain composure. She stared at the antique-style ring, an oval diamond surrounded by a halo of much smaller diamonds and set in a white gold band. Nothing flashy or over-the-top.

It was perfect.

"How long have you had this?"

"A few weeks. Since before Thanksgiving."

"I can't believe you were keeping this from me," she said, glancing at the ring.

"I thought about doing something big and public, but the truth is, Cam, I just wanted it to be me and you. For as long as we both shall live."

"It's perfect, Luke, thank you so much."

Luke took her hands. "I've never been so sure about anything in my life. When I imagine myself five, ten—even fifty—years from now, you're there."

"How do I look?"

He laughed. "I'm serious. I don't want to wait. I want to marry you and make decisions with you and have kids with you."

She smiled. "So, are you going to ask me a question?"

Luke straightened, not looking away from her. "Campbell Jane Carter, will you marry me?"

Her face flushed with heat as he took her face in his hands, wiping a tear from her cheek as he drew her closer to him.

"I thought you'd never ask," she said.

He closed the gap between them, his lips covering hers and reminding her how quickly she could lose herself in him. In seconds, she'd forgotten all the disappointment leading up to that moment and let herself get a little lost in the depth of his kiss.

Luke pulled away and held her gaze. "Is that a yes?"

She nodded, unable to pull her eyes away from his. "That's a huge yes."

# FORTY-EIGHT

*Lila*

When Lila left Adele's house, her heart was full. She couldn't remember the last time she'd had such a joyful, laid-back Christmas celebration, and in her current state, she needed it.

The best part might've been meeting Charlotte's family. Charlotte and her husband Andy arrived with their three kids in tow, and Lila greeted them in the entryway.

"Lila, this is my family," Charlotte said. "My husband Andy."

Tall, yet somewhat stocky, Andy had a kind face and a nice smile. He shook Lila's hand, then Tom's. "Good to meet you both, and thanks for having us."

"And this is our son Drew and our girls Julia and Maddie."

One by one, Lila shook their hands, and when she got to Maddie, the little girl smiled at her. "Thank you," she said.

Lila glanced at Charlotte, who watched Maddie with pride.

"For what?"

"For getting tested," Maddie said. "It's what I wanted most for Christmas."

Lila's throat swelled and she bit the inside of her lip to keep from crying. "I'm happy to do it, Maddie. I'm praying we can get you all better."

Charlotte's family had fit right in, and Lila began to imagine getting together with her sister after she had the baby. Charlotte had even talked about renting a cottage in Sweethaven for a week this summer or flying down to Macon after the baby came.

The idea of it, which would've sent her into a frenzy only a few short weeks ago, warmed Lila's heart and made her think maybe she actually had a chance at a normal family.

"What do you think Mama and Daddy did today?" Lila broke the silence with her unintentional question.

Tom glanced at her, then back to the road. "Do you want to go find out?"

Lila played with the ring on her left hand. "I feel bad for them, Tom."

"That's good."

She gave him a puzzled look.

"You've changed. A year ago, finding this out about your parents, well, you would've written them off once and for all. But here you are, thinking about them and feeling bad for them. It's good."

Lila stared out the window. Tom was right. All these years, she'd been the person her mother had raised her to be, but there had been so many other influences—Suzanne and Adele and Jane—people who taught her what unconditional love looked like. Perhaps she'd become more like them than she realized.

Perhaps she'd always been more like them and less like Mama.

"Can you take me there?" Lila asked.

"To the lake house?"

She nodded.

"You sure?"

"I think so."

Her parents might not even be there. They might have gone back to Macon after they found out Lila and the baby were both going to be fine.

Tom made the turn into the driveway and Lila realized she was holding her breath. The empty driveway gave nothing away. Daddy would've put the car in the garage. She wouldn't know if they were home until she knocked on the door.

"Wait there, the driveway looks slick," Tom said, turning off the engine. He walked around to her side of the car and helped her out. The fall at the Whitmore fresh in her mind, Lila clung to his arm. With his strength behind her, she felt solid and strong.

Those feelings waned as soon as she rang the bell.

Moments later, the door opened and Mama stood on the other side of the glass.

"Can we come in?"

Mama didn't say a word. Instead, she opened the door and allowed them to pass by her, into the entryway.

"Is Daddy here?"

"In his study."

Lila called for her father, who appeared in the doorway, a shocked look on his face.

"Are you here to apologize?" Mama asked. She stood, glaring, arms crossed in front of her.

Lila's nerve dwindled, but Tom's hand on the small of her back reminded her why she'd come.

"I came to tell you that I forgive you both."

Mama's brows shot upward. "*You* forgive *us*?"

"Parents can do wrong by their children, Mama." Lila pressed her lips together. "Some of them even say they're sorry." She was careful to keep her tone calm. She hadn't come for a fight—she simply knew if she didn't get it out, the only person it would harm was her.

Daddy took a few steps toward her, but one glance at Mama and he stilled.

All these years, she thought Daddy had the upper hand, but the scene in front of her painted a very different picture.

"I've realized something the past few weeks," Lila said, her voice shaking. "I'll never be good enough for you, and that's okay."

Mama looked away, an annoyed expression on her face.

"Because I'm not supposed to be who *you* want me to be. I'm supposed to be who God made me to be."

"Now you're going to bring God into all this?" Mama scoffed.

"God made me to be different from you—both of you. And while I hope one day we can get past all of this, I know that the family I have with Tom is what's really important now. I'm going to make my own mistakes, but I can promise you, I'm not going to repeat yours."

"You sound more high and mighty than ever."

"Cilla, let her talk." Daddy's face had turned to stone.

Mama opened her mouth to say something but quickly closed it.

"The truth is, I want you both to love me, and I want you to know our son."

Daddy's eyes widened.

"It's a boy." Lila let her hands rest on her stomach where her son grew. "But you already have a grandson, Daddy."

Daddy frowned.

"His name is Drew and he's very sweet."

Mama stiffened. "You've *met* him?"

Lila nodded.

"How could you do that to us, Lila?"

"I didn't do anything to you, Mama. I did it *for* me. I want to know my family. I want to try to save my niece's life. Something you should've done." Lila took a deep breath.

Neither of her parents said a word. Daddy seemed lost in thought and Mama looked like she might explode.

So far, this was going exactly as she expected. Why couldn't she just forgive them quietly—by herself?

"I'm not saying this to hurt you. It's just what needed to be said so I could move on."

Mama leveled her glare. "I hope you're happy with yourself. Because of you, our family has fallen apart. We can't go back now— all *we* can do is pretend none of this ever happened."

Lila's heart sank. Mama hadn't listened to a word she said. She glanced at Tom, who'd stayed silent by her side the whole time. Even without her parents, she knew she could count on her husband. "We can go, Tom."

"That's all you came here for?" Mama asked.

"There is somewhere to go from here, but on the outside it won't look all pretty and wrapped up in a red bow. It'll mean coming clean with Charlotte—making things right with the *whole* family. Admitting your mistakes." She stared at Mama. "Why I thought you could do that, I'm not sure."

"Thank you for coming, Lila," Daddy said.

Lila glanced at him, a shell of a man. His lies threatened to unravel him.

"Come to the Christmas Eve service," Lila said, walking toward her father. "Charlotte brought her family, and Tom and I will be there. We want to spend Christmas with you."

Lila detected a hint of hopefulness in his expression.

"You can go now, Lila," Mama said. "We're spending Christmas Eve here."

Lila's eyes pleaded with Daddy's—to make the right choice, to make things right not just with her, but with Charlotte and his grandchildren. The thought surprised even her, but she wanted that—for all of them.

"It starts at midnight."

As soon as Lila and Tom cleared the door, her mother slammed it shut behind them and Lila burst into tears. Tom wrapped his arm around her waist and steadied her down the slippery steps.

"Why did I think anything I said would matter?"

They walked around to the other side of the car where Tom made sure she got in safely. Once they were on the road, he took her hand. "I'm proud of you for standing up to her like that."

"It didn't do any good."

"You can't change her, Lila. The only thing you can do is get yourself right. You did that today—for maybe the first time ever."

Lila let his words hover in the air, winding their way into her heart. He was right. She wasn't retaliating or trying to wound them with her words. She said what she needed to say to move on. To forgive them.

And something about that freed her in a way she hadn't expected.

FORTY-NINE

*Lila*

The Sweethaven Chapel had never looked so beautiful. Candlelit and glowing, the little church beckoned, like the safe haven it had always been. What better place to celebrate Christmas?

Still, despite the beauty, Lila's eyes were as heavy as her heart. She hadn't fully recovered from her talk with her parents, but she discovered her sadness wasn't for herself. It was for them. Their inability to move past the sins of the past held them captive—frozen exactly where they were, where they'd always been.

It hardly seemed fair, but clearly she couldn't get through to them.

That would take a miracle.

Again, she clung to Tom's arm as she headed up the walk. The cold air nipped through her, biting in the dark.

"Makes you miss Georgia, doesn't it?"

Lila glanced up at the chapel. Luminaries lined the walkway leading to the door. The building had been outlined with white lights, and as someone up ahead walked inside, she caught a glimpse of the candlelit sanctuary.

"No, I think it's perfect that we're here for Christmas," she said.

Inside, she saw the cluster of her friends, all circled around Campbell with grins on their faces.

Tom caught Campbell's eye. "He must've finally asked her."

Lila looked at her husband.

"He came to me over a month ago and told me he wanted to marry her. Felt he should run it by me first." Tom smiled. "Made me feel like a father."

Lila took his hand. "You're going to be a wonderful father. You are a wonderful father."

They moved toward Campbell and Luke, handing out their congratulations and eyeing her ring. Months ago, Lila would've found a way to criticize Campbell's smallish diamond, but this new version of her could find nothing but joy for Tom's daughter.

They'd purposely arrived early, and now weariness swept through Lila like a gust of wind. "I think I need to sit down," she told Tom.

Moments later, Charlotte and her family arrived and joined the others in the right section of the sanctuary. People began to filter in, candles waiting to be lit, quiet murmurings filling the little church.

Adele scooted in the pew in front of them, Henry at her side and beaming. "Lila, you didn't tell me your mother was coming," she said, sitting down, head still turned toward the back of the church.

"I invited her but she said no."

"Looks like she changed her mind."

Lila turned and saw Mama standing in the back, scanning the crowd and looking a little lost. She sighed. "This can't be good."

Tom followed her gaze to where Mama stood. "Maybe she'll surprise you."

Not likely.

Lila met Mama in the small lobby. "You came?"

She lifted her chin ever so slightly. "Can I talk to you?"

People filtered through the lobby like it was command central. Lila spotted Jane coming out of a room down a narrow hallway.

"Hey, you're here," Jane said when she reached Lila. "I'm getting ready to go on stage to welcome everyone."

Lila smiled. "Is there a room back there? Somewhere private?"

Jane's eyes darted to Lila's mother and then back to Lila. "Of course. There are Sunday school rooms. They're all empty, so feel free."

Moments later, Lila found herself face-to-face with her mother in the solace of a small room decorated for preschoolers. The tables sat low to the ground with kid-size chairs pushed underneath.

"This won't take long," Mama said.

Lila nodded. She hoped not. She didn't think she could withstand another verbal beating from her mother. Only a few hours had passed since the last one.

"I've been thinking a lot about what you said. Not just today, but over the past few weeks—ever since that woman appeared in our lives."

"Charlotte."

Mama looked away. "You were right."

"I was?"

Her mother nodded. "Your father was married when we met. To Charlotte's mother."

Lila's eyes fell to the rainbow-colored rug beneath her feet.

"What you didn't guess was that it wasn't in your father's nature to step out on his wife. At least, it wasn't until he met me."

Lila looked up.

Mama turned and walked toward her reflection in the dark windows. "I guess you'd say I seduced him. I knew I was beautiful. His wife was pregnant and we all know what that does to a woman."

Lila met her own reflection, set apart from her mother's. She couldn't deny she looked less than attractive.

"Getting him to stray was easy, but that wasn't enough for me. I wanted him for myself—at least, I thought I did. So, I let myself get pregnant."

Lila tried to process this admission. "I was a trap?"

Mama turned to her. "Yes. You were. And once your father left his wife and daughter, I had exactly what I thought I wanted."

Lila sat down in the only adult-size chair in the room. It was even worse than she thought. Being an accident was one thing, but being a trap was something else entirely. "But it didn't turn out to be what you thought it would be."

Mama's gaze fell to the floor. "I was crazy about him, Lila," she said, wistful. "I fell in love with him and made it my life's ambition to make him fall in love with me. But the more time we spent together, the less he seemed to want to be with me—with us. And I started to feel like I was the one who was trapped."

"Because of me." A lump formed in Lila's throat.

Mama pulled her shoulders back. "I think I always resented you for that. I thought if I never got pregnant, he never would've left them and I'd have been free to move on."

Lila had no words.

"And I came here tonight to tell you . . ." Mama pressed her lips together. "I'm sorry for that." When their eyes met, Lila saw sincerity waiting for her for the first time. "All of this, it is my fault. As much as I hate to admit it."

Lila watched a discomfort come over her mother. "I know it was hard for you to come here."

"Every time I tried to say anything about it, I lashed out at you instead. It's how I deal with my own disappointment, I suppose."

"I've been known to do the same."

Mama shook her head. "No, Lila, in many ways, you've always been your own person. When you forgave Tom, I was amazed by you."

"I thought you were disappointed."

Mama's eyes filled with tears. "I was proud."

Proud? Mama had never in all her life told Lila she was proud of her.

"Mama, I'm not going to lie. What you did—stealing a married man, trapping him into marrying you—it's terrible."

Mama looked away.

"And I think it's affected every relationship you have."

"It has," Mama whispered.

In that moment, Lila glimpsed the shame Mama had been living with all these years. She didn't need Lila to tell her what she'd done was wrong—she'd been telling herself that ever since Lila had been born. Over forty years of living with the pain of a regret Lila couldn't fathom.

Lila stood. "Mama, I accept your apology, and I do forgive you, but you have to forgive yourself now."

Lila watched as her mother dotted her eyes with a tissue before any tears could fall. And in an instant, the Cilla Adler she'd always known had returned. Poised and put together. "I don't think that's going to happen. All these years, I've stayed in a marriage with a man I didn't love just because I felt guilty. How could I steal him away and then walk out? It made no sense. Besides, I had a right to him—so I put up with all of it. I decided that was my punishment."

"But you did love him once."

Mama looked pensive again. "I did. Very much."

Lila thought of Adele and Henry—how they'd found each other again after all this time. It could be the same for her parents, couldn't it? "Why don't you start over? A new slate—with everything out in the open."

She cocked her head and looked at Lila. "When did you get to be such a hopeless romantic? Things don't work out that way in real life."

"They did for me."

Mama took a breath but didn't say another word. Lila imagined she'd just bitten back a remark—and that was progress.

"I brought you something." Mama opened her oversize designer purse, pulled out a small box and handed it to Lila.

Lila took the lid off the box and her body filled with warmth. A small gown filled the box, next to it a little bonnet.

"It was your baptism gown. I thought you might want it for the baby."

Lila picked up the outfit and imagined putting it on her baby—her son—on the day they dedicated his life to God. "Thank you, Mama." She put the gown back in the box and held it to her chest. As she did, her stomach got a kick from the inside. Lila gasped.

"I think I just felt the baby move."

Mama's eyes widened, and for a brief moment, she looked excited.

The fluttering in her stomach came again, this time like butterfly wings. "That's amazing," Lila said.

"I forgot how amazing," Mama said.

Lila met her mother's eyes. "None of this will be easy, you know."

Mama nodded.

"But it will be worth it. Forgiving you and Daddy will be worth it. Forgiving yourself will be worth it. Not being so angry all the time will be worth it."

Mama started to say something and then snapped her mouth shut. "I'm going to do my best."

The sound of "Silent Night" drifted in from the sanctuary. "Will you stay for the service?"

Mama sighed. "I don't know, Lila. I know Charlotte's in there."

Lila didn't want to pretend that Charlotte would accept Mama—maybe not ever—but they had to at least try, didn't they?

"Everything isn't going to have a fairy-tale ending, you know." Mama's eyes held an age-old sadness.

"I know, but it's Christmas. Tonight, more than ever, we have to at least try. Maybe a little of the Sweethaven Magic will help us out."

Mama was quiet for a few long moments. "All right, Lila," she finally said. "If you want me to come in, I will."

Lila smiled and considered pulling her mother into a hug. She decided against it, telling herself instead that they'd take this one day at a time.

They left the Sunday school room and walked into the lobby, which was glowing with a circle of candles around the perimeter.

"I sure hope the fire department is on call," Mama said.

"I'm glad to see everything about you hasn't changed," Lila whispered.

They stood in the back, peering in through the windows as the congregation stood, singing "Silent Night," led by nothing but Meghan's acoustic guitar. Lila smiled at her old friend. Who would've thought either of them would end up in a church this way?

The Christmas special had surely worked its magic, solidifying Meghan's place in America's heart. Lila marveled that she didn't feel even a twinge of jealousy—only joy—toward her friend.

A chill rushed through the lobby and Lila turned to see the door opening. Daddy appeared from outside, still looking broken and tired.

He looked startled to see the two of them standing together. For that matter, it still surprised Lila. With his eyes, Daddy seemed to ask for permission to approach them, so Lila gave him a slight smile.

Mama turned away and Lila saw the shame behind her eyes. All these years, she'd mistaken it for pride.

"Clean slate," Lila whispered.

Mama shot her a look just as Daddy reached them. "Are you girls going in?"

"I think we should," Lila said.

Mama nodded.

Before Lila could pull open the door, Daddy stopped her with a hand on her arm. She turned and faced him, both she and Mama waiting to hear what he had to say.

"I'm going to do better from now on."

Lila saw his pride break in half and Mama stiffened at her side. She wrapped an arm around her mother and smiled. "We all are, Daddy."

He nodded and took a deep breath. How hard it had been for him to say even that.

Lila led them to the pew where Tom waited for her, mulling over how long it would be before her family resembled *healthy*. But at least they'd all agreed to try.

For once they were headed in the right direction.

As she moved past Tom, taking her place next to Charlotte, Mama and Daddy scooted in on the aisle. In front of her, Campbell and Luke held hands, their candles flickering in front of happy faces. Jane stood on the stage next to her husband, and Meghan sang, eyes closed in front of the microphone.

Adele, directly in front of her, turned around and surveyed the pew, then met Lila's eyes with a smile. "Merry Christmas, darlin'," she said.

The music swelled.

> *Silent night, holy night*
> *Son of God, love's pure light*
> *Radiant beams from Thy holy face*
> *With the dawn of redeeming grace.*

Lila closed her eyes and said a prayer of thanks for that redeeming grace. Where would any of them be without it?

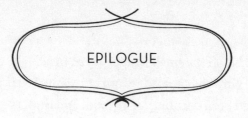

EPILOGUE

*The following June*

Campbell stood at the back of the Sweethaven Chapel in a room reserved for brides. Out the window, she could see their guests filtering in, sitting in the white wooden chairs they'd set up earlier that morning. Underneath a white canopy, Graham stood, Bible in hand, and in just a few seconds, the music would start and she'd walk down the aisle to meet her groom.

Tilly Watkins, her mom's best friend from Chicago, appeared in the doorway. Her gasp turned Campbell around. "You look so beautiful."

Campbell caught her reflection in the full-length mirror. She'd never been a frilly girl, but she had to admit, she did feel like a princess in her dress. The strapless gown had just enough tulle to be special without being too much.

She'd grown her hair out, and after it had been curled and sprayed, the stylist had pinned it up, leaving a few tendrils hanging around her face and securing the veil underneath the gathered hair.

"Thanks, Tilly."

Tilly walked in and handed her a small box. "This is from your mother."

Campbell stared at it and then found Tilly's eyes. "My mother?"

Tilly nodded. "She wanted you to have it today." She pulled Campbell into a hug. "See you out there."

After she'd gone, Campbell sat, careful not to wrinkle her dress, and took the lid off the small wrapped box. Inside, she found a hand-made book. On the cover, the words "I wanted you to know . . ." The cover had been decorated with paint and flowers and, of course, Mom's gorgeous hand-lettering.

Campbell opened the book and found that the pages were envelopes, each decorated with Mom's unique style. On the first envelope, Mom had written the words "On your wedding day . . ."

Campbell turned the page and saw that the envelope had been sealed, and on the next page, she saw the words "When you find out you're expecting your first child . . ."

The book continued like that, milestone after milestone documented and accounted for. Mom's way of having her say even after she'd gone. Campbell blinked to keep the tears from ruining her makeup. Carefully, she opened the first envelope and inside found a handwritten letter.

*Dear Campbell,*

*I can only imagine how beautiful you look today. I can only imagine how special a man you found if you've agreed to make him your husband. I'm so proud of the woman you've become. As you know, I never had a wedding day, but if I did, I would've made sure to enjoy every second of it. I would've danced until my feet ached and spoken to every person who came to celebrate with me.*

*I would've fallen in love all over again.*

*Don't let this day pass by too quickly, and remember that while a wedding is important, it's the marriage that really matters. Treat him with kindness always, and don't ever be afraid to let him know how much you love him.*

*I know my death may cause you some confusion, but if there's one thing I will never regret in my life, it's the people I've loved with every fiber of my being. Knowing I don't have much time left, those are the relationships I cherish most.*

*Forgive easily. Give freely of yourself. And love with your whole heart.*

*Even when you have to say good-bye, you'll find it was all worth it in the end.*

*I did.*

*I love you, Campbell.*
*Mom*

Campbell reread Mom's words and wondered how her mother had known exactly what to say.

"Campbell?" her father's voice startled her. "You okay?"

Campbell glanced back at the book, tucked the letter back in its envelope and put it back in its box. She'd never cherished anything more. She nodded at Tom.

"They're ready to start the music."

Campbell checked herself in the mirror one last time and then took Tom's arm, walking outside to the back of the wide yard behind the church.

"You look beautiful," Tom said. "Your mother would be so proud."

Campbell looked up toward the sky as if to acknowledge her presence, and for the briefest moment, it almost felt like her mom was right beside her.

As she stood at the back of the rows of chairs, sprays of tulips lining the aisle they'd created, Campbell scanned the crowd. Old friends and new turned toward her, smiles on everyone's faces. Adele sat beside her new husband and old love, tears falling faster than she could wipe them away. Campbell smiled when she met her eyes.

Jane, equally weepy, sat beside Adele, and while Campbell would know the woman's kind eyes anywhere, her body had been completely transformed. Healthy and strong, Jane had done what she set out to do—she'd taken her life back, and inspired many other people to do the same.

Lila beamed in the front row, cradling her one-month-old son, Thomas Jr. Now that he'd been born, she would finally be able to donate bone marrow for her niece Maddie. Lila glanced down at her son, smiled, then looked back at Campbell.

"You guys seem so happy," Campbell said to Tom.

His face lit up. "We are so happy."

Somehow, Campbell and her father had managed to work everything out, in spite of the secrets of the past, and she knew in her heart that her coming to Sweethaven wasn't a mistake. In fact, it was the biggest blessing of her life.

"Looks like it's time." Meghan, dressed in a simple sky-blue dress, looked less like a bridesmaid and more like a star. Finn and Nadia would lead the way down the aisle where Campbell would finally say "I do" to the man who'd stolen her heart from the second she arrived in Sweethaven. She glanced at Luke, who looked more handsome than she'd ever seen him in a gray suit and blue tie.

When Luke saw her, his expression changed, and Campbell thought his face could've lit the night sky.

Looking out over the scene in front of her, Campbell whispered a prayer of thanks. For the scrapbook that led her there. For the friends she'd met there. For the life she intended to have there.

This little town had done more than given her a place to live. It had stolen her heart.

And she knew she would never be the same.

## AUTHOR'S NOTE

Dear Reader,

For me, Christmas has always been such a magical time of year, especially the older I've gotten. It's a time to slow down, to enjoy, to be thankful, but it always flies by so quickly. This year, I hope you take a few extra moments to rest in the magic of the season . . . and I hope a visit to Sweethaven helps you accomplish that goal.

This book was more difficult to write because I knew it was the final book in the series, and in some ways, it was hard to say good-bye to these women who have found their way into my heart. It's my hope, though, that their stories and the lessons they're learning stay with you long after you close the book.

This final installment of the Sweethaven series has reminded me of the redeeming grace of our heavenly Father, something I've relied on time and time again (because I'm stubborn and tend to make the same mistakes over and over).

It's my hope that no matter who you are or what mistakes you've made, you can rest in knowing that God's arms are always open and His grace is always sufficient. Run to God when you are weary and He will give you rest.

Thank you for taking the time to read the conclusion of this story. I can't properly express how much it means to me, but please know that it is a tremendous blessing. If you, like the women in the Sweethaven Circle, want to preserve your memories through the pages of a scrapbook, I'd like to invite you to visit me on my blog (CourtneyWalsh.typepad.com) where I share crafting tips and tricks and also tell the stories of my life.

Your notes and e-mails are a huge bright spot in my day, so feel free to contact me via my Web site CourtneyWalshWrites.com.

And may God richly bless you this and every Christmas.

Courtney Walsh

## ABOUT THE AUTHOR

Courtney Walsh is a published author, scrapbooking expert, theater director, and playwright. She has written two papercrafting books, *Scrapbooking Your Faith* and *The Busy Scrapper*. She has been a contributing editor for *Memory Makers Magazine* and *Children's Ministry Magazine* and is a frequent contributor to Group Publishing curriculum, newsletters, and other publications. She has also written several full-length musicals, including her most recent: *The Great American Tall Tales* and *Hercules* for Christian Youth Theatre, Chicago. *A Sweethaven Christmas* is the third novel in the Sweethaven Circle trilogy, along with *A Sweethaven Summer* and *A Sweethaven Homecoming*.

Courtney lives in Illinois with her husband and three children.

We hope you enjoy *A Sweethaven Christmas,* created by the Books and Inspirational Media Division of Guideposts. In all of our books, magazines and outreach efforts, we aim to deliver inspiration and encouragement, help you grow in your faith, and celebrate God's love in every aspect of your daily life.

Thank you for making a difference with your purchase of this book, which helps fund our many outreach programs to the military, prisons, hospitals, nursing homes and schools. To learn more, visit GuidepostsFoundation.org.

We also maintain many useful and uplifting online resources. Visit Guideposts.org to read true stories of hope and inspiration, access OurPrayer network, sign up for free newsletters, join our Facebook community, and follow our stimulating blogs.

To order your favorite Guideposts publications, go to ShopGuideposts.org, call (800) 932-2145 or write to Guideposts, PO Box 5815, Harlan, Iowa 51593.